THE
TOMORROW
PEOPLE

By
JUDITH MERRIL

I0616865

ARMCHAIR FICTION
PO Box 4369, Medford, Oregon 97504

MYSTERY FROM THE RED PLANET

It was supposed to be a great day. A manned rocket was sent to Mars with three brave crewmen inside. But something went wrong; it never came back. Not wanting to give up easily, it was decided a second attempt would be made. This second expedition went hurtling through the wilds of space toward the Red Planet. And it did meet with greater success—but just barely. Only one of its crewmen came back alive. That crewmember's name was Johnny Wendt, and the knowledge he brought back with him could prove to be decisive in a desperate international race for superiority in outer space. Unfortunately, that wasn't the only thing that Wendt brought back with him!

CAST OF CHARACTERS

JOHNNY WENDT
The world's first Space hero, until something affected him on Mars—then he became an alcoholic drifter.

LISA TROVI
She went to the Moon to help Johnny—but found something there more important than love.

PHIL KUTLER
His job was to find out what Space had done to Johnny—and see that it didn't happen again.

CONGRESSMAN MCLAFFERTY
He was out to grab the Space program for himself—and his dreadfully effective weapons were headlines.

DR. PETE CHRISTENSEN
He had built a successful moon station, but why was someone running a smear campaign against it?

THAD BOURGNESE
Surrounded by beautiful scientists, which one did he fancy the most?

PROLOGUE
June, 1973—January, 1976

They sent two men out through unknown space to a far, cold place, a place whose very name was fear, the name of the cruel god, the god of war. They shot two men off the Moon—out from the sun and away from the earth—in a new great ship with a shiny hull and a miracle fuel.

The ship went out with a blast and a prayer. After three years it came back with a sigh, unpowered, fuel-less, floating in slow-spiraled orbit through empty sky around the Moon. It came back with its hull scratched and dented and darkened from the dust and debris of space, the wind and sands of Mars. It came back with one man in it instead of two.

Johnny Wendt was the one who came back.

CHAPTER ONE
January 1976—June 23, 1977

Rockland, N. Y.—Thursday, June 23, 1:30 A.M. (E.D.S.T.)

He woke up screaming again.

Or else he dreamed the scream?

But when his eyes started to open, they closed reactively against the light. So Lee was up. And so it was no dream.

Sweat tickled his neck, but he lay still, breathing evenly, eyes shut. He would talk to her in the morning. Not now. In the morning it would be better, but not *now...*

He opened his eyes a slit to make sure. It was her light, all right. She was sitting up, watching him.

"Sorry, darling," she said. "I couldn't get to sleep, I didn't think the light would bother you..."

"Huh?" He blinked his eyes open wider. She was sitting, but with a pillow propped behind her back, book on her lap. "No, 'sarigh'," he mumbled. "Go 'head. Light don' bother..."

She'd been reading...*She had been up first!* He shook his head, clearing it, got her in focus. The flicker of frown on her forehead was apology, not worry...

So it *had* been a dream?

"Hey," he said. "Was I...?" He twisted his neck cautiously, felt for the knot in back with an exploring hand. "I feel like...Was I keeping you up, babe? Thrashing around, or...anything?"

"No. It was just this damn book. I got started reading it and I kept thinking and I couldn't sleep—I'm sorry, darling," she said again.

She closed the book with a snap and reached for the light switch.

No!

"Don't quit on account of me," he said quickly. "Light doesn't bother me." *Jesus, what a dream!* "Anyhow, I'm up now." He rubbed at his neck, groped under the pillow and found his handkerchief. "I guess I was dreaming." He wiped sweat from his forehead and neck and face. Then he swung his legs out of the bed and stood up. "Coffee?"

Lisa hesitated, shook her head: No.

Johnny found his shorts on the floor, pulled them on. There was sweat on his thighs, too. Sticky and drying. *A shower*, he thought...*too damn hot in here.* He peered at the thermostat; it said 68, but the room was hot. He turned it down. *Check it out in the morning,* he thought. Couldn't be working right. A drink and a shower would do it, all right. Then he could get back to sleep. Just one drink...

"Maybe a brandy..."

It took a moment to register—she meant for *her.* He looked down at her, grinning. "Hey," he said. "Don't you think one lush around here is enough?" She smiled and he leaned over, meaning to drop a quick kiss on her hair. Then it hit him again: the incredible fact of her presence, right there, in his house, in his bed...the look and shape of her, the curve of shoulder, the *aliveness* just below her skin, the way her cheek curved with her smile...smiling light in her eyes, and all for him...*for him*...even while the faint line of frowning...for him, too...lingered above. The cloudy feel and fragrance of her hair, and the strange blend of scents on her skin; soap, grass, sex, something else, something sweet and delicious and way-back in memory.

"Oh, *baby!*" he said and sat down to do an all-out job of kissing her. "Maybe I *don't* want that coffee—Nope!" He stood up, abruptly aware of dried sweat on his face, in his hair, "The lady wants a drink, that's what she gets!"

In the kitchen, he got the bottle and two glasses and went straight back, not giving himself time for the quick one he would have had while he mixed his coffee. He gave Lisa the bottle.

"Pour me. I'll be right back."

And what the Hell do you think you're proving? he jeered at himself as he turned on the shower. All the answers he could think of sounded more like Phil Kutler's brand of idiocy than like any of his own. He stepped impatiently out of the air blast and wrapped a towel around his still-damp waist. *Well,* he thought, *any way you look at it, it's your own damn fault!*

He went out, took the glass Lee held out, and belted it fast. He filled it again, leaving the jug carefully on her table, not his own. Then he walked around the bed and sat down, leaning against the headboard.

Sip it, he told himself. Lisa leaned back beside him. He watched her breasts move under the fullness of the thin nightgown: rising, as she settled into place, and again as she raised her glass to her lips; falling when she lowered it; shifting again when she turned to smile at him. Her hair was freshly brushed, he saw, and her lips newly, lightly, rouged. There was a trace of perfume, too, that had not been there before—and the other smell, the special one he couldn't quite place, was lost under it. That was when he remembered something she'd said before.

"What's with the morning bus?" he asked.

"I have to be at the studio at ten. They're taping the Bartok. Didn't I tell you Hal called…?"

"Yeah." She *had* told him. So okay. One more thing he didn't remember. He looked at her again. *What the Hell is that smell, anyway…?*

"Lee…" He could sense her tension, her shrinking from what he was going to say. "I could go down too…while we're there…we could see about that license, you know?"

"Oh, *Johnny…*" She paused, and because he did love her, he didn't wait to make her say the rest.

"Okay, doll. Listen…" *No good.* "Oh, Hell! Just don't forget old Johnny did his best to make an honest woman out of you!" What the Hell should *he* care? If that's how she wanted it…

She'd do anything for him, he knew. Anything—except marry him.

Okay! "Better get some sleep," he said stiffly.

"Mmmmm?" She emptied her glass, squashed out her cigarette, and slid down on her pillow. Her hand hovered over the light switch while her eyes questioned his.

"Hand me the jug first," he said. *Jesus! What a dream!* He filled his glass again, setting the bottle down on his own table. The Hell with it. This time he needed it.

"Jesus!" he said. "What a dream!" He laughed but it didn't sound right. "You know how words can get all mixed up? *Choke* and *artichoke*. First somebody's pushing my head in, then they're pulling me apart. Just like an artichoke—Christ! You know, you take off one leaf at a time and dip it in butter and suck all the good part off and throw it away and pull off another one. Then you get down to the heart—just sitting there naked with all the leaves off, and you can't even yell for help, who the Hell'd ever hear an *artichoke…?*"

The goddam glass was empty. In the dark, the gurgling sound of pouring was too loud.

The Hell with it!

Lisa didn't say anything.

Well, what *could* she say?

What the Hell did he want her to say?

"There's a moon tonight." That's what she said.

"*Is* there?"

The Hell with that too!

She shouldn't have put on that perfume, he thought. Then, startled, he found that his hand had gone out to the switch, and the wall that had been milky glass before turned transparent. A near-full moon, heavy and low on the hilltops silhouetted the silvery birches and tall pines: brought them so close he could feel the night breeze outside. He shivered, suddenly and uncontrollably, then remembered he'd turned the conditioner down before.

He reached for the panel light. Lee stirred in the bed, turned her back to him. *Fooled you!* he thought with childish malice as he found the light...but no more childish than her back when she thought he was going for the bottle again, he decided. She moved again, and he saw she was propped on an elbow, staring out. A current of air, from her back maybe, carried that scent again—what in Hell was it? An old smell, a happy one, something from back when the Moon was a moon, and the man in the moon was a joke, and not Chris, and Mars was an orangey spot in the sky, with no man in it anywhere.

His hand on the thermostat wavered. He stood up, dropped the towel, and shivered again.

"Mind if I light the fire?" His voice sounded harsh in his ears. Hell with that *too*...

"Mmm..." That could have meant anything. He crossed the room, set a match to the kindling and crouched at the fireplace, hugging the warmth, while he watched flames leap up. Smell of pine burning, the crackle of pitch, and then he remembered...

Vanilla!

A year...more than a year now...fourteen, fifteen months, that flavor, the scent of it on Lisa's skin had been haunting him. *The smell of vanilla!* He laughed. She made and inquiring noise and he looked around.

The moon was gone. The milky wall was black. His panel light glowed for a moment, then she moved toward his side of the bed and stretched out her arm and the small glow died. Firelight leaped up, warming him through.

"Hey, babe!" he said. "Oh, baby, I love you..."

The Moon—January, 1976

Across the broad pockmarked face of the Moon, like blue-tinged boils on chin, cheek, and forehead, three air-filled pressure domes gleamed in the hard rays of the naked sun.

Largest and best advertised of these was the joint military and astronomical observatory base of the United Nations World Peace Control and International Scientific Congress, nestled appropriately, or at least hopefully, inside a hilltop between the great dry "seas," *Tranquilitatis* and *Serenitatis.*

Flanking it, at distances of about 800 miles each, were the Low-atmosphere and Low-temperature Laboratory of the Soviet Union of Asian Republics, and the All America Laboratory for the Investigation of Extra-Terrestrial Phenomena.

In both cases, the official designations of the smaller domes stated something less than the whole truth. Certainly, valuable scientific researches into the properties and effects of near-zero and near-vacuum were being pursued, eagerly, in the Red Dome. Just as surely, extra-terrestrial phenomena were being studied with active interest inside Dollars Dome. But the primary purposes of the two national labs were somewhat less academic than the "pure" scientific research which, for the most part, motivated the mixed crews of physicists, chemists, and astronomers in the big World Dome.

There was just one objective that could have induced either the USAA or the SUAR to finance and maintain experimental scientific bases more than a quarter of a million miles out from under the quivering noses of, respectively, the Congressional Committees and the Politburo. In his stronghold far out of sight beyond the Lunar Appenines, some 1500 miles from the United States of All Americas Dome in Playfair Crater, Dr. Chen Lian-Tsu was occupied just as busily as was Dr. Peter Andrew Christensen in Dollars Dome with the application of known physical; chemical, and astronomical data to the specific political-economic-imperial requirements of practical space-flight (tomorrow...for our side).

In the surface matters of dress and taste, preference in food, sport, and language, as well as national allegiance, the two men were worlds apart. In the basics of personality both of them were so well suited to the similar jobs they held that they were almost absurdly alike—even to the fact that neither (though both were in their mid-forties) had ever married. They were the kind of men who "marry their work" but, unlike others *almost* of their own type, both had avoided entanglement in arid marriages to which they could bring no real emotions. Their passions were already committed, wholly and without reserve, to the great dream of Space: of *man* in Space.

For these two, the immediate physical world, the Earth, was already abandoned; and from the perspective of an inward life based in the universe-at-large, either one could see with tragic clarity the narrow limits and uses of the old, little, world. They understood well enough the need of *other* men for competitive glories. They understood profit-and-loss and its importance to other *other*-men. And they knew perfectly well that for the non-imperial realities of the UN or the ISC there *was no* economic; political, or social need for space flight.

So they had cause to be loyal nationals, each to his own.

And each took care, as he had all his life, that no breath of suspicion sully his name or place in doubt (by a wary government) his suitability for the work he had to do. And if on rare and most private occasions, either one of them thought briefly, wistfully, of the advantages of a united approach to the Dream—he knew well enough that for *other* men. Space was no dream at all, but a prize enhanced—if not created—by competition. The isolation, security measures, and endless duplication of research and planning were, *realistically*, necessary.

This attitude was of course easier to maintain on the Moon than on Earth. Fifteen hundred miles of rugged lunar terrain, and the exigencies of rocket fuel economy, kept physical contact between the domes down to a minimum. Two hundred fifty thousand miles of empty space, and the economics of human existence on the Moon, kept political contact with the home governments down to a minimum too: on the Moon, a really rigid security could be sustained with almost no worry about infiltration, no possible worry about associations, and no petty fogging annoyances from suspicious, ambitious policemen or politicians.

The prevailing state of by-mutual-consent *laissez-faire* isolation was such an inherent fabric that Dr. Chen and Dr. Christensen had never even met personally. There had simply been no occasion. For that matter, up till the day of Johnny Wendt's return, the men on either staff who had even seen the other dome could be counted on two hands; none had ever been further inside the other than the landing lock—and that only on the occasions of the inevitable minor emergencies that called for humane sharing of survival (*not* scientific) equipment. With the exception of these instances, USAA ships made it a point not even to fly inside a line-of-sight of Plato Crater, and Red pilots stayed equally clear of Playfair.

The only modification of this "natural security" status that had occurred between the times that the two domes went up, in '69, and the orbiting of the *Moon Messenger* in '74, was when an outraged AA Congress learned that the Reds had succeeded in sending a ship to Mars without any previous knowledge at Dollars Dome.

But even then, no real attempt was made at an Intelligence network operating directly between the domes; it just wasn't worth the waste of oxygen on a Dome resident doing less than a full-time job of research or development. The money authorized as a result of the indignant Congressional Investigation went into tightening and improving existing infiltrations on Relay Station, the 400-mile Earth satellite, and at World Dome.

Undoubtedly, counter-espionage was strengthened correspondingly—and with just as little effect on the Red Dome itself as the USAA move had on life at Playfair. Not till the orbiting of the *Messenger*, the giant wheel of space that rode the great ellipse from a 12,000-mile orbit around Earth out to the convenient dropping-distance of the Moon, carrying shuttle-ships of all three domes, was there the kind of inter-grouping that breeds espionage. In eighteen months of operation, the *Messenger* had already started to acquire an aura of the sort of glamour that once permeated Istanbul, Paris, Lisbon, and Rome, complete with agents, counter-agents, and double agents.

Congressional apprehension had increased sharply when it was finally admitted, less than a year after the *Messenger* went up, that the whole spectrum of psychogenic and psychosomatic ailments plaguing the dwellers on the Moon could be relieved by nothing less than a month-long quarterly rest leave on Earth. For a time, there was even talk of "rest camps" and "recreation centers" where top-secret Moon Dome scientists could take their rehabilitation leaves on Earth. But public distaste for the idea prevailed—and the original Congressional fears dissolved almost out of shape when, 32 months after its unheralded departure, the *Lenin* failed to make its scheduled return.

By that time—Christmas, 1973—the *Colombo* was six months out, en route to Mars. And when a strenuous Intelligence effort confirmed that the Soviet ship was really lost (and not just secretly arrived), Dr. Christensen did not hesitate to remind the genial Congressmen that he *had* Told Them So, three years earlier, when he explained his failure to alert anyone to the possibility of a Red Mars-trip in the spring of '71.

The fact was he had assumed his opposite number would wait, as he was doing, for the next A-orbit date, in June '73, so as to gain the advantages that might accrue from the results of the ISC Observatory's studies during the close Mars opposition of '71. *After* the fact, he remembered that Chen had been faced with an extra intangible that had not troubled him: the history of Soviet "firsts." From Sputnik I on up through the first Moon-landing, SUAR (or USSR) rocket men had been first. The Party Chairman desired to keep it that way—so the *Lenin* left first.

But the *Colombo* came back.

It came back with no news of the Red ship.

And it came back with one man instead of two.

Dollars Dome—January 12, 1976

Johnny Wendt was the one who came back.

They met him with cheers and rejoicing, welcomed him home with music and medals and speeches on worldwide video beamed from the bunting-draped central square of the United States Moon Dome.

They sent relays of shuttles up to the big ship, with fuel and ship-to-base radio and an ace pilot, encased in the newest and Safest of protective gear, to guide her down. The first shuttle took Johnny off, while official cameras recorded for all time the opening of the historic lock and the return of mankind's first space-traveler to Terra's Moon.

The cameras kept grinding inside the shuttle while Major Wendt was bathed under batteries of ultraviolet, and a medic in Geiger-suit looked down his throat, checked his heartbeat and pulse and lungs, looked at his insides under a fluoroscope, took smears and samples and ran off fast lab checks—then smiled and handed him a brand-new uniform, one they could trust to harbor no alien virus or unknown seed.

The camera followed him out of the shuttle, into the dome lock. Another camera, and the live video scanners, picked him up inside the dome. But in the lock, for the sixty-nine seconds it took to bleed air, no record was made. And Chris was there, alone, to meet him first.

He pumped Johnny's hand, grinning with triumph. *"Man!"* he said. "We made it, man!"

Then his grin faded. *"You* did," he corrected. "Johnny—what happened to Doug?"

"I don't know," Wendt said.

The inner door opened. Cameras swung into action. General Harbridge stepped forward and shook Johnny's hand.

"Congratulations—Colonel!" he said, and pinned the new eagles onto the new uniform. But when they were under way, out of range for a moment of audio pickups, he asked anxiously, "Wendt—what happened to Laughlin?"

"I don't know," Johnny said, "sir." Then, wearily: "Everything I know is in the Log, sir. I brought it down with me. I figured you'd want it. The doctor's got it."

Harbridge nodded and said nothing more. But his smile when he led Johnny up to the platform on the Mall was a shade forced. And as soon as he decently could, he whispered a word to an aide and ducked out, leaving the assembled Dignitaries to welcome the space hero home.

Nobody missed him. The Ambassadors and Senators pinned a whole chestful of medals on the new uniform, and found a few for Dr. Christensen and his staff too. Then the VIPs and the cameras followed the new colonel to his first meal. The staff conference room had been turned into a banquet hall. Johnny was toasted and feted and fed.

They asked him to speak.

He stood up and looked at them all and his face was grim. Chris, sitting next to him, knowing him almost too well from five years of training and planning before the trip, stood up quickly beside him and grabbed the mike.

"Boy's all choked up," he said.

While the room laughed he managed to cover the mike for a moment. "Just tell 'em thanks, Johnny."

When it was quiet again, Wendt looked around, indecisive, looked down at Chris and grinned painfully. "I'm not much of a speaker," he said. "I... Hell, I'm glad to be home!"

"Thanks," Chris said.

When it all broke up, Chris took him up to his room.

"Thanks?"

"For keeping your mouth shut. Whatever's bugging you…"

"You seen Harbridge yet?"

"No. He took off during the speeches."

"I know." Johnny smiled the new one-sided smile again. "He went to read the Log."

Pete Christensen looked at the stranger who had been a friend. "All right," he said. "What the hell happened?"

"It's in the Log, Chris—all *I* know about it. Ask Harbridge." He paused. "Hey," he said. "You got something up here to drink?"

Everything on the *Colombo* was tested and touched (and in some cases tasted too) by teams of two: a scientist and an Intelligence officer. Johnny had done his job all right, and Doug apparently had completed his before he disappeared. The boxes and bottles, tubes and jars, notebooks and tape recorders and camera films were all filled and filed, packed with the answers to centuries of human questioning.

Yes, there had once been intelligent life on Mars.

No, it was there no more.

There were pictures of crumbling ruins, a very few carefully packed fossil remains, atmosphere samples, terrain maps and photographs, wind charts, rock samples, analyses, assays, and boxes of "Mars-Earth," from seven different "canals," alive with one-celled life-forms that made planet-life possible in the dry air above ground. The record of Laughlin's work on the symbiosis between the moisture-retaining "Mars-bugs" and the sparse photo-sensitive lichen of the "canals" were there too, neat and in order, properly filed away and labeled in Doug Laughlin's hand. And Johnny had finished the job; he'd brought back all the pictures and records and readings, the answers they sent him to get. Nothing was missing, not a thing out of place— nothing but Laughlin himself, one specially designed sand-caterpillar-tractor, two oxygen cylinders, and the four pages torn out of the Log.

Daily, sometimes hourly, press releases were beamed down to Earth, telling it all to a waiting world—all but the last bit, about the Log.

The teams of two went through the ship of space.

The semanticists, psychers, and medics went to work on the Hero, and on the Log he brought back.

The last entry before the torn-out sheets was in Laughlin's hand, dated April 26, 1975, roughly a month before scheduled takeoff for the return trip to Earth: a routine report on routine existence, noting temperature, wind, and moisture readings; cataloguing the men's whereabouts and accomplishments during the twenty-four-and-a-half hours that made one Martian day; listing lab findings of the past several days. Nothing remarkable in any way—except that it broke off in mid-sentence at the end of the page.

No clues or hints, no intimations, no cryptic allusions to Doug's impending act—not in that entry or any previous one. Presumably, the missing pages *did* hold some such references; but they were gone—presumably wherever Laughlin himself had gone.

Handwriting experts, called in by the Psych staff, agreed that Laughlin's last entry showed signs of emotional upset. But both men's handwriting showed a slow increase of tension throughout the Log, mounting sharply after the landing on Mars, and more swiftly again during the month since the sampling and mapping were finished, until the day of Laughlin's departure.

The next entry, after the missing four pages, was Wendt's, on April 29, at 1816 hours: "Laughlin gone out alone without notice. No signals from sand cat. I do not believe he plans to return. Tire tracks visible from cargo lock point N39W. Going out in heli now, no flight plan, will follow tracks. Carrying four hours fuel, standard 24-hr oxy-water etc. Figure two hours tot. flight time, unless I find him in trouble. Tape 237, a-6."

The next notation, at 2129 hours, said briefly: "No luck. Lost tracks in hills. Saw what looked like sand cat dust trail at N32W on other side. Going out again now, with six hours fuel. Oxy-water, 12 hrs. Tape 237, a-9."

Then: "4/30/75, 0110-Dust storm, 50 mi. past previous flight limit. N32W dust cloud could have been storm approaching. Any tracks will be covered now. Will commence standard search pattern, 3-hr. flights, when storm passes."

Half an hour later, at 0048: "Thought I'd catch a nap till storm let up, but might as well get the story down, as much as I know, before I forget anything. Doug left the ship sometime between 2315 (approx.)

last night and 0650 this morning (Mars-time. eq: 1108 and 1754, 4/29/75). Most likely he left just before I woke up, say between—"

Here, the Mars time had been written in and scratched out, and Earth time (which was Standard Log procedure), written in instead.

"—1745, say, and 1754. This is hunch mostly, I think the sound of the airlock might have been what woke me, since I did not actually go to sleep till an hour or more after 1108, when I went to my bunk, and I was surprised to see the time when I woke. Usually sleep longer. Was not aware of what woke me (if anything) at first, and did not take special notice of Doug's absence. Assumed he was sleeping. Got dressed, started making breakfast, then noticed panel signal that a sand cat was out—but no beeps coming in. Checked Doug's bunk, which was empty. Checked Log, for his trip plan. Found missing pages. Checked time; then 1812. Found dust cloud that could have been cat trail on scope at N37W. Proceeded on first search, as noted, at 1816.

"Throughout first search, I kept helmet radio tuned for automatic signals from cat, except for a five minute waveband search every half-hour after trying helmet-radio calls. No signals received.

"Storm seems to be mostly past now. Will now commence search pattern." Fuel and oxy-water data and signal tape reference numbers followed.

Laughlin had then been gone at least seven hours. Longer trips than that had been made before—but not by either man alone. Nor were *any* trips—prior to this one—made singly by either partner without advance arrangements. If one of them went out alone, the other was required, by operating procedures established beforehand, to stand by and maintain continuous radio contact. When they left ship together, the same continuous radio contact was maintained, one-way, and automatically taped on board the ship. Both sand cats, the helicopter, and the small plane were equipped with radio transmitters that operated automatically, sending signal directions, as long as the vehicle was in operation. There was no switchoff on the devices, and there was a secondary system designed to cut in if the primary were damaged in any way.

No direction signals had been recorded from Laughlin's cat at any time. Wendt's immediate reaction, written before his first search, "I do not believe he plans to return," had appeared filled with sinister import when the log was first examined. On consideration, the quick conclusion seemed a natural one, in view of Doug's failure to inform

Johnny of his trip plans, or to file a route plan, plus the absence of any direction signals from the cat (which pointed toward deliberate dismantling of the automatic equipment), and, finally, Johnny's discovery of the missing pages in the log book.

The next entry, made several hours later, debated the advisability of further search. The first effort had turned up no trail of any kind. The rule against simultaneous departures from line-of-sight had to be considered. Everything pointed to one extreme likelihood that Laughlin's departure had been planned and purposeful, and that no amount of searching would be rewarded. Nevertheless, Johnny continued to search for five more days, two or three flights a day, until the search pattern was finished, the flight coordinates adding up to a circle whose radius represented a narrow margin of safety above the flight limits imposed for one-man trips.

The final entry on the search was brief:

"I do not believe there is a possibility that Laughlin is still alive. He did not take any extra oxygen cylinders with him. At minimum usage, the two standard tanks in the cat, if full when he started, would have been stretched to 95 hours. He has now been gone from the ship for at least 127 hours. I have seen no sign of him, or of any ship's equipment, or of any trail he might have left, on any flight since the second one."

There were no further entries except for routine daily temperature and atmosphere reading, until the one that gave the calculations for takeoff and homeward orbit. Doug Laughlin's name was not mentioned again, nor was any reference to him made. No opinion was volunteered as to why he should have left the ship.

They went back to Johnny again.

"I don't know," he kept saying.

"Why did you tear those pages out of the Log?"

"I didn't."

"Who did?"

"I don't know."

"You think Laughlin did it?"

"I know *I* didn't."

"Why would he do a thing like that?"

"I don't know."

"What made you think he wasn't coming back?"

"I don't know. I just thought so."

"How did it happen that you weren't aware of his going?"

"It's all in the Log."

"Now look, Colonel Wendt..." (or "Johnny" or "son," depending on who did the questioning) "...you must have had some idea why he went..."

Silence, usually. If the interrogator was friendly, a quiet curse.

"What happened to Laughlin?"

"Search me," he said.

So they did. They searched him with "truth" drugs, which only confirmed what he'd told them. He did not know what had happened to Doug Laughlin. He did not know what had happened to the missing pages of the book. And he had no knowledge of having had anything to do with the loss of the man or of the material from the Log.

Meantime, reporters and commentators, interviewers and feature-writers from every corner of Earth fraternized restlessly in a well-appointed suite at Mexcity's best hotel where a Public Relations man in Space Academy brass buttons smilingly poured drinks, dealt out freshly-inked mimeographed sheets from a cardboard box, and made sure the free-lunch was kept replenished.

Security would be lifted, and Colonel Wendt would be personally available, as soon as the ship was completely unloaded, he told the reporters.

How long would that be?

Well, it was hard to say...

Soon...

Mexcity, U.S.A.A.—February, 1976

They brought him back to Earth, on the next downswing the *Messenger* made. Security would have preferred to keep him on the Moon till they had something—anything—on Laughlin or on the missing Log pages at least. But the M. I. squad had to have expert consultants and some psych equipment which Dr. Christensen irritably, arbitrarily, would not grant shuttle space. And the Psych man attached to the team was insisting they'd never get anything out of John Wendt till they let him go home, back to Earth.

So, twenty days after the feasting and medals, Colonel Wendt and an escort of nine guards and questioners left Dollars Dome. Five days later, they landed on a snow-swept concrete prairie in the Andes. The landing and clearance routine seemed to take an absurdly long time; it was after dark when a plain helicopter finally left the spaceport, carrying Johnny and two "bodyguards" from Security. By the time the reporters got wind of the hero's arrival, he was already installed in his prison-of-honor—a whole floor of luxury in the tower penthouse of the same hotel where, nineteen floors down, in the pressroom, free lunch and free drinks were still passing around.

They showed Johnny through the place and explained politely, very pleasantly, that it would be best if he stayed in his rooms for a while. Adjustment period. Psych tests. All that sort of thing. Then they posted a very polite, pleasant, guard at each door to keep unauthorized visitors out—and Johnny in. Just as politely, and very firmly, they told the clamoring press:

"Not yet..."

When the records of the trip had been fully examined, when all the films and test-tubes and tapes and sample-boxes had been classified and examined, Security could be lifted completely...

How long would that be?

Well, it was hard to say...

Soon. Very soon...

One after another, different men of eminence in different schools of psychiatric practice came up to the hotel penthouse. Johnny met them politely and listened—at first with interest, and then with indifference—and agreed, passively, to the succession of exhumative techniques they proposed.

They explained to him how a man's memory worked, how the brain stores and holds memories, how a memory block occurs, how the subconscious mind can dominate a person's consciousness. Johnny nodded patiently, and remembered nothing more than before.

"You can remember if you want to," one man said.

"Yeah." Johnny grinned, and looked embarrassed. "But what about if I *don't* want to?"

They told him that the information he withheld—from them as well as from himself—would probably make a difference of years in sending out another ship.

"Okay," he said, with the same one-sided grin. "Do yourselves a favor. *Don't* find out."

He made it very clear that he himself fully intended to spend the remainder of his days on Earth; and that he was quite convinced any man in his right mind would do likewise.

Pete Christensen came down to see him. Chris was a friend, twice: not just Johnny's friend, but Doug's too. It had been his job to choose the men for that trip. The training and planning that had prepared them had been by his orders, and much of the time at his hands. And they had all shared the dream...

He said, "Listen, Johnny, *we've got to know!*" He talked about Congress and the new appropriations bill, about the dream that was dying in a morass of reaction and funk; and added, "There's nothing in your Log about the *Lenin* either."

"We never saw it."

"All right, you never saw it. So now you come back, without Doug, and something happened, but you won't talk..."

"Chris, if I *knew* anything..."

"Okay, but you know these Mexcity characters, four pages missing from that damn Log, Doug missing, the *Lenin* missing. And now you not only *won't* talk, but what they're saying is, you *can't*. You see what I mean? Christ, you read enough science fiction and horror stuff to see the picture. And you can believe me, they've got lobbies working nights painting the pic. Not just in Mexcity, either. You should see the Sunday supplement trash on tri-di!"

"I've seen it. What do you mean—lobbies?"

"The Undersea Dome crowd, Arctic reclamation. Half a dozen of 'em. Mostly the Undersea bunch, though."

"Undersea? I thought that bunch was so rich they didn't *bother* with Congress?"

Chris laughed. "You think that means they don't want public money to work with?"

Wendt shook his head and grinned: a nice young boyish grin, rueful, amused.

"Okay, look," Chris said. "They've got a bill going in now to cut *all* Space money outside of routine Lab funds, only for maintenance, see?, and some work on the stuff you brought back. But no new ship.

Not even a refit for the old bird. No Venus job. You know what that means?"

Johnny nodded. He still smiled; but now it had twisted to the new one-sided kind.

"Damn it, they're *scared,*" Chris said. "And damn it, you scared 'em! Johnny, you know even pressure from a group like Undersea wouldn't work if those guys didn't know all the folks back home were scared right out of their pants too?"

"That's right."

Chris looked at him, shook his head. "What the *hell* is out there?" he asked. *"What made you feel this way?"*

Wendt stood up and paced the length of the big room and back again. "Okay!" he said. "You want to know what's out there? I'll tell you...all right, I'll tell you, and you can have a good laugh and forget all about it. Forget it until you manage to wheedle some more dough out of Congress, and send some other poor goof out there. Then if he gets back alive and tells you the same thing, you might even start to believe it.

"I'll tell you what's out there: *God,* that's what. Mars is heaven, see—just like it said in the story—only different—and God lives there. So if you know some guy holy enough to meet up with the Hot Shot in person, send him on out. Otherwise, you better forget the whole thing."

Chris stood up stiffly. "Okay," he said. "I know when I'm licked."

"What's the matter?" Johnny said bitterly. "You're not laughing. Don't you think it's funny?"

"No. Maybe I haven't got any sense of humor. You know how us dedicated souls are. Anyhow, the joke is on me."

It was only after Chris left that Johnny realized the older man hadn't believed that he meant it. *Score one for the psychers,* he thought; at least they could tell when he was not kidding. *They'd* believe that one all right: believe that he meant it; what would bug *them* was trying to figure out what he meant by it.

Which was a good question too, when you thought of it...

It was some hours later that he realized he couldn't answer that one for himself—because it wasn't really his idea to start with. It was something Doug had said, in that bad month, the last month, before he went...

Okay, he thought grimly, *let's see how long it takes for them to dig that out...*

By that time, it was a game with him, a bitter game, to see how much he could throw the psychers off without actually telling a lie they could spot.

Mexcity—March, 1976

Phil Kutler would never have gotten a crack at the Wendt case, except that none of the big men in the field had gotten anywhere, and that Johnny and Phil happened to have gone to school together. And when they examined the tapes that carried a record of every word Johnny Wendt had spoken in his luxury-prison, they realized that the most revealing thing anybody had gotten out of him—if only they knew what it revealed—was his bitter little speech to Pete Christensen. So they asked Kutler to come from New York, and sent him up, not quite sure himself whether he was there as friend or doctor.

Johnny greeted him suspiciously. They ordered some beer, and yakked for a while about things they'd done and places they'd been since they saw each other five-six years before. Mostly Phil's places and people and things; Johnny found he could damn near enjoy himself when someone else did the talking.

Finally Phil said, "Look, I'm a doctor. You know why I'm here. I got a big pep talk downstairs about all the stuff I'm supposed to find out for the sake of Progress and the Human Race, and a pile of high-minded stuff like that...

"Don't get me wrong, man. I've got nothing against noble abstractions. I'm all for the human race, and I guess progress is real peachy too. But like I said, I'm a doctor. We all get our kicks different ways, and I get mine curing sick people. And man, you're sick. Maybe I'm not supposed to come out and tell you like that, but it's sticking out all over..."

"Sure," sure," Johnny said quickly. "How do you want to do it? Sometimes they want me to lie down. Sometimes I'm supposed to shut my eyes. One guy brought up a little tank of CO_2, and there was one with some vitamin guk, and they tried scop, or something like it, a couple of times and—"

"Okay, chum." Phil stood up and stuck out his hand. "I'll tell 'em it looks promising and maybe they'll let me come and see you again some time."

"Not on your life," Johnny said. "They've got every word of this down on their magic spy rays."

"Oh?" Kutler looked around the room curiously, then with visible irritation, and finally with explosive fury: "The stupid brassbound idiots! What in God's name are they trying to do to you? Take a guy with the most obvious case of exposure fears any half-assed medic ever diagnosed, and sit him in a great big glass house with the whole world looking in..." He broke off abruptly. "Well, they got me on record now, too," he said quietly.

"You mean they sent you up here without telling you that?" Johnny asked.

"How come they told you?"

Johnny shook his head. "They didn't. I just figured it. Things the wrong people know about. Stuff like that. Yeah, sure, I know, it could all be—what do you call it?—'projection?' Eyes and ears in the wall? Stuff like that?"

Kutler looked at him thoughtfully. "Have you asked anyone about it?"

"Hell no!"

"Why not?"

"What difference would it make? Like you said, I'm in a glass box anyhow. Maybe I felt good knowing something they didn't know I knew... Well I shot *that* wad, now, didn't I?"

"Yeah." Kutler sat back in the soft chair, picked up his beer, stretched his legs, and watched Johnny pacing from piano to windows and back. "Yeah, you sure did. If you're right, then they already have it..."

"What did you mean, 'exposure fears'?" Johnny broke in. He stood tensely, halfway from the wall to the piano. "Don't you think I *want* to get out of here?"

"Huh? Oh, no. I meant—just what you said. 'Eyes and ears in the wall.' Only now I'm not sure which came first, the chicken or the egg— Listen, John, do you want to find out? Right now?" He got up and went to the phone, but he did not pick it up, waiting for Johnny's answer.

"I don't give a damn one way or the other!"

"Oh?" He took his hand off the phone, half-turned away. "Of course if you don't think you'd feel better knowing you're right, then maybe you'd just rather not take a risk of being wrong. Oh, hell! Who's kidding whom anyway?" He turned angrily back and picked up the phone. "*I* want to know."

"Okay, okay. Go ahead. I told you I don't care…"

New York City—March-May, 1976

That was the beginning. Kutler came up every day for a while, just to talk. He was the only personal visitor Johnny would admit; and he himself refused to consider the visits professional in the bugged apartment. By the end of the week, a compromise agreement had been reached all around. Kutler had him for a patient, and his patient would come, like any other, to the doctor's office for treatment. Johnny was moved to a new hotel penthouse in New York.

Three months of probing, plus Wendt's agreement, finally, to the use of hypnotic recall technique, told them what they didn't want to know: which was, essentially, that they already knew just as much as he did.

Oh, they gained a few details, but none of any importance. The fact remained simply that Doug Laughlin had walked out of the ship one day while Johnny was asleep. He hadn't come back. He had taken nothing with him except what he wore on his back, and the food and equipment normally kept in the sand cat, plus, presumably, four pages out of the Log. Nowhere in the detailed memories of the days before Laughlin's disappearance, or the months after, was there slightest evidence that Wendt had torn those sheets out, nor that he had even read them at any time. Nowhere was there anything to relate Laughlin's disappearance, or the mutilation of the Log, to the Soviet ship, *Lenin*. Nowhere was there any shred of cause to believe that either of the two who went out in *Colombo* had seen or heard anything at all of the other ship.

The objective facts of the case, as far as Johnny Wendt knew them, or ever had known them, were exactly as stated before. But, adding Kutler's findings to those of the men who had preceded him, and to the evidence of conversations on tape, they could at least form an opinion on which it was just barely possible to rest a theory.

As far as Johnny himself was concerned, the final official verdict was that he was guilty of nothing but guilt itself. The two ideas to which the guilt was most frequently attached were—

a) the obvious possibility that he had in some way been personally, directly, responsible for Laughlin's death: and

b) the completely suppressed (except under hypnotic recall) fear of remembering that for a time, before Laughlin's disappearance, a strong homosexual attraction had apparently been developing between the two men.

In neither case was there any reason to believe that Johnny's self-accusations were based on anything other than fearful fantasies.

As to what had actually happened to Doug—it was still anyone's guess. The best guess seemed to be that he was suffering from the same developing fear of inversion that had afflicted Wendt; that he had been even more horrified at the idea than Johnny was, and had chosen deliberate suicide in preference to involuntary surrender to "degeneracy"; and that, perhaps, he had written something into those four pages that he thought might be revealing, and so removed them before he left.

It hung together. As a theory, it made sense. The only trouble was, if the theory was correct, then the wrong man had come back. The same psychiatrists who formulated the theories swore up and down that psych-tests on both men before the trip made it absurd to think that Laughlin would have reacted in this way. If anyone did, it should have been Wendt; and that would not have made much more sense.

But the theory was all they had. The only way they would ever know more was to go back and find out—and the very fact that they *didn't* know more was enough to whittle down the chances of going back, any time soon, almost to the vanishing point.

The great All American public was scared.

Earth—May, 1976-May, 1977

When they were satisfied that Johnny had told all he knew, they let him go home—which was no place in particular. He didn't like having a lot of people around, so he skipped the big whirl he could have had in New York or Washington or Buenos Aires. He bummed around as quietly as possible for a while; found that liquor helped, and women, mostly, did not; set himself up as a kind of roving consultant in engineering and design, and found that work could help, too, for short spells. If it happened to catch his interest.

Getting jobs was easy; the name of Johnny Wendt was enough, even though his qualifications could be equaled by any number of other bright young cybernetics engineers. But *wanting* to get jobs was tougher. He had all the money he'd ever need; and if he needed more, after the lifetime pension and bonus pay, there were always advertisers clamoring for his endorsements, and manufacturers for the use of his name.

He could get money, jobs, liquor, women. But what he wanted, he couldn't get, and didn't even know a name for.

The therapy had helped. But not enough. He knew for a fact that he hadn't killed Doug; but between fact and belief there is a world of difference. He knew, too, that he hadn't done any of the things he'd been afraid even to think about, before the therapy. Now he could think about them; and did. Now he knew what he'd wanted to do. Now he couldn't forget.

After a while he met Lisa, or rather, met her again. He didn't really remember her from before, but she remembered him. When he first went up to the Moon, one of the beglamoured selectees from the Space Academy, to train for the Mars flight, she was one of a crowd of worshipful and willing girls—young actresses, models, dance students—the whole gang dated. In the intervening years, she had made a name for herself on world-wide tri-di—which would have disqualified her from Johnny's cynical viewpoint ("The higher they get, the easier they fall," he was fond of saying just then), except that he met her quite unsuspiciously during her twice-a-week stints as dance-therapist for a group therapy clinic of Kutler's.

Oddly, she had remained just as worshipful, and just as willing. And Johnny found, after a bit, that he was reassured by some special warmth in her willingness; later he was fascinated by the calm pleasure she took in knowing that a million people were watching her when she danced on tri-di. Later still, when fascination and reassurance progressed far enough, he found at least a partial answer, with her, to some of the questions he was still asking himself about Johnny Wendt.

Rockland, N. Y.—Thursday, June 23, 1977, 2 A.M. (E.D.S.T.)

She watched him straighten up and come back to the bed. There were two women in her. One woman was glad because it would be all right now: he wouldn't drink any more tonight. The other woman, watching as he came to her, was just glad...

He sat on the bed and pulled her against him with both hands. "Oh, baby," he said, and lowered his head to her breast. His hands moved up her back to her shoulders, pulled down the straps of her gown. "Oh, Lisa, Lisa," he murmured against her skin. His lips moved down and encountered the crumpled gown again. "What's *that* doing there?"

His head came up again, with the good smile, and he was still smiling as his lips met hers; while his hands pulled the gown down and off her hips.

When he was asleep again, she knew it really was going to be all right this time. He lay on his side, a faint smile on his face still, his breathing even, untroubled, one hand cupping her breast. He looked *so young...*

Now, the lines smoothed from his face, he could almost have been the same man she had first met five years, and a world, ago.

She lay quiet under his hand. *Oh, Johnny! If you could just...*

But she stopped the thought. *No pushing,* she reminded herself. *No pulling. He'll come through his own way.*

But this time she didn't believe it. It was taking too long. And the truth was, it didn't get better. It only got worse.

Would it help if I left?

That was the hardest part, to know if she herself did more good or more harm...

She tried to lie still and the effort defeated itself. One by one, the muscles in her leg, her arm, her back and neck, stiffened to unsustainable tensions. She moved warily and he mumbled, his fingers tightening. Then he came up a little out of sleep, muttered "Sorry," and rolled over, freeing her to move.

But now she was afraid that if she moved at all, the tears would spill out, so she lay still again. Not till his breathing was quiet once more did she start edging over, an inch at a time, to her side of the bed. Then, holding herself balanced, as one might handle a bowl of hot soup, she shifted her weight till her feet touched the floor and her body was erect. She crossed the room, one silent padding footstep at a time, nudged the door noiselessly closed behind her, went through the shadowed living room to the kitchen, and closed another door.

Coffee, she thought. She put the percolator on, remembering he'd offered her coffee to start with. But she'd thought that if she drank with him, he wouldn't drink more than she did. Not much more, anyhow...

Well, it worked, she thought, and added: *this time.*

The pot bubbled on the stove; Lisa sat on a stool and cried. No one heard either sound.

After a while she got up and rinsed her face at the sink. She poured her coffee, took it into the living room, and sat restlessly. Got up and went to the bedroom, tiptoed in and got the book from her table.

It was a good thing he hadn't looked to see what she was reading. She had grabbed the first thing at hand when she woke up. She laughed softly, remembering his righteous engineer's horror the first time the subject of ESP came up. Now he could joke about it, mostly... *You better watch out—my girl can read minds. She studies up on it...*

But in the ugly aftermath of the dream, if he had noticed, he would have seized on it furiously.

Well, it had all worked out.

This time.

She opened the book and read, sipping at coffee, till she felt ready to sleep again. Then she went back to bed.

CHAPTER TWO
Thursday, June 23, 1977

New York City—1 P.M. (E.D.S.T.)

He was only ten minutes late. *Pretty good—for me,* he thought ruefully. The image of Doc Bronski came alive again behind his eyes, the pink-cheeked old man listening and nodding while a much younger Phil Kutler talked importantly about his future plans. *Good!* the old doctor said. *Good!* Then at the end, straight-faced: *Good! For you it's right. Only once a day you got to get someplace. The rest of the time, your patients worry about being on time...*

Usually, he made sure to keep it that way; he did not ordinarily go out for lunch. But on Thursdays, one to three was free and—for some reason he had not yet examined—he had been very reluctant to have Lisa come to the office.

Halfway down the block, he saw her in front of the restaurant. She was wearing green, a startling sea-green with a soft full skirt that seemed to float around her legs. She stood alone, very straight, with the dancer's solidity under her slenderness that always took him by surprise. He noticed, too, that in her flat green sandals she somehow had the posture of a woman in high heels; and that she stood without any impatience; and that something about her kept the other people who hurried heedless along the sidewalk, from bumping or brushing her.

She's a good waiter, he thought.

Whatever had held her attention across the street released it. She turned and saw him, took a step forward as he hurried up.

"I'm sorry," he started. "You know how—" He saw her smile start. "You didn't have to wait out here. I had a table reserved."

"I was enjoying it." She glanced across the street. "They're gone now. There were two girls waiting for someone over there—just kids, they looked like—and three boys came down from the loft building next door here and kept watching them. Then one of them went across, and the girls wouldn't talk at first, and I guess they were mad at their dates or whoever they'd been waiting for. Anyhow, they got together, and—" She laughed, and took his arm. "—I'll tell you this, you almost lost me. The third boy looked so *lonesome*—"

They sat down and ordered drinks. "I ordered lunch before," he told her. "They make a good *cacciatore* here, but you have to wait if you don't give them notice."

"Fine!" She talked on, still glowing, about the girls across the street and the ragged old man who had tipped his hat to her as he passed: the way the whole city *tingled* on this kind of June day.

She had always loved New York. And she didn't get down much these days. Like a kid, on a holiday, he thought—or more like a kid playing hooky...

"Does Johnny know you're out?" It started light, but by the time the words were on his lips, he had to work at keeping it that way.

She laughed. She had a good laugh, but this time it had lost the spontaneity of the sidewalk. "I'm not...an escaped prisoner," she said. "Johnny thinks it's great I'm doing a little work for a change."

A few more minutes of holiday would have been nice, Phil thought irritably. Not *escaped*, no...

She went on, "He just flew me down, and I had a recording date at the Center. That's what made me think of calling you—I knew I'd be in the neighborhood." The waiter set frosted martini glasses in front of them. Lisa lifted her glass and held it toward Phil in a smiling toast. She sipped slowly. "All right, mastermind, you're way ahead of me. No, he does *not* know I'm out—" she set the glass back on the table with care—"with *you*."

Abruptly, the cloak of detached relaxation that had enveloped her, held her apart from the sidewalk crowd, fell from her shoulders. It was, perversely, like watching another woman take off a too-tight dress, sighing out of girdle, stockings, brassiere, into naked comfort. Lisa seemed almost to vent the same sigh of relief as she stripped the practiced, professional, surface of calm from the coiled tense energies inside her.

"In fact, I almost called you to call it off," she said. "After I called yesterday, I realized Johnny wouldn't—Well, I guess I was sort of peeved. He was being silly about this morning. Oh Hell! I don't have to explain it to you." The edge of brightness in her voice was sharp.

Phil leaned back in his chair, his hand twirling the stem of his glass on the cocktail napkin, making wet circles. Across the table, Lisa sat straight on her chair, her lips moving with taut animation, shoulders tensing a little with each new sentence. "You know, when we first started—seeing each other—he used to talk about you all the time: 'Phil said this,' and 'Phil told me that' and 'the way Phil explains it...' It got to where I was actually jealous of you for a while there..." She hesitated.

"Fair enough," he smiled. "I was kind of jealous myself..."

"I bite," she said. "Of whom?"

"'And to which, and with what?'"

This time her laugh was genuine. "Hey, Doc, remember me? I'm not a patient. I'm just your lunch date. The rule book says you have to answer my questions."

"Well, I did. *Both* of you, if you've got to know."

She was embarrassed; he knew why, and let himself enjoy her confusion a moment before he explained:

"First of all, I kicked myself six times around the block for letting *anyone* else walk away with you. And then I noticed this little cloud, see? Absolutely no bigger than a man's hand. You know what it was? *Professional* jealousy. My psychiatrist explained it all to me. I was sore because you could get things out of Johnny that I couldn't." He grinned. "And we *won't* go into anything about my choice of words, either—"

Or anything about why a girl who's as miserably "in love" as you are, should feel sorry for me for being single... "Did you say a recording date?" he went on aloud. "A new show?"

"Well, not exactly a *show.*" She tasted her chicken and nodded approvingly. "They're doing a tape series—Bartok—tri-di. We did the first movement of that percussion and celeste thing this morning."

"A series?"

"Well, I haven't *committed* myself after this one. I didn't know— This chicken is marvelous, Phil."

"Was this the recording or just rehearsal?"

"Recording. I did most of my practice at home. Only had to come down a couple of times."

"Well," he said neutrally, "it'll be good to see a new Trovi tape. You haven't done much recently."

She looked at him with brittle amusement. "That's like saying, 'Johnny took a long trip.' You know damn well I haven't done anything for the last year, almost. Since we moved up there." She stopped, waited, hoping he'd pick it up, give her an opening.

Not yet, he thought with faint annoyance, and fed her a question instead about the morning's work. He ate slowly, watching from under half-lowered lids as she talked just a little too briskly about the session: musicians; dancers; cameramen and their idiocies. The dark shadows under her eyes and strained set of her mouth did not match the bright narrative. She caught his eye, and her talk trailed off.

"Okay," he said. "So you got over being jealous of me. And Johnny does not know you called me. And you're back at work. Maybe. And you haven't been sleeping. So?"

"So—Well—Actually, it was sort of silly, I guess, calling you. I was feeling kind of low, and I—well, Johnny was drinking a lot again and—in spite of what I said before, I guess he didn't like my taking this job too well. He may have to face up to *something* he won't like, soon, though…" she added, half to herself. "Actually, things are much better now. I almost called you up to call it off, and then I thought it would be good to see you again anyhow. I'll probably tell Johnny when I get home." But her face tensed again when she said it. Then she broke into a smile: "Only, I think I might better say I just bumped into you? If your conscience will let you back me up…?"

He nodded. Inside him a slot opened up, and like letters, the thoughts that were not spoken slid safely into a waiting-room of his mind where he could pick them up, open them and spell them out at his leisure.

"Phil, the truth is, he— The way it is now, he *hates* you! He hates so many— Oh, I'm *sorry*, Phil! Does everyone treat you like this? Like a piece of furniture or something? As if *you* had no feelings?"

Not everyone, kid. Just my patients. "If I'm lucky they do," he said, laughing. "That's how you can tell your friends from a psychiatrist. Sure, Johnny hates me, Lee. He's got reasons. How would you feel about a doctor who told you what was wrong with you, and then wouldn't cure you?"

"Wouldn't? Oh. I guess he does feel that way."

"I'm not sure he's wrong, Lee. I've been over that file fifty times in the last year if I've looked at it once. And I still don't know why it fizzled. Which makes it pretty sure that the blind spot's in me."

"But nobody else got anywhere at all with it!"

"That's just what I mean. He had some good solid frontline defenses. I got through. Period. Then I got lost somehow. I'm the guy who's peddling road maps, see? And I didn't have one for him. So he found his own way out. Period and exclamation point." He ate a forkful of high-priced sawdust, and added, "Also crazy-mixed-up metaphors. But you dig me, kid."

Only you don't, he realized with an unanticipated pang of dismay. *You used to, but now you don't. Lee, honey, can't you think anything any more but Johnny Wendt? Or see, or hear, or feel.*

Ah, cut the crap, Kutler! he told himself. Of course she couldn't. Wouldn't. Shouldn't. He knew that beforehand. He had it all planned for them. *What the hell, Doc? You wrote the prescription yourself!*

So open up. Take the nice medicine.

Mexcity—12 M. (C.S.T.)

It was not excessively hot, for late June in Mexcity. But four blocks, from the air-conditioned Government office to the cool stone walled interior of the club left Chris sweat-sodden and near exhaustion. He was a big man, with a powerful frame, who tended to run to flesh. He was conscientious about exercise; he had to be, more than most of them. They came up, mostly, for six months, a year— maybe six years. He had gone up with the first crew to work on the Dome; he had every intention of dying there—or farther out.

But meantime, he thought (as he thought every time he came down) he ought to come Earthside more often; his muscles were in good condition, and the regular centrifuge workout topside kept the giant gravity down here from overcoming him. But his heart pumped too hard; his blood rushed too much; and the unfiltered air out of doors clogged his nostrils; the sun bursting out from behind clouds seared his eyeballs; clouds hiding the sun obscured his vision. It was always too bright or too dim, too damp or too dry, too cold or too hot, when you were used to Dome-regulated atmosphere.

Today, it was—for him—steaming hot.

And, when he entered the cool lobby of the club, it was clammy cold.

He went up to his room, switched on the air conditioning and lay down. After a while his heart stopped thumping, and the sweat on his neck and back dried. He got up, peeled off the sticky clothes, called down for ice cubes. A tall drink and a quick shower, and it was twelve-thirty. He might still catch Harbridge for lunch.

The General was out, the Decagon switchboard said. He should be back by two.

Chris left his name. "Please have him call me as soon as he gets back," he said.

It was a relief, in a way. He ordered lunch sent up, and ate in comfort in the room, without having to venture out into the street again. As he ate, he pulled out his notebook and pencil, and started figuring. A small smile settled on his mouth, while his second cup of coffee cooled in the pot. His pie sat forgotten on the back of the tray. Names and figures and layouts and lists of equipment filled page after page, as Dr. Christensen practiced the day-to-day magic of modern science: fitting five pet projects into the money allotted for one.

Twice, he stopped to make calls out: the first to New York, the second to St. Thomas.

He was smiling grimly over a column of figures when they buzzed back, and he reached for it unthinkingly. He had already flicked the switch when he thought of his rumpled shirtsleeves, and the messy lunch tray still in view. Too late...

It wasn't Harbridge anyhow; it was Kutler, from New York.

"Phil, for krissake! How've you been?"

"Mostly good. I got a message here to call you back—what brings you down to Earth? I thought you took vows up there?"

"Damn near." He laughed. "Only thing I come down for is begging trips. Say, what's the chances of getting together while I'm here? I've got a couple of ideas I'd like to toss around with you."

"What's on your mind?"

"Couple of things. I'll tell you, I'd just as well not do it on the phone. Any chance of getting you down here?"

The other man hesitated, looked down at something on his desk. "Over the weekend, I guess," he said. "What's your schedule?"

Chris shook his head. "I have to be at the base tomorrow afternoon." But there was nothing really to keep him in Mexcity till then. He didn't mind traveling: flying was more comfortable lot of ways than sitting still, and he had enough vanity left to relish his VIP's privilege of a seat on the Mexcity-New York mail rocket—thirty-two minutes, pad to cradle. "Suppose I make it up your way?" he suggested. "Could we get together for a couple of hours? Tonight, maybe? Or tomorrow?"

"Tonight would be better," Kutler said. "I don't see where I could squeeze anything in at all during the day. Look—can you give me any idea what's on your mind?"

"Well, this much at least: I need a psycher to do a job for us. It's a big job. And I think you might be the right guy. There's nothing secret about it, really, but it just happens to be tied up sideways with a Security problem, so—that's all I can say on the phone."

"I see." He was thoughtful. "Then it has nothing to do with—our mutual friend?"

"Friend? Oh—Johnny? No."

"Have you been in touch with him lately?"

"No. What's up?" He asked it casually enough, but in the time it took to say the three words, a whole new set of possibilities and probabilities opened up. The whole wild plan with Harbridge could be thrown out...maybe even the lab transfer bit wouldn't matter...though that was going to be necessary anyhow...unless, of course, Kutler—or somebody—*could* solve the leave problem...

Slice it any way you liked, if Wendt was about to come out of his funk, the whole picture changed—for the dam-sight better.

"I don't know exactly," the doctor said. "I was sort of hoping when I got your message that *you'd* heard something. I just had lunch with Lisa—"

"Lisa?"

"Trovi. The dancer. You know she and Johnny are—engaged?"

"Oh. Yeah. I knew about it. Didn't know her name." He dug back in memory. "I thought they were married by now."

"Sort of." Kutler smiled.

"Oh. Well, *you're* in touch then?"

"Not really. I had lunch with Lisa, but that's the first I've seen either of them in six months. You know Johnny quit on the therapy? He wouldn't consider analysis, and we'd about had it with anything else."

"Oh. Well how does it look now?"

"Offhand, bad. But I don't know. I know Lee pretty well. She used to work with me, you know? Dance and music stuff with a clinic group I had for a while? She—well, just say, she's not the panic type; but she was pretty shook today. I figured things were just getting worse. Then I got back and found your message, and thought maybe you'd heard from him, and that got me wondering if whatever's up with them could be just—call it *crisis*. You follow?"

"Yeah." *All the way. In fact, I'm way out front.* And better slow down, too. It could be nothing. But it could be—"

He did not let himself pursue it further.

"...any chance of your seeing them while you're down? I know you're busy as hell, Chris, but I can't go myself; I'm the last one he'd talk to right now. And I don't know who else would even know what the difference was, if anything's happened at all—one way or the other. Lee's a good kid, but I can't rely altogether on what she says. You're not in love with the guy." He paused, and added: "This is pure hunch, Chris. I haven't got fact one to go on, but I've got a feeling, that's all. I think maybe this is the time that you could get through to him."

"Through, how?" he asked cautiously. Prayers don't get answered like that, on the phone.

"I wish I knew. I don't. I couldn't tell you where or what or how or even who. I just think that something's about to bust there. Could be just her, and you'd be wasting your time. But—I think it's a good time for you to see Johnny. If you still want him back that is?"

"Yeah. We could use him." *Want him? Jeeeeesus!* "Okay, I'll tell you what. I'll try calling him. See what happens." He thought quickly. "Suppose I get hold of him and call you back? See how his time stacks up—if he'll see me at all. Then you and I can work out some time to get together."

"Good. I'll juggle my time if I have to, for this."

"Right."

After he switched off, he sat and thought for a while. Then he moved the tray, combed his hair, got his jacket back on, and tried Jed again. He got through this time.

"Say, don't you get any phone messages there?" he demanded.

"Sure, but I never get to make any calls. There's always one coming in."

The general and the scientist grinned at each other.

"I take it you made out?" Harbridge said.

"*I* didn't. You did," Chris told him. "They were all ready to let me out the back door with a pat on the head and a promise of a box of old clothes for my little Mars-bugs as soon as they had some to spare. But lab facilities down here for Earth-normal environment studies? Sorry! So...I told them, very sincerely, that I thought perhaps General Harbridge could be persuaded to handle the Earthside part of the project—and we sat down and talked."

Jed looked very innocent. "You know," he said, "sometimes I wonder what we ever did to make them so—*touchy* over there?"

"It's a long story," Chris said, and then, soberly: "Look, I still got troubles. It worked out about the way we figured some personnel money, and maybe a bit for supplies. Okay, we can run some good studies on the bugs down here, which we need to, but they won't even consider transferring the whole lab setup down till the September report. After elections, that means. It was a stone wall, Jed. We're already shut out."

"Not *quite,*" Harbridge said. "But—" He didn't have to finish it; they'd been all over the ground the night before. "Well?" he said finally. "What do you think? You want to try it the hard way?"

"I don't know, Jed," Chris said slowly. "It looked good last night, but— Let's say, if it looks necessary, a month from now would be soon enough. Don't you think?"

"Better," the General said. "Silly season."

"Yeah. Okay. Hell, I hope we don't have to— I've got a new line to try, anyhow."

"Something good?"

"I don't know. Phil Kutler just called me. You know—the psycher? I was telling you about him last night?"

Jed nodded.

"He's been following up on Johnny Wendt. Thought I ought to see him, about now." He saw Harbridge's wary glint. "If there's anything to it..." he said prayerfully.

"Well, if you get Wendt, you won't need—" He broke off again.

"What I was thinking—I'm going to call Johnny now. If I get anywhere, I'll let you know." He smiled. "Or if I don't. Either way, I'll talk to you tomorrow before I take off."

"Right. Good luck, Chris."

"Thanks."

He made several rapid calls, checking on the routine of the trip. Then he built himself one more tall drink and switched on the phone.

"I want Rockland, New York," he told the operator. "The residence of Colonel John Wendt. I don't know the number. It's person to person for Colonel Wendt..."

Rockland—4 P.M. (E.D.S.T.)

The phone chime couldn't compete with Beethoven. He didn't even hear it till it rang once in an interval. Then he tried not to hear it. But when the music began again, he was listening for it, and at the next chime he got up and went inside, turned the volume down and switched the phone onto audio only.

"Yes?" *Lisa!* She was never this late...

"Colonel Wendt? Hold the line for Mexcity, please."

Mexcity? Not Lisa, anyhow. *Colonel* Wendt? Who the hell—? What did Mexcity want with him anyhow, at this late date?

"Colonel Wendt?" The voice was familiar.

"Yes?"

"Johnny—hi! This is Chris."

"I'll be damned! I thought you were away up there."

"Was. Will be. Tomorrow. Don't you ever answer your phone? I've been trying to get you for the last half hour."

"What's on your mind?"

A moment's silence, after which Christensen's voice came through just a bit too loud and too jovial: "At the moment: dinner. What are you people doing tonight? I thought maybe I could talk you into coming down to New York for the evening. I'm planning to hop the mail rocket there right away."

"Anything in particular, Chris?" *You're not calling me just for love, ole bud!*

"Several things." The voice was more normal.

Okay. Backslapping gambit rejected. "How about tomorrow?" Johnny said. "I'm not sure I could, but—?" He let it dangle.

"I can't tomorrow. Got to be in Denver by three."

"Hate to miss seeing you," Johnny said evenly. "Next time around, maybe?" *Yeah, next century.* Perversely, he reached out and switched on the video. After all, it wasn't Chris' fault. He'd been pretty decent, all round.

"My God, you look comfortable!" Christensen said. "It's miserable here!"

So go back up where you belong... "Yeah," he said. "Hate to go into town myself." The perverse impulse swept him again. "Listen, why don't you come up here instead? Why don't you eat with us? You know Lee, don't you?" *No, you don't.*

"Only from watching her. Matter of fact, I'd like to. If you really mean it?"

"Right. You can pick up a heli in New York, fly right in here. Just north of Nyack. Our strip is number seventeen. You can't miss it."

"Okay. If I have any trouble getting on the rocket, I'll call you back. Otherwise—let's see—I guess I should make it about seven?"

"We won't eat till eight, probably."

"I'll see you."

"Right."

He switched off, and snapped off the player angrily. Well, it was his home and his dinner, after all. He didn't have to listen to anything he didn't want to.

And where in Hell was Lisa?

After four, now.

He went outside and got the coffee cup from the grass. Took it in to the kitchen and poured it down the sink. Scrubbed the cup by hand, and filled it up again, with just coffee. Got out another tape, a new piano boogie revival and started the player again—loud.

He went into the workroom and sat down at the drafting board, with its half-finished sketch. Lisa would be in any minute now. He got up and opened the door from the kitchen. Make her feel good to find him working...

He stared at the sketch, trying to feel like a man who was working. Then something hit him—the ghost of an idea. Or the memory of one? There was a picture in back of his mind of what the sketch *should* be.

The memory was of a time when the pictures were always there, waiting, ready to go onto paper, into wire and contacts and complex machines.

This picture was not shiny-new, the way they used to be. This was remembered, a legacy from himself. But it was sharp and clear. It was good design. It would work.

He ripped the old sheet off the drawing board, pinned on a fresh one, and started sketching.

The coffee got cold between sips. The boogie tape came to an end, and began playing over. After a while, the kitchen door closed, or almost did. He looked up. Lee was home. Going to start supper, he thought, didn't want to disturb him.

Hah! That's a good one! He looked at the drawing. What the hell had he been trying to do? *What for?*

But he felt good.

He went out and watched her move, wifely, around the room. When she came within reach, he grabbed her and pulled her down on his lap. Laughing, she told him about the morning session, about the pickup she'd watched on Sixty-third Street, the weird redhead salesgirl at Best's that afternoon.

Something nagged at his mind; then he remembered. It wouldn't be one of their good nights at home after all.

"Oh, I should have told you before, I guess. Pete Christensen called. You know, Moon Lab guy? He's coming for dinner—?"

"*Dinner?*" she pushed away, and stood up. "What *time?*"

"Seven-ish." He looked at the clock. It was almost a quarter of. He grinned. "Well," he said, "I forgot. I'm sorry, babe." Then he pulled her back on his lap, and kissed her.

Rockland—9 P.M. (E.D.S.T.)

"I heard about this place," the big blond man said slowly. "But I don't think I really believed it before."

I like him, she thought. And he *really* liked the house. Lisa piled the last of the dinner dishes into the conveyer, and followed Christensen's gaze out across the patio to the pink and purple glory of the fading sun reflected in the river far below. She hadn't seen any of it this way for a while. The house, the river, the sheer brown cliff on the other side that was the twin of the one on which their house stood. The food, the furniture, the porch on which they sat. All this, through the stranger's eyes, re-acquired meaning.

Christensen was saying something, a question, about the conveyer. Lisa opened her mouth, but Johnny was answering him. Well, that was something; at least he could still talk about his own bright ideas.

The flashing hostility of the thought shocked her. *I'm over-anxious,* she told herself. She was being foolish about the whole thing. He just didn't want company. He'd been working, and he didn't want to be interrupted, that's all.

Just the same, she was glad Chris was there. If they were alone, no matter how much his mind was on what he was doing, sooner or later Johnny would have looked at her sharply, questioning. *Where'd you go, babe? What took you so long?*

Sooner or later, she thought again. He still would ask: tonight or tomorrow, or next year. Sooner or later...

I won't think about it. I won't worry.

It had been easy enough not to mention Phil before. She had just talked all around it. The sense of shock returned as she realized that was why she'd gone shopping, why she had stayed so late. Luncheon was incidental to him by this time; it was the afternoon that bothered him.

I won't think about it! She sat back in the chair, half-listening to Johnny's explanation, and concentrated on visualizing what was happening behind the conveyer door. Soundless, sterile processing of dirty dishes: along the perforated belt where floods of hot water rinsed the food particles down the drain into the grinder; then into the washer, where detergent foamed around them; then out again along the belt, through the rinsing spouts and the drying jets, and at last through the side opening of the long shelf in the kitchen, still neatly racked, ready to use.

Lucky Lisa. *Lucky, lucky Lisa.* Nothing to do. The dinner cooks itself, cleans up after itself. *Next week we put in the automatic digester. Then there'll be nothing left for Lisa to have to do except sit and stew about Johnny. And Lisa.*

She stood up. "The view is really better from the living room this time of day," she said. *The girl speaks her lines well,* she thought idiotically, and watched the characters move to the new set, rearranging themselves with just the sort of almost-right staging that was inevitable without a really *good* director.

The Successful Scientist said something to the Ex-Rocket Jockey. Ex-Rocket Jockey replied, rather shortly.

Both look at Girl. S S smiles successfully. E-R J smiles X-ly. *(Crookedly? I suppose)*

Girl: (Smiling girl-ly) "Mmmmmm? I was daydreaming."

S S: "Just looking at your book here. I used to be fascinated with this stuff myself, but I haven't done any serious reading outside the job since—I don't know when."

E-R J: (Points to Book) *"Serious?* You too, Chris? Well, I'll be damned!"

S S: (Embarrassed, but genial) "Oh, I don't know. If you'd brought back a couple of telepaths, now, instead of just bugs, we might have got somewhere."

Oh, God! she thought. *Oh my dear God!* That did it. *Okay, here goes nothing!*

"It is fascinating," Lisa said slowly. "They've done a lot of work on it the last three or four years, you know."

Chris shook his head. "I didn't know. Anything really new?"

"This fellow—what's his name?—Potter," she went on, as Chris held the book jacket up to the light. "He has a theory that all the different kinds of psi powers that have been proved to exist so far—"

She offered the bait consciously, deliberately.

"—all boil down to some form of PK…"

"Proved to exist?" Johnny asked coldly, taking the bait.

"All right, *demonstrated?"*

"Not to *me."* He took the hook too.

"Well, they've run enough experiments to show at least—all right, to *indicate—"*

It wasn't hard to do. Easier than if he'd had a chance to sit there reacting to the mention of the trip. Why in hell hadn't she remembered beforehand that Dr. Christensen was the one who'd been in charge of the whole trip? "Moon Lab" just meant some vague kind of research to her. But of course—

If she *had* connected, what good would it have done? It was too late to stop him from coming.

"—to *indicate* that there *are* people who are—well, *sensitive—"*

What was the book doing out there anyhow? She'd left it in the bedroom.

"—and others who can control—All right, who *seem* to be able to control—"

She saw his smile loosen up a little bit, and found she could breathe again without thinking about it.

"—to control the motion of inanimate objects—"

Damn! She'd done it herself. She'd left it—No she hadn't. She'd left it in the *kitchen.* Johnny must have picked it up during the day… Then he'd been reading it himself?

"—'non-physical' isn't the right word," she said, still floundering half-deliberately. "That would put the whole thing right back on a mystical plane."

"Which is a fine place for it." Johnny stood up. "Your glass is empty, Chris. *Lee?* You ready?" She shook her head. He went out to the kitchen with the two empty glasses.

"You worked yourself into a hole," Chris said, laughing, not knowing what had happened, or what had almost happened—maybe—either.

"Back up about ten sentences, will you?" he asked. "You started to say something about Potter's theory?"

"Well, I haven't finished the book," she said. "Actually, I just got started on it last night. I wouldn't want to try to explain it." Her smile looked less nervous than it felt, she hoped. "Do you get down often?" she asked, stalling until she could come up with something better. If they could get onto something safe before he came back...

"Not often enough, I'm beginning to think." She liked the way he smiled: he *meant* it. And he meant what he said. All the time. "You said something before about 'PK,' and I've been trying to remember—"

Oh, no-o-o-o!

"...I told you, it's been years since I followed the literature on this. PK is teleportation, isn't it? Stuff like that?"

All right, she thought recklessly, *the hell with it!* Let Johnny have all the fits he wanted to. This man was really interested: he *meant* it. And she liked him. And liked talking to him.

"Psychokinesis is what it actually stands for," she said. "That's control of physical objects—Well, actually, any psi activity that involves application of energy, rather than just perception." Damn if she was going to keep floundering, either. She wasn't setting up straw houses now. "And Potter's approach basically is that perception involves an energy transfer, too. Light rays have to strike the eye, or sound waves hit your ear, before you see or hear. Even internally, the message goes to the brain through a series of impulses that he claims work like a radio condenser. I mean, he says the nerves don't actually *touch*, but energy stores up in one end until it sort of sparks to the end of the next one. So—wait a minute, let me find it here."

She reached for the book. He had been studying the back jacket. "This man, Potter, is a neurologist," he said thoughtfully. "Got interested in this stuff from working on neural exchange process. You know, that's goddam interesting. Say, Johnny, this is right up your alley, you know? Thanks." He took the full glass. "I never thought of it that way before, but if anyone ever does crack this nut, I'll bet it's a cybe man who does it!"

"Wouldn't surprise me," Johnny said drily. "Some of the squirrel tracks they're following now are no nuttier."

The silence did not really last long. Christensen said mildly, "Which set of tracks did you have in mind, John? Cybernetics or parapsychology?"

"Take your pick. I was thinking of some of the commercialized, excuse the expression, *robots*. But if you want to drag para- or any other kind of psychology into it, that's okay with me."

The X-smile again, Lisa noted. *I ought to do something.* This could get out of hand with no trouble at all. Everything she could think of seemed too absurd. It was quite evident that neither of them wanted coffee. Or music, or cards, or a look at the Moon.

What the hell am I doing here? He knew the answer to that one, too well: there were dozens—or hundreds?—of men who could handle the job he wanted Wendt for. Handle it better than John could, from the looks of things. But none of them were named *Johnny Wendt: Space Hero.*

And he, Peter Christensen, didn't *owe* anything to them, either.

Oh, crap. You don't need a new conscience, chum. You just need headlines. Go fetch!

Then he saw that the glass in the other man's hand was empty again.

Already? Things were worse than he'd thought...

"Hey, Johnny, wait up!" He drained the glass, and decided he'd been moralizing too damn much. If he didn't have to fly back tonight, he wouldn't mind tying one on himself. He followed his host to the kitchen.

"What are you working on, now?" He asked, then chuckled. "Or have you got an idea-conveyor-and-processor to do your designing jobs too?"

The answering grin was almost like a guy he used to know named Johnny Wendt. "Not yet. Matter of fact, I got into something today that's been half on my mind all evening. I keep forgetting to be sociable. We don't have much company here, you know..." He trailed off, and eyed his drink. Then abruptly: "Got nine-tenths of something on the drawing board," he said, "if you want a look?"

"Sure. I'd like to."

He turned to follow and saw Lisa, halfway through the door, stop herself fluidly in midstride, and melt back into the living room.

Smart girl, he thought. He stepped into the study.

It was a good room, well designed, like the rest of the house, arranged for comfort and use as well as looks. And it was Johnny's room, beyond a doubt. If he'd been brought here blindfolded, Chris thought, he'd have known this room belonged to John Wendt. But there was also something that *didn't* fit: something you couldn't quite put your finger on. It bothered him.

He started for the drawing board but Johnny waved him to the couch instead. "Nothing worth looking at," he said. "Not yet, anyhow."

Chris sat down obediently. Anything he said was going to be the wrong thing. Let Wendt keep the ball.

After a while, Johnny said, "Okay, let's get it over with. *What* didn't you want to talk about on the phone?"

"I don't know if you'd be interested," Chris said slowly. "I just finagled some dough for an increase in personnel. There's a job I thought you might do for us, but..." He waved a hand to include not just the room, but the house and the river, and the life it stood for. "Why should you?" he finished.

"Yeah. Why should I?"

More silence. Chris looked around still trying to pin down the elusive wrongness of that room.

Then he got it.

There was a gilded football on a shelf from Johnny's college days. There were old books, and a couple of photographs: on the wall that couldn't have any meaning except in one person's memories. There were new things, too. But there was nothing, nothing at all, in this room, or anywhere in the house, to remind Johnny Wendt or anyone else that the man who lived here had spent most of five years of his life off of Earth: on the Moon, on Mars, inside the *Colombo*.

Involuntarily, Chris shivered, as a child shivers in the ghost-filled dark. He stood up, feeling tired. He had to get up early tomorrow morning. He ought to be leaving.

"Okay, so you changed your mind," Johnny said. "What were you...? A—ah, never mind. Skip it." He picked up his glass. It was empty again. He stared at it, then put it carefully down, still empty. "I'm sorry, Chris," he said suddenly. "I'm being damn rude. I get— jumpy. Sit down for krissake, and tell me what's on your mind. You came all the way up here to see me. I can at least listen to what you want."

"Okay," Chris said. "But do me a favor?"

"What?"

"Get the jug." He caught Wendt's eye and held it. "Then we can *both* settle down. All right?"

It was close. Johnny wavered, then grinned crookedly and went for the bottle. *All right.* There wouldn't have been much sense even in trying to talk if Wendt was lushing so bad he couldn't admit it. *All right*, Chris thought: *Here goes nothin'...*

He talked steadily for half an hour. Wendt sat and listened, arms folded across his chest, legs crossed, lips pressed in, his whole face narrowed and closed. When he spoke at all, it was in monosyllables. More likely, he would just grunt a reply to a question. But he listened.

"Damn place has turned into a bio lab," Chris said.

Johnny shrugged, didn't smile. The man was a guest in his home; he'd been childish enough already.

"Those damn bugs you brought back..."

Johnny lifted his glass to his mouth, barely sipped, put it down. *So I brought 'em back. All right. We've made that point now. Let's drop it, hey, boy?* He folded his arms across his chest, sat listening.

"Look, before I get into this any more—this is so new, some of it, I mean, it hasn't even been classified yet. But they'll probably top-secret it out of habit. For that matter, it might be pretty big. If you'd rather not hear—?"

"It's okay with me," Johnny said. "Who the hell would *I* talk to?" And cursed himself for an idiot. There went the last chance to get out from under the whole damn fool thing gracefully. *Well*, he thought, *maybe I like to suffer...*or maybe it was time to find out how bad it was to sit through this kind of crap. Some day it had to get to where it just didn't make any difference. It wasn't *his* ball game now. He was off the team. He was too old for it. If the kids still wanted to play, why should it matter to him if they babbled about it?

About time, he decided, approvingly, biting his fingers into his biceps across his chest.

"Okay. Well, you remember those freak results on the first chromosome charts?"

He nodded. Doug had—*Hell with that bit!* Listen to the man...

"Well it got even freakier when we got some good clear micropics and tried it again. Turns out all seven varieties had the *same damn charts*—let alone the same crazy number of genes."

"Yeah?" This time he allowed himself a small smile. It was getting just too damn silly. He knew where the damn bugs came from, and what they did, and they were no more related than—

The Hell with it! Nobody's asking you anything. Just listen, that's all you have to do—listen!

After that he managed to sip and hear, hear and sip, and not think at all, mostly.

"...maybe different parts of a cycle, or even mutated species of the same bug? And we had just about decided we were dead wrong, when this crazy new thing comes up—

"Understand, now, we had these things under twenty-four hour-a-day observation, cameras on the microscopes around the clock, and not a damn one of 'em ever did anything except make more of the same. No meiosis, no conjugation, nothing to account for the diploid chart or make any use of it. No mutations—but, *none*, see? That's about the only thing that kept anybody interested.

"We figured at first maybe the lab is *too* clean. So we x-rayed a few batches, and *still* no mutations. Then some bright lad pops up with figures showing that the increase in cell *deaths* under radiation corresponded to what you'd expect statistically for total of deaths plus mutations in protozoa down here. So these damn things would rather die than change—they're just not *capable* of adaptation. It says here.

"We had a couple of bio men around who thought this was the most fascinating thing since the original rib job, and I was kind of tickled at the idea of getting whatever those cells were using to resist radiations with—or I was until those statistics popped up to show it wasn't resistance, it was just complete lack of flexibility.

"So one of the bio boys gets the bright notion of trying a culture in Earth-normal atmosphere. I think he was chasing some notion about mutations being a complex result of radiations and some elements in the atmosphere. And the first reaction looked like high score for him, because the damn bugs went wild. Not one friggin' one of them stayed the way it was. *Every single one* changed at least slightly.

"So they started all over again, and when we ran off the first rolls of film, we found out we were not only getting meiosis and conjugation, but getting it between what were supposed to be different species—which was what we'd figured all along. The only thing we *weren't* getting was mutation!

"Johnny, every damn one of those changes could be charted on the maps! And every damn one of 'em came out the way they were supposed to. Some of 'em were wild but not wild, crazy—just wild, way-out. You'd get a bacterium conjugating with an alga—or what we had figured for bacteria and algae, and the one of the products mixing with one of the water-retentive fungi, maybe, while the other one went into symbiosis with an unchanged alga and wound up like a new lichen—oh, some of those things mixed and matched seven or eight times around before they were done. But it all settled down into a group of five different types perfectly adapted to the environment they were in, and just as viable in it as they'd been on Mars."

It seemed to be time to say something again. Chris looked like it was time for an answer. It was damn sure time to wrap the whole thing up.

"So?" he said. "What's the scoop?"

"I've just told you essentially all we know so far. What I came down for this trip was to dig up some extra dough fox a big program on it. Frankly, I'd hoped I could get all or most of it transferred to Earthside Labs. I think I'll be able to get that come fall. Right now, it's all upstairs, and if you feel the same way you did, I guess there's no point in asking—but let's put it this way: I have a hunch our best approach to this will be with the math and, if we can do it, with analogs. I don't think straight bio experimentation will ever crack this—unless we can set up the labs on Mars."

All right, man, all right, get to it, will you? The answer is No!

"So the first thing I need is a hell of a good cybe man, and you—"

"Lots of good cybe men around," Johnny broke in evenly.

"Yeah. You realize, that part could just as easily be done down here? Christ, no reason you couldn't work at home—don't blame you not wanting to swap a setup like this for—"

"Ready for a refill?" Johnny asked. "Wish I could help you out, Chris, but I tell you, I've got my hands full right now. I—"

Chris *was* eyeing the bottle and glass in his hands. *Why so eager, son? I thought I was the lush...?* Then he got it. His hand tightened on the bottleneck as he poured...*I've got my hands full,* he'd said.

"Yeah," he said out loud. He handed the glass back, and poured himself one. "Yeah. Well—luck."

"...*really* a pleasure. It's a lovely place..."

Too smooth, too polite. Whatever he came for, he didn't find, Lisa thought. She was sorry.

"Too lovely, maybe," she said suddenly. "I think sometimes we forget we're still part of the human race."

Shock raced around the room, bouncing off each of them to boomerang on the others.

Johnny's grin was a social grimace. "Her trouble is just not having things tough enough," he said. "When we were still putting the place together, she didn't have a gripe in her. Now I think she'd be jealous of the dishwasher."

Laugh, she told herself. *Go ahead. The man made a funny.* Chris was laughing: a polite laugh, too. Surely she ought to do as much.

"Frankly, I think it would get me that way," Chris said. "You know, this is the only place I've ever been on Earth that has all the comforts of home. And right now, I'd give anything to have, say, a week, with nothing to do in a joint like this— Just lie around in the sun and listen to music and boss the servos around. But I'd bet I'd be half-nuts in three days—" He stopped short. "I'm sorry. I didn't mean..."

"Well, why don't you stick around...?"

"We keep talking about taking a camping..."

They broke in at once, both broke off at once, and for some reason the tension was gone.

"Well, any time you think you can stand a day or two of it," Johnny said, "just give us a couple days' notice..."

It wasn't what you'd call wild enthusiasm; but for Johnny, it was an effusion.

"Thanks," Chris said, and meant it. He *did* understand. "I'll take you up on that one of these days. Right now—Look, how about turning that around? It wouldn't be as uncomfortable as camping out, I'm afraid, but at least it's *different.* Changed a lot since your time, too, Johnny—You ever been up, Lee?"

She shook her head. She could feel the pinkness of her cheeks, and her own quickened breathing. She tried to see Johnny's face, but he moved back a step into the shadow. She couldn't even tell if her own feeling was more excitement or apprehension.

"We'll think it over," Johnny said. "Might be an idea." His tone was completely flat.

"You understand," Chris said. "This has nothing to do with what we discussed? I'm talking about just a visit."

"Carfare's pretty high, isn't it?"

"It's on the company. The boss has *some* privileges."

"Well, we'll think it over." And this time, she thought, he really *meant* it. He *would* think about it.

What did Chris say to him? What did it?

They stood outside together, and watched the heli lift.

Johnny switched off the landing lights, and the Moon jumped out of the background and hung like a lantern right over the patio wall.

Lisa stared up with a new fascination. After a while she became aware of Johnny's eyes watching her, with mixed amusement and tenderness.

She moved closer to him. And broke the spell. "Nice to see Chris," he said abstractedly. "Maybe we ought to take him up on that some time—if you want to, I mean. But I—well, Hell, I wish he'd picked some other time to come. I was only half here tonight. Look, babe, you mind if I sit up some? Got a little work I've been thinking about—design stuff I was working on while you were in town today."

Mind? "Go ahead," she said, and made a face at him. "At least I'll be able to finish that book of mine without giving you bad dreams."

Mind? She watched him till he disappeared through the kitchen door, reading the angularity of his shoulders, the swinging of his hands, the forward thrust of his head, and delighting in what she read. *We should see more people*, she thought. But Chris was special.

She got ready for bed slowly, and lay there a long time, with the book open in front of her, but not really reading. *What a day!* The dance session—Kutler—Christensen—and maybe even a trip to the Moon! And on top of it all, Johnny working again.

After a while, a sentence caught her attention, and she began reading. It was after two when she finished the book, and turned out the light. She fell asleep almost instantly, and dreamed of cute little fat viruses, teaching her telepathy, so that she didn't have to wait for her baby to talk before she could communicate with it.

Her baby...

Dollars Dome—10:30 P.M. (C.S.T.)

Her name was Rita. She stood immobile behind the high counter, head bent in a posture of reverie—almost of prayer—to the microscope eyepiece.

His name was Thad. He was holding two culture plates, which he had just carried up, from the Mars lab. He intended to set the plates down on a rack at the end of room. But when he saw her, he stopped.

Her new lab coat was spotless white, and she had pinned a stiff white square of cloth around her head to cover her hair. The way she stood, only the shoulders and collar of her coat showed; the folds of the headcloth draped so that the coat and cloth framed her face with the suggestion of a robed and cowled young nun.

She was not pretty. But the serenity of her fresh-skinned cheek, emphasized by the furrows of concentration on her brow, gave her so much the look of the eternal virgin that he could not, at first do anything but stand and stare.

He had seen her before, of course: in the cafeteria, several times; on the Mall; at a party the week before; in the projection room, yesterday. It was a month, at least, since she came up. They had been introduced at the party, and again yesterday, watching some films. He could not have seen her less than fifteen-twenty times, altogether. And each time he had noted, without interest, only that she was new, quiet, plain-looking; and of course goggle-eyed and stumble-footed, like all newcomers.

Now he wondered how he could possibly have thought her *plain;* or why, when they met, he had registered only her name, Rita Donovan, and her background—a *summa cum* type from Johns Hopkins. He had not been concerned enough to learn if she were married or single, or otherwise unattached.

It might have been half a minute that he stood watching her. Then he walked on and set his culture plates down. Neither his stillness nor his action penetrated the distant focus of her concentration. He walked around back of her counter, and noticed she had damn good legs, too.

"Something good?" he asked.

She started, and looked up.

"Good?" She laughed. "Every time I see these things—They're just *fantastic!"*

"Right out of this world," he reminded her, smiling.

"Oh, of course." She flushed faintly and her laugh held a note of embarrassment. "I guess I'll get used to it too. Some day. But—"

"Not very damn likely you won't, if you're working up here," he said. "Not at the rate *these* babies are going. We get to where it all seems almost normal, downstairs—every once in a while, that is. Then somebody comes up with something like Hendrickson's idea on controlled evolution, and you know you haven't even scratched the surface yet!"

"Have you seen his films?" she asked eagerly.

"Not the whole thing. I caught part of the run this morning. They're showing 'em again at sixteen hundred." He glanced at the big wall chrono, pleasurably aware that until his eyes moved, the pink lingering in her cheeks had been, in part at least, a (pleased?) response to the way he was looking at her. (Yes, pleased, he was sure, when he looked back.) There was an hour to kill before the showing. "Got anything cooking you have to stick with?" he asked. "We'd have just about time for some coffee before they start."

She looked around carefully, checking. "I guess nothing special..." Her hesitation was not about leaving the lab; he was sure of it.

"I'll help you check out the cameras," he said, and headed for the far end, brushing her arm as he passed. The intensity of joint awareness startled—almost stopped—him. He debated suggesting his room for the coffee: but only an hour...

"Why don't we go up to my place for coffee?" she said. The words broke the bubble of tension surrounding the touch.

He grinned. "I'm with you," he said fervently.

"What's Hendrickson getting at anyhow?" she asked. "I didn't hear him the other night, but the way it looked in the *Abstracts*, he's hypothesizing what amounts to *intelligent* choice when he says 'controlled.' Did you hear his talk?"

"I missed it too. There's so damn much all the time, you never know which one to go to. But I got hold of him last night, and he won't put it that way of course, but it seemed to me that's how it added up."

53

They left the building and went outside into the bright glow of "afternoon sunlight," diffused from the dome-top lights during the lunar night.

"But that means you also have to accept the idea of—I mean, what does the *deciding?*"

"Well, I guess that's why he won't use the word, 'intelligence.' He keeps saying his theory is purely pragmatic—a description of behavior, he says, not an explanation. So you can't pin him down." The most fantastic thing of all, he thought contentedly, more startling even than the stuff you worked on up here were the people you worked *with*. She had taken off the white kerchief, and out in the "sunlight," her hair shone a rich reddish brown and her face glowed with something quite other than the austere intensity in the lab.

They entered the dorm building, and she started up the stairs. "Wait a minute!" he said. "Anyone showed you the *right* way to go upstairs here yet?"

She laughed. "You mean 'giant steps'?"

"Yup. Race?"

"You're on." They both knelt to remove their shoes. "Three flights," she said, and they set off together, bounding up four, five, six steps at a time under the light gravity of the Moon.

Rockland—2 A.M. (E.D.S.T.)

Across the patio, a glow of light from the opaqued bedroom wall showed him Lisa was still up. He thought about that, and decided against it. Too much of that. Too much liquor; too much Lisa. Too much mash, too much mush. Half the drink was still in the glass. He stepped outside, and slowly, carefully, quietly, let it trickle over the edge of the tilted glass, till it was all gone, back to the soil. *Asses to ashes and alcohol to earth.* He lit a cigarette, and looked up again at the looming deceitful lure of the Moon. He wasn't going there. He wasn't going. *Anywhere.* He'd done all his going. And all his coming. Yeah. Too much.

He looked at the drawing board. The design that had seemed so good, so right in the afternoon now looked dead and clumsy. Hell with it. Hell with—Damn him! *Damn him!* Coming in here with his talk and his problems and his five-year-old daydreams, throwing everything out of whack. Tilting the machine… Great big blond baby who didn't know it was too big to be out there. Nice safe little Moon base.

Hell, the Moon was part of Earth, didn't they know that?

Took all the know-how they had to make out even there... And they wanted to go to Mars! All the big babies, like Chris, out of the yard for the first time... Stand on the curb screaming blue murder to get across the street.

Well he'd been across the street. And back. Back for good. If they wouldn't listen to him, that was their tough luck.

What he needed was a drink.

He went back and filled his glass. The bedroom light was out. Good. For once, there was nobody watching, waiting, listening, to see what he'd do. Nobody...? He walked through the living room and pushed the door open, suddenly, silently. She was asleep, sound asleep, sprawled on the bed like a kid. She was smiling a little bit. She was beautiful. He closed the door just as softly, and padded back to his workroom.

Work room! That was a laugh. He laughed. *Haw, haw!* The sound came out, too loud and not funny.

What does Johnny Wendt want with a workroom? Used to work. Don't got to work now.

What for?

Money? Smile once for a whiskey ad. That's money. Science? That was a laugh, too, but he didn't try it this time. Science is a big blond bastard, fixing it for everybody to go the way Doug went.

Which way? Which way did you go, Doug?

Doug, for chrissake, where are you?

Come back, Doug.

Doug, migod! And you stand on the dry dust with your suit all around you to keep you safe in the thin air, and miles away, whichever way you look, is nothing, nothing at all.

Better have another drink. Put the bottle down, now. Careful. Might spill.

CHAPTER THREE
Friday, June 24, 1977

Rockland—8:30 A.M. (E.D.S.T.)

He woke with a twist in his neck and his shoulders and arms stiff and sore. Faint sounds somewhere took on shape and meaning. Lisa, in the kitchen. Breakfast. His stomach turned over, and settled down to hunger.

He'd decided to go to the Moon. *Why?*

Who knows? He shrugged. *What's the difference?*

He'd decided something; that was an accomplishment right there. Yeah, big deal: go see ole buddy Chris and get yapped at some more. Okay, he'd *decided,* hadn't he? Give Lee a kick anyhow.

Lisa Goes To The Moon. He started to laugh, but he coughed and half-choked instead. He was thinking of the magazines when he was a kid. Too bad Lisa couldn't wear one of those bubble-type outfits the girls on the magazine covers had. That would go over big, in the Dome! He could just see them, Chris's crew of tame scientists, goggle-eyed.

Spent two damn years up there and never saw a babe worth looking at. *All* goggle-eyed.

This time the laugh almost came out right.

If it was a magazine story, though, Chris's little Mars-bugs would turn out to be secret-super-intelligences with invincible powers, from Betelgeuse.

Or Arcturus.

That would be nice, he thought. Let it turn out poor old Doug was just a rabbit mesmerized by these snakey protozoan *intelligences.* Pretty soon they'd take the whole world over, too—except for The Hero, who'd dash in and save everyone just in time.

Singing: "I'll be glad when you're dead, you amoeba, you."

Lee was making breakfast. He wasn't ready to see her yet.

He found the coffee jar, and made himself some, boiling scalding hot, turned the outside wall to full light and transparency, and propped himself on the couch with the hot coffee and the hot sun shining on him.

When he was ready to go out to the kitchen, he found her just finishing her breakfast, wearing yellow shorts, *very* short, and a bright purple halter top, looking about sixteen years old.

"Hi, hon." Grinning made his face feel cracked and a million years old. "How come you look like that when I feel like this? I worked late," he said. "Lay down to think something out, and I fell asleep."

"Sure," she said.

He looked straight in her eyes for a moment, and remembered she wasn't really a kid. She was two months older than he was. He hated her for knowing what he wouldn't tell; and blessed her for not trying to make him say it. He sat down and patted her hand.

"Hey, babe?"

"Hmmmm?"

"I seem to have made a decision."

"Yes?" But there was something scared in her eyes.

"I have some recollection of deciding last night that we would go to the Moon."

She surprised him. Last night, he was sure she was all hopped up about it. And even now, the scared look left her eyes. *Scared? Why? What of?* She looked pleased, all right. But she didn't say a word.

"That is, if you still want to go," he said stiffly.

"I—well, yes, but—Let me think about it a little. All right?"

"Sure." He stood up and went and looked in the warmer. Bacon and toast. *You goddam lucky bastard,* he thought, *You're so used to her doing things your way, you think you have to get sore if she doesn't climb all over you and yell Hallelujah!*

He made a sandwich out of the bacon and toast, and went back to the table.

"Whatever you want, baby," he said softly.

New York City—6:15 P.M. (E.D.S.T.)

"Well, I'm sorry," Kutler said. "I guess it was a bum hunch."

"I don't know. You weren't too far off—I don't think. But damn if I knew how to get through. You're sure there's no way you—?"

The doctor shook his head. "I wish I could. I've tried a couple of times. I'll keep on trying. But—" He shrugged, and finished his drink.

Pete Christensen cleared his throat. "What do you say to some dinner? This place serve any food?" *Damn it, the guy actually gives a damn!* You didn't find many like that any more... *Any more...?* Damn fool thought. Never was more than one in a million who did— outside his own yard or his own pocketbook.

"Well, they serve it," Kutler said. "Nobody in his right mind would eat it. Tell you what—there's a place down the street here— You like Swedish cooking?"

"Grew up on it."

The doctor nodded, pleased. "Okay, let's get out of here." He caught a waiter, paid the check, and they walked down Lexington toward the Swedish place, talking trivia about the city and how it changed. It must have been seven-eight years, Chris thought, since he'd seen this part of town; yet some blocks, you could go back twenty years after, and nothing changed at all.

"I used to love this damn town," he said, surprised, because it had been so long since he had even thought about New York, let alone *looked* at it. Kutler was good for him; the man *cared*. It was a little painful even to visualize all the things he seemed to care about. Like a wheel hub, with another spoke reaching out every part-turn. "I guess," he said slowly, "I've put it all into one." And then thought, *That was dumb.* Then: *But he knows what I meant.*

"Rockets only go one way at a time, don't they?" the doctor said.

Chris cleared his throat.

"Here we are," Phil said.

As soon as they'd ordered, Chris plunged in. "Here's what I wanted to see you about, Phil. You know, we've had a personnel problem up there all along that's a little unusual. I suppose you know the background—I'm sure you do, because we fed you this stuff when you worked with Wendt. Our psychogenic troubles?"

"Yeah. Fascinating stuff, too. I figured if you wanted me, it would be something to do with that. But you want a good psychosomaticist, Chris, there are a hell of a lot of 'em better than me. I've always been interested, but it's not really my field."

"I don't need just a good psychosomatics man," Chris said. "We've got the problem under control from the point of view of our people's health. Nothing to it. Every damn contract calls for one month Earth rest leave after each working quarter. Three months up, one down. Keeps 'em healthy as hell. Any good psychosomatics man will tell you that's the only answer, short of an all-out training program that adds up to something like studying yoga, f'krissake!" He dipped into heaven-scented pea soup, and broke crisp bread. "Phil, what I'm after is someone who'll look at it from the point of view of a new environment that men damn well can live in. I do. Have, more than ten years now. Some of the others could, if the contracts let 'em. I don't know how you feel about this. Maybe you'll take the same stand the others do: we're asking for something 'unnatural,' and we have to pay the price. I just had a hunch you might—feel differently."

"Because of Johnny?" the doctor asked quietly.

"All right." Chris let himself look at the other man for the first time since he'd started his speech. "Because of Johnny. But I mean it a couple of ways."

"Relax, will you?" Phil looked as if he could take some of his own advice, too. "Who's kiddin' whom? I know I feel guilty about Johnny. So what difference does it make if you know it too? But that doesn't mean I'm going to throw up a good practice here and go tromping off to Outer Space to offer myself up in his place."

Chris finished the pea soup, looked at the other man, and laughed. "Damn it, I've got to get down more often," he said, and laughed again. "I keep saying that. When I'm down. Now look: first of all, I said it was a *couple* of ways 'because of Johnny.' Sure, that was one of them. The other is, you *did* get somewhere with him. Or come to think of it, that's just one other part of it. You got through to him; nobody else could. That means, the way I see it, you maybe speak our language some? You don't start with the idea that being off of Earth is 'unnatural.' Am I wrong?"

"I don't think so," Kutler said slowly. "Hadn't really looked at it that way. Maybe so— What's the other bit?"

"Obvious. Just that you've had some experience with our kind of nut."

"Oh *now!* Just because two guys have been to the same place, and both come back sick doesn't mean—" He stopped short. Chris grinned. "Yeah. I see what you mean," the doctor went on, slowly. "Nine times out of ten, it does mean just that. Only," he finished, "Johnny didn't get sick on the Moon."

"Well, frankly, I didn't mean it that strongly anyhow. You're way ahead of me, as usual. But—let's just say, if I've got a sick horse, and I can't get a vet—because nobody's invented veterinary medicine yet—

I'm damn well going to try to find a doctor who's at least worked on a horse before."

"Even if it died?"

"He's not dead," Chris said drily. "Far from it. You seen that layout up there?"

"Not since it was finished."

"Well, you've seen the girl."

"Yeah." Kutler looked at him levelly. "I saw her yesterday. He's not dead. Yet."

"He's sick. Okay. You *still* know more about—horses—than a man who's never opened one up." Kutler started to speak, but Chris went on. "At least, *I* think so. So here's what I'd like to ask you to do—"

He opened his briefcase, and pulled out the folder of case histories and medic reports. "Here's the background stuff. If you can find time to look it over, and you think you're willing to consider the idea at all, what I'd like to do is start sending my leave people in to see you. Not for treatment," he said hastily, as the doctor tried to stop him again. "Just interviews, sort of. Get your own histories on them. See what ideas you get. This thing is wide open, Phil. I don't know if what we need is a man on the job up there, or a consultant, or a whole staff and program, or what the hell. I figure you can at least give us a push the right way. Will you hire on as consultant for now on that basis? Then if you think you're not the right man, find us one. Or a dozen. Or tell us what we need. Or tell us you can't even do that. But give it a whirl, will you? I don't know where else to start with."

Kutler hesitated, still. "How much time do you figure I'll need for that 'month'?"

"You decide. Give it what you can. Take what time you need. Bill us at whatever your hourly rates for government jobs are. We're used to cost-plus," he added drily. "Don't stint yourself on the expense account. When you've got a yea or nay or maybe for me, let me hear it."

The doctor was silent a moment, and Chris held his breath, almost. He'd had the right hunch this time. If Kutler took it at all, he just *might* actually crack it—because if he took it, he'd kill himself *trying*.

"I can at least look over the literature," Phil said finally. He grinned. "Which in English means, all right, so you've got me curious. Or hooked?"

Chris passed over the envelope with the folder. He saw Phil's eyebrows go up.

"What's this bit?" He was indicating the red-stamped TOP SECRET.

"Christ, I get to where I don't even see it. Every damn thing we do up there—But on this job, they mean it. Only reason I got funds for anything as—way out?—as this was Security has fits about these people going up and down all the time. Anything to keep 'em up on the farm, the way they see it. Frankly," he added, "that was another reason for wanting you. You're cleared already. God knows how long I'd wait before they found another man they'd put their gold star on."

Acapulco—7:30 P.M. (C.S.T.)

"What do you think?"

Brigadier General Jedro Arthur Harbridge, USA, ASF, turned from the bar cabinet in the study of his country home with an air of some satisfaction. He carried two palest-gold martinis to the desk, handed one ceremoniously to his Press Secretary.

"Hard to say," Prentiss answered. "Thanks. Well—here's luck!" He sipped appreciatively. "Okay, you win. The Dutch gin is better." He picked up the memo he'd been looking at while the General mixed drinks. "I can't see anything in here that will make headlines—that's sure."

"Okay." Harbridge settled down in an anachronistically solid-comfortable leather chair. "What *are* you going to make 'em with, then?"

Al Prentiss shrugged one gray dacron shoulder. "What's the rush?"

You wouldn't understand, boy, if I spelled out every word! This particular rush had started a *long* time ago—for some people. For others, including all or damn-near-all PR men, the General thought, there was no rush: just the crush of the crowd.

"That's my problem," he said heavily. "Now your problem is getting the Dome in the papers, and getting it in good."

Prentiss studied his chief's face, and nodded. "Okay. So let's take it from One. How much of this stuff has been released before?"

Harbridge frowned. "Just the general background. Nothing on the genetic structure at any time. Seems to me, the only thing that went out was a film made up from their lab micros, with a very basic sound-track—you know, the little Mars whachahoosies in their natural habitat?—the symbiosis stuff, or fission or fusion, or whatever these dingusses do instead of screw—that kind of thing. That's about a year ago, I guess, little less. On the other hand, I think the only stuff mentioned here that's been officially classified is the chromosome chart stuff: or anything that was done before June 1, come to think of it, unless it's been released. That was the last full regular report, and *they* get stamped before they're read."

"So I'm stupid," said Prentiss, "but what's such hot news about chromosomes? We all got 'em." He stood up abruptly. "Damn it, sir, you just can't make good copy out of what a bunch of amoebas do for sex—even if they come from Mars." He held the papers fanned out, and looked at them with scorn.

Harbridge took the sheets, and held them in his lap. A slow smile spread on his face. "All right, Al. I'll give you a story to write. Two of 'em. First one is the bugs. Just what's in here, but no details. Leave out the chromosomes: they might not be copy to you, lad, but they're hot, believe me. Now let's see."

He put his drink down, picked up the papers again, and reached for a clipboard and pencil. Then he went through carefully checking and crossing-out.

"Use this, you can quote this bit direct," he said, as Prentiss came around the desk to look over his shoulder. "'...startling adaptation syndrome, which does not conform so much to the concept of mutation as of controlled evolution.' Hey, you know this stuff is pretty jazzy, Al. Come to think of it, we better leave out the last bit— What the hell does he mean, 'controlled' evolution? Who's doin' the damn controlling—? Never mind. Just make it, 'does not conform entirely to the usual concept of mutation.' Leave out all this part about the Earth-normal environment—that's *really* secret. Here, this bit won't hurt anything, '...genetic relationships between species...'and if you just change this about capacity for cross-breeding to something about experiments at cross-breeding—make it sound like Luther Burbank or something—you follow all this?"

"From a distance," Al Prentiss said dourly. "Or maybe through a glass, darkly."

"Okay. Now this chromosome chart bit I guess is pretty touchy too, but there's no reason we can't say something like 'unusual' or 'unanticipated' chromosome count. What do you think?"

"I'd hate to say—*sir*. But if you mean, do I think I can write a story out of this that sounds like telling something without actually anything classified—sure. Just let me run home for my trusty old bio notebook, so I know what I'm talking about, and I'll whip right out— one, two, three."

The General put down the memo, stood up, and laughed. "In your own unpleasant way, Al, you're a good boy. Drink up, you're too slow." He took the empty glasses back to the bar, and immersed himself once more in his elaborate martini ritual.

"I take it," Prentiss said thoughtfully, "that when I get this written, you'd like to see it in print somewhere?"

"Probably."

"I see. Following the same thought, I come up with the notion that you'd want to see it—if you did—in some paper whose publisher does not play golf with you?"

Harbridge nodded solemnly. "Not even the editor," he said.

"Right. I assume then..."

The phone buzzer sounded. Harbridge lost all interest in the bar. He picked up the phone, leaving his inscreen dead. "Hello."

"Jed? Hi. Listen—"

"I've got company," Harbridge said. "I think he'd rather not know who called. What's the word?"

"No dice. I spent five hours and had a lovely time. Nice wife. Or whatever she is. But no dice. Stone cold dead, I'd say. You better take the ball."

"Okay. You know this can get rough?"

"I've got calluses."

"You're on, man." He hung up, wondering just how sure young Prentiss was as to Chris' identity: and whether it mattered.

"In short," said Prentiss smoothly. "I assume that once the thing's planted, we never *heard* of it. Do I dig you, sir?"

"Right where I live," said the General. "And, by the way—I do want to see it in print, for sure."

CHAPTER FOUR
June 28-August 4, 1977

Rockland—Tuesday, June 28

For four days, she'd been waiting for Johnny to leave the house: leave it long enough so she'd *know* she had ten minutes' time all alone.

It was hard to believe it could have gone that far; but when she thought back, it must have been going on quite a while now. Unless they went somewhere together, days—or weeks?—might go by till Johnny found any reason to go even down the road.

They had built the house in the exact center of their own thirty-five acres: no near neighbors to plague them—or to gossip with or play bridge, or borrow lawn-mowers, or any one of the things that might take a man ten minutes' walk to the next house.

The place was provisioned and stocked for every possible need. They marketed once a month—together.

On rare occasions, if the heli needed work Johnny did not want to do, he'd fly down to Nyack; usually, she went along, anyhow, and they'd have dinner out, take in a show, spend an evening pub-crawling, something like that.

But the house had everything that he wanted; most of all, it had *her*. Up till now, that knowledge by itself had been enough to allow her to overlook, not-notice, or never-mind all the rest.

But now, for four days, she had wanted to make one single phone call without him around: and there had never been a time she could be sure he wouldn't wake up, or pick up an extension from some other room, or—or *some*thing.

The whole thing was ridiculous. Most of all, her own feeling about it was all out of proportion. She kept telling herself that.

Just pick up the damn phone and call! He was in the shower; how was he going to hear her from there?

But, again, she jittered around until, just as she reached for the switch, he came out.

Damn!

"Hi, babe." He came over and kissed her. And at the touch, the easy relaxation with which he had entered the room vanished. "What's the matter, babe?" He sat down and put his arms around her; tilted her face up with one hand under her chin.

"Nothing," she said unconvincingly, and tried to smile a response to him. That was not very convincing either. She saw the small muscles in his jaw tighten up, and start knotting. *Oh, Goddamn!* "Probably just—time of month, I guess," she said.

He bought it. He grinned and patted her on the head sympathetically; his face relaxed; he stood up with the confident nonchalance of masculinity, not prey to nervous cyclic emotions, and went into the kitchen. A moment later, he called back: "I'm going out and see what I can do about that door handle." The door slammed.

She saw him cross the back lawn toward the hangar. She watched till he went inside. With her eyes still on the window, she switched on the phone.

"May I speak to the doctor?" she asked the pert nurse who answered.

Dr. Aaronson looked harassed as usual, but his smile was beatific: "Everything's fine," he said. "All down the line. Don't give it a thought. You ought to come in, say, oh, two-three weeks?"

She tried to look as she thought she ought to feel. "That's wonderful," she said. "Look, I've got a problem."

"Hmmm?" His eyes were watching something else off the screen. His manner said clearly: *I already told you, you don't have a problem.*

"It's just—well, is there any reason—" It sounded so *silly*, when you came to ask it. "—reason I shouldn't take a trip to the Moon?"

"How far—" he'd started to ask before she finished. His eyes swiveled back sharply. "Well!" It was the first time she'd ever heard him laugh out loud. "Well!" he said again, satisfied, "I thought I knew *all* the questions by now! Offhand, let's see—I can't see any reason not to, in the shape you're in. When did you plan to go?"

"I'm not sure—two or three weeks? A month, maybe?" He nodded thoughtfully. "Well, I'll check up, but I don't see why not. Stop in for a checkup before you go."

"Thanks. I will. I'm sorry if I interrupted you—"

"Nonsense. It was a pleasure, believe me. I think that's the first new question anyone's asked me in fifteen years."

She switched off and sat there a minute, her eyes at last off the window, her whole self composed for the first time in days.

He found her half-asleep in the sun at the edge of the pool, her orange swimsuit with the tigerish black stripes a splash of color on pale green tiles. She lifted her head and squinted at him from some faraway place inside herself.

"Hi, handsome," she said.

"Hello, babe." He dropped into a chair, looking down at her. She was okay now. She started lifting herself up from the tiles, backbone first, as if someone had tied a rope around her torso, and was pulling her up. He watched, fascinated; incredible, what she could do with herself!

"How's the water?" he asked lazily.

"Good." It looked good too. He went inside for his trunks, and she called after him to switch the player on.

"There's a tape on already," she said. "That new one you got."

The soft beat of African drums was beginning when he came back out. Lisa sprawled in the grass past the pool, and with each beat, she raised herself higher, till as the tempo grew furious and swelled into crashing crescendos she was moving swiftly in a whirling ecstasy of liquid orange flame and streaked black shadow.

It was a long time since she had danced for him this way, he realized abruptly. She danced by herself, or unselfconsciously in front of him, all the time; but this was a performance—planned, staged, presented for his pleasure. He sat back and let the poetry of her pervade all his senses.

When the dance was done, she fell in a huddled heap at his feet, the fingers of one hand outstretched to almost-grasp his toes. She lay so still that he hardly dared breathe, while the memory of sound died.

Then she opened one eye, half-raised her head, grinned, and winked at him.

"Swim?" she said.

"You're on."

As they climbed out of the pool, she asked, casually, as if it was something they'd just stopped talking about, "Still want to go to the Moon?"

"Sure," he said quickly. "Why don't we make it a honeymoon trip?"

He saw the tautness begin in her face, and he had to do something: "Christ!" he said. "What a tin-pan-alley bonanza. Song called 'Do You Want a Moon Honeymoon, Honey?' We'll make a million, babe!"

"Get a good old-fashioned Turkey In The Straw type tune for it," she came back, "and the callers can say, 'Everybody rise an' shine, for

Moon Honeymoon, Honey—"" But the troubled tension was still there. And he could feel it stretching the skin on his own face now. "—On the other hand," she said, too lightly, "I always did want to live in sin with a Man in the Moon."

Okay, let it go, the kid's trying... "You mean you'd rather have the wedding *after* the honeymoon?" he persisted compulsively. "It's kind of—unconventional, Lee—" *Stop! For Chrissake, stop!*

"I never commit myself to more than one drastic action before four P.M.," she said primly.

Commit yourself? Well, that was that. *Neatly done, babe,* he thought. And then remembered that *he* was the one who had started the Moon bit.

Okay. Okay, they'd go. What the hell? The Moon was just part of the Earth's backyard, that's all. Right across the street, nothing else.

Okay, they'd go.

"Okay, babe," he said, stepping toward her. "But if you won't have me, I don't know what I can do about it, except for *me* to have *you...*"

Rockland, N.Y.
July 25, 1977

Dear Chris—

You guessed it, I suppose, as soon as you saw the envelope. (I suppose this is what they really mean by a 'dilatory correspondence?' I've gotten to feel as if I've known you for years, just through exchanging delaying letters—)

Turns out now we can't do it on the 31st. Johnny got some sort of (hush-hush) job onto the drawing board today, and they've got to have it Aug. 3, he says. Has to take his first plans in Saturday; and then he could leave, if they like what he's done, but he won't go until he sees the final blueprints, so—

Frankly, as you realized (from what you said in your note last week), I can't really say I'm sorry to see him so wrapped up in new work. But must confess I am getting kind of wistful about the trip up too—

Anyhow, I rearranged my own schedule as soon as he told me about this last night, and have now got things set so the recording series will be finished by Aug. 5—working all next week like mad—so that *I* won't have any dates I can't break, and I'll be free to pick up and go any week after this coming one, any time Johnny can tear himself away from the drawing board.

Did Phil finally make it? I know he's been champing at the bit the past week or so, since he made up his mind to the trip.

(Just phoned his office, found out he took off yesterday.)

Tell him hello from us, and I hope the whole thing works out. He never said whether it would mean his staying up there or not, but I gather this trip is just a visit anyhow? Maybe we'll make it up before he leaves—?

Do give him regards, anyhow.

Very best, and from J.,
Lisa

P.S. Will assume any date after the 31st is okay, unless you let us know otherwise... L

Mexcity—July 27, 1977

"I guess they're not going to pick up on it," the General admitted.

"You can't win *every* time," Prentiss said.

"I know. But how many battles lose a war? Any bright thoughts?"

"Only complicated ones."

"Okay. Even not-so-bright. Something is better than nothing."

"Well, it's not *that* complicated, I guess. Just tricky. Pick up on it ourselves."

"You mean plant it?" Harbridge was thoughtful. "No," he said. "Too risky. If we got caught out on the first plant, so we're devious bastards with something up our sleeves. If we didn't do the first one, and got caught on this, we're not so devious, and it's obvious we're out to get Christensen. If we got caught on both, it would smell real funny—and too many people have good noses in this town—hey!"

"Something?"

"I think so. This thing is a windfall to anyone who's after Chris' hide. Or it ought to look that way, if they were just looking. I think you did too good a job, Al. They just didn't realize there was anything there *shouldn't* have been in that article." Which shows just how much *any*one is worried about what goes on up there, he thought. Chris used to keep an eye on his public relations, but he's been out of touch too much. Well, let's give a push—"I think—let's see, that Dartmouth boy we got shoved at us, what's his name?, Jennings?

Yuh. He's Andy Jennings' son?" Prentiss nodded. "Okay. That's it. I *think* this kid is just dumb enough so if you clucked at him about the kind of leaks that let important stuff like that get out, he'd be very likely to go home and tell his pop. And in view of the fact that Andy Jennings just bought himself a small interest worth a half million dollars in Undersea, I think we might just get our work done for us."

"You think Jennings can remember a whole sentence that long? I mean, get home and tell it straight?"

"Well you better make it *very* clear." The General laughed. Prentiss went out to find young Jennings, and Jed sat down to write to Chris.

Dollars Dome—July 28, 1977

NESNETSIRHC .RD said the lettering on the translucent plastic door and then, underneath it, ROTCERID HCRAESER. Nature's own idiot, spelled backwards, the Director thought. Peter Andrew Christensen, Big Brain. If you're so smart, why aren't you a University President? Or Research Director for General Atomics? Or a respectable dues-paid master plumber, maybe?

Irritably, he flipped the reader switch and swung his chair ninety degrees to the glowing screen beside his desk, where Lisa Trovi's ragged typing explained, as adequately as possible, why the visit had to be postponed *again*. He flipped the frame, and got Jed Harbridge's carefully composed message on the screen. Might as well start writing answers—get them on the shuttle back. He sat, thought about what to tell Jed, and flipped back to Lisa's note. Switched on the Dictaphone, and thought some more.

Knock on the door. "Come in!" The shadow behind the panel moved, and the door opened. "Oh, Phil." Good. He turned off both machines.

"Busy? I can come back..."

"You couldn't have picked a better time. I've just been sitting here stewing in my own juices—such as are left. Sit down. What's on your mind?"

"Questions. mostly."

"Like...?"

"Like, to start with, what's in *your* mind?"

Chris grinned briefly: "You decided I'm a case too?"

"Sure. What of? If it's all the same with you, I haven't had an agoraphobic in a long time..."

"You know, I might've been better off that way." He laughed. "What can I do for you outside of that? I don't suppose you've had time enough yet to have any idea..."

"Pretty damn good idea," Phil broke in cheerfully. "I'll do you up a proper report when I get back down, but I can tell you offhand now that I think any kind of half-decent psych staff up here could solve most of the problem, without half trying. In fact, the most interesting damn thing, about it isn't the diseases, but the patients. They *don't want* to be sick. I've never seen a more co-operative group in my life. It's a headshrinker's heaven, man!"

"That right?" Chris thought it over. "Well. Of course, I guess it helps to start out with a high IQ level and—" He broke off at the doctor's amused headshake.

"Chris, if you asked me before I came up here I'd have said you *couldn't* take a batch of human beings, selected for ability rather than stability, and shut 'em up in an enclosed system where the environment violates every bit of early conditioning, and expect any thing but Trouble, with a capital T. You did it. Which proves only that my preconceptions are as useless as yours or anybody else's."

"You think we're in pretty good shape, then?"

"No. *Astonishingly* good shape. I have never seen a group of human beings working with such a high integration of aims and abilities; or expressing their own emotions so satisfactorily, with so little apparent hostility—or in such good physical shape, for the most part, considering the unfamiliar conditions."

"Well, of course, those rest-leaves have a lot to do with it," Chris conceded.

"I'll bet. If it wasn't for that, I couldn't honestly even consider taking the job. I've been counting noses, and I figure there are enough of 'em ready to try giving up their leaves so I can count on a few cases, anyhow..."

It finally penetrated. "Say! Do you mean you've decided?"

"I haven't decided anything. I just want to know: where and how do I apply for employment around here? And *which* is more to the point?"

"You mean it?" The depression that had weighed on him for the past week, and had hung so thickly in the air all morning that it immobilized him, began to lift. "Damn it, that's great! Never mind the employment office, you're hired! How much do you want—?"

"Who-a-oa... Like I said, first I want to know what I'm hired *for.*"

"*How* do you mean?" Chris asked slowly. "We went all through that to start with...?"

"That was the official request. Now suppose we lay it on the line for each other. I don't think you'd sacrifice any work-time up here just to solve the pro-tem personnel problem. And I frankly would not be interested in giving up a fairly well-established and moderately lucrative Earthside practice, just to solve your hiring problems. You've got your own reasons, and I've got mine, but I think what we're both interested in is finding out how to make human beings tolerate life off of Earth—here, or on Mars, or in a starship or any other place. Do I read you right, friend?"

"Well—I'll—be—damned!" He looked across the desk at the young doctor with a new respect. "Am I all *that* transparent?

Phil smiled. "Let's just say I'm a trained observer."

"No, I mean it," Chris said earnestly. "Does it all show right out there on my face? I mean, I can see where you'd know what was going on—but I'd hate to think of some of these Decagon jerks or the buggers down in Accounting knowing everything I thought about—"

"Relax, man! No, it doesn't show that much, Chris. Like I said, I'm a trained observer, and—" He broke into laughter. "Don't worry, Chris. Unless you go around feeding the Decagon boys the same stories you gave me, I doubt they'd be fretting about your intentions. You gave it away when you dragged Johnny into it. Or rather, you got *me* hooked that way, so it wasn't too hard to figure maybe you *meant* what you said. I don't know if I'd have read it the same way at all, if I didn't have this jazzy old Johnny-monkey on *my* back—so to speak."

Well, what in hell did you say to something like that? "Oh! By the way—I have another note from Lisa today. Begins to look like they won't make it at all, the rate he's stalling." He had a sudden worried thought. "I hope that wasn't what you were counting on—?"

"Noooooo. Tell you the truth, I never figured that was better than an outside chance. Last I heard, he still was flipping his lid if anyone even *talked* about space. I don't know how he'd face up to the trip out here."

"Yeah, I know." He was thinking of Lisa's frantic efforts to control the conversation that one night at their home—to keep away from *any*thing that bothered John. He scowled. "As a matter of fact you could've knocked me over with any handy feather when I got that first letter from him, but I guess—dammit!" He cut himself off, and switched on the reader speaker briefly.

"Note: If John Wendt comes up, he is to have sedation for full trip. Copies to all Earth launch sites. Request special handling. Full sedation, delivered as much as possible according to pre-*Messenger* routine, without comment, as if still normal procedure. That's all.

"Excuse me," he said to the doctor. "I've been meaning to get that notice out ever since he said he was coming. Didn't want to forget it again. I just don't want to take any chances."

"Good idea," Phil nodded, then, explosively: "Damn it to hell anyhow!"

"That boy really is under your skin, hey?" He watched the doctor's face with interest; it was the first time he had seen the professional mask completely gone.

"Well, hell, we were old buddies, and—That's not it, though, really. I used to be fond, of Johnny, but I don't think that's even specially true any more. It's just—well, put it this way:

"Suppose a patient comes in and tells me he keeps imagining that he's chained to the floor of a dungeon and that a gorgeous babe comes in every evening to give him a good time? Chances are, I'll nod my head like a wise old doctor and start explaining about erotic fantasies, masochism, and all that. *But*—

"Supposing, for instance, this guy really *is* getting chained up every night, and this gorgeous doll really is raping him each time? It's so damn unlikely, the guy might even think he was dreaming if it did happen. Right?

"*Or*—supposing this fellow was sure enough imagining things, only he wasn't having erotic or masochistic fantasies at all? Like, let's say he works in a bicycle chain factory, and hates his job, and maybe there's a supervisor who's a beautiful dish, and she's always giving him a hard time. So maybe his fantasies are fear and revenge instead?

"Okay, so this I'd find out a lot easier than I would anything about the guy who's really getting tied up. But that's because everybody talks about their jobs and bosses, on the couch or off it. So you take Johnny Wendt, and Doug Laughlin for that matter, too. Here are two guys who got psych-tested inside out and upside down before they left. They also got all kinds of training and preparation for the things they might encounter, and I've taken the trouble to find out—you probably already know—that homosexuality was an eventuality the training program prepared them to cope with. Plus, neither one of them showed any appreciable tendency to panic over anything like that, if it *did* happen."

"Okay. I know all that," Chris said. "It still happens to be what *did* happen. So, like with the guy who really gets the chains and the babe, maybe there was something in the psychological—I don't know—atmosphere?—that we couldn't prepare for and don't know about, and—Hell, whatever the reason was, at least you found out *what* happened. *Why* is something else."

"Sure as hell is," Kutler said wryly. "And maybe you're right that what Johnny—or rather, Johnny's unconscious—thinks happened *did* happen. Only I don't think so. I find it easier to think there was something in the *physical* environment which was just so completely different and new and unprepared for that maybe neither one of them could even perceive it fully; and to the half-assed extent that they were aware of it at all, they interpreted it by association of some kind and—I just wish to hell Laughlin hadn't torn those pages out! If we knew what *he* thought was the matter, it might—Well, hell, forget it. I just thought you might like to know what's pushin' *me.*"

"Yeah. Thanks." There ought to be something better to say, he thought. "Tell you what: you get the money for the next trip, and I'll see to it you get to go in person."

Kutler shrugged and smiled. "It's a deal. Meanwhile, suppose I start on my elementary school work up here? Your people have problems people on Earth don't have. Maybe they have nothing to do with Johnny's troubles. Or maybe they do. But the principle is the same. When you already know five languages, the next three are easier to learn. If I find out what one-sixth gravity and Dome atmosphere do to people, maybe I'm that much closer to what one-third and a Mars atmosphere can do?"

"I take it," Chris said slowly, "that what you mean is you want the job, and you'll do what you're hired for, but with the understanding that you expect to be free to do more than that, too?"

"Man, you dig me the most!"

"Okay. Let me lay it on the line now, and make sure we both know what goes on. When I first thought of you for the job, it was mainly because I knew you were bugged about Johnny. Well so am I.

But a different way. Frankly, if we never find out what happened to Doug or to Johnny, it don't make no never mind for me—just so we can get the next guys back alive—and get 'em *there*, to start with."

He stood up and walked around the desk; turned and went back and stood at his own seat looking at the doctor across the desktop. "Listen, Phil, you talk about me being 'a case.' Well, I am one, all right, and I guess you know it as well as I do. Johnny was my friend. So was Doug. But I'd send 'em again, even if I knew it would happen the same way again—unless I knew some *better* men to send. And I figure I owe Johnny a whole lot now—but that comes second with me. If it came first, I'd leave him alone, I guess."

"I think you might do a lot more for Johnny by not leaving him alone," Kutler broke in.

"Good. Only it's still secondary. I've been busting a gut to get him back on the job with us, but you know as well as I do *why* I want him. It all comes down to Congress, the Care and Feeding Of."

"I know," the doctor said slowly. "Okay, so while we're showing our cards, let me add this: that's one of the reasons I want this job. *Another* one of the reasons. I know what you're trying to do—but I don't want to see Johnny fouled up any more either."

"Okay, so stick around and keep an eye on me. That's all right too. The way it is right now, Kutler, I can see a good chance of every damn thing we've done so far going right swoosh down the drain for God only knows how long—another ten, twenty, thirty, years, maybe. Unless the Reds make it, that is—"

"Yeah, that's something else. What's with them over there? You've had these bugs Johnny brought back and the other stuff to work on—I take it the bugs get the most attention now?" Chris nodded. "So what are they doing there? They run shuttles up and down, and from what I saw coming up, and the scuttlebutt hither and yon, there's enough espionage going on to support a half dozen space programs. So what are they *doing?*"

"I wish to hell I knew! About the only thing I'm pretty sure of is, they haven't got anything big going out soon. If they *did*—well, frankly, I'd be the last to know. But the Decagon boys would know all about it before the New Kremlin did, I'll guarantee. Then maybe we'd see some changes here too. *Maybe, hell!* That's the *only* thing that would get us off the ground again, the way it is now."

"A *la* Sputnik?"

Chris nodded. *"And* Muttnik, and Lunik, and Mechta and the *Lenin,* for that matter, Frankly, Phil—" He hesitated. It was tempting to talk to this man; it would be a damn big help to have *someone* to talk to. But—"I wonder if some of the big-scare reaction to the whole *Lenin-Colombo* bust wasn't—encouraged a little? After all, Johnny *did* bring the ship back. It *went* to Mars. It came *back.* He's alive, in one piece, sane—as much as anyone, I guess?"

Phil nodded, smiling.

"So why the big scare? The way it adds to me—bearing in mind that I'm a wild-eyed scientist, see? Not a politico—" He grinned. "I keep thinking, the *Colombo* puts us one-up. As long as they don't make another move, we stay one-up. As far as the politicians go, that means the Space Program has done its bit for God and country—for now, anyhow. And meantime, for this new Undersea Corporation... And the Arctic Circle crowd has some big money behind it too. So why throwaway the taxpayers' hard-earned loot on spaceships? No profits, no porkbarrel, not even any damn propaganda value. See?"

"That figures," Kutler said thoughtfully. So?"

"So I don't know. I'm just trying everything I have. Or can get. Including—" He hovered on the brink of filling in the rest of the picture, and decided against it. Not till he knew Phil Kutler a little more. And not till Harbridge was fully committed. "Including you, and Wendt, and the psych program and the bug research, and anything else I can dream up that might either be some *real* help, or might work to push Congress the right way, or both."

"But right now if you have to make a choice, what counts is the propaganda end of it?"

"Frankly—yes."

"Okay." The doctor stood up. "I just like to know what I'm doing when I do it. Where do I sign up?"

Chris stood too and held out his hand. "You just did. I'll get the contracts and stuff taken care of. When do you think you can start?"

"Hard to say for sure. As soon as possible—could be two weeks, could be six. I can't make the move till I get my patients settled with other men. Call it three-four weeks, with moderate luck."

"From when you go down?" Chris frowned. Add a week and a half, and it was going to run right into September anyhow.

Kutler nodded. "Is it too late to catch the *Messenger* back this trip?"

He hadn't thought of that. "No. The passenger shuttles don't leave till evening anyhow. But don't you need more time—?"

"What for? I had my case histories before I came up, and I'd already seen twenty-five per cent of your people. I've seen enough up here now to know there's a job to do, and I want to do it. The rest can wait."

Chris nodded. *Damn it, I like this guy!* He thought. Then he remembered. He switched on the deskreader and flicked back to Lisa's letter. "Say, I almost forgot, Lee sent you all kinds of regards."

He was ridiculously conscious of Chris' eyes on his face as he read, and of his own determinedly neutral expression.

The note was typically Lisa: the wording, punctuation, even the typing, held that quality of—what?—mock-effrontery?—that had drawn him so strongly that day in front of the restaurant.

Then he got to the bottom, and smiled. Great little intriguer *she'd* make—like real subtle messages, hey?

"I take it she thinks I should haul out of here before Buster gets on board," he murmured.

"Well, you thought so too, didn't you?"

He nodded and glanced at the other man's face. *Just what is it that girl's got?* he wondered again. *And what difference does it make? Never mind her...what about him?*

"Looks like *some*thing's going on with our boy, anyhow," he said carefully. "Maybe my hunch wasn't all the way off after all. I'm glad you got up there, Chris. Maybe you scared him back to work at least." *Unless she meant "sideboard" where she wrote "drawing board."*

Chris switched off the screen. "That's quite a gal," he said a shade too casually.

"First time you met her?" Phil asked.

"Yup." *Very* casual now. "What's with those two, Phil? I mean..." He let it trail off.

Phil shrugged and refrained from smiling. "I guess the girl knows what she wants," he said noncommittally.

"I mean—well, hell, what's the deal? How come he doesn't break down and propose?"

This time he let himself smile. "He does. Every day and twice on Tuesdays, the way I hear it. *She's* the one who won't play."

Chris looked up sharply. "What the hell—?"

"Look, I'm not telling any stories out of school; I would have thought you'd know that much anyhow. Don't your people keep any tabs on Wendt at all?"

"Not *my* people," the other man said bitterly. "Just Security. And what they don't tell me would—would probably launch a thousand spaceships, come right down to it. Hell, I wouldn't even know as much as I've told you if I didn't take that trip Earthside last month."

"Oh?" *Well, you've got some connection, then...* He caught himself up, astonished at his own hostility. *Well, something new has been added!* Only it wasn't new at all. The only thing was that Chris had joined the club. Phil Kutler grinned inside himself, not pleasantly. *Strange bedfellows,* he thought—*goddam strange!*

Mexcity, Thursday, August 4

The General dictated the last letter of the morning, dismissed his secretary with a tired pleasantry, and buzzed Al Prentiss.

"You seen the papers yet?"

Prentiss was in a good mood—and a good thing, Harbridge thought. He himself was beginning to think again wistfully about the pleasures of retirement.

"Only the *Times,*" he said warily. He hoped Al's good humor was not the fine edge of battle. This would be a good day not to get clobbered by anything.

"I'll be right in." *Click.* That's the trouble with civilians, Harbridge thought. No damn manners. Al came bursting in, three folded newspapers under his arm, all early afternoon editions.

"Like a charm," he said, spreading them to the marked articles.

MOON DOME ADMINISTRATION
SCOURGED BY CONGRESSMAN
McLafferty Will Investigate
Dome Security Practices

Iquique, Aug. 4: Representative Ramon E. McLafferty (I., E. Ch.) announced today that he was in receipt of 'evidence of incredible sloppiness' in the handling of what ought to be Top-Secret space research projects at Moon Dome.

The Congressman, who is newly appointed Chairman of the Security Subcommittee of the Joint Space Affairs Committee, declined to reveal his sources, but promised an 'immediate and vigorous investigation.' Asked if his statement was connected in any way with his interview earlier today with Andrew Jennings, a close neighbor and friend of Rep. McLafferty in the northern mountains, the Industrialist Congressman refused to comment...

That was the gist of them all, except for one columnist's item: "Ray McLafferty will gain a lot of momentum for the Senatorial elections this fall, if the Moon Dome hearings turn out half as popular as you'd think. Not to mention a well-known neighbor of Ray's who has what you might call a small interest in persuading Congress that some of the Space Research funds could be better applied under water..."

Harbridge chuckled. The day was not going to be so bad after all. "I hope it doesn't get *too* rough," he said.

"It's what the man ordered," Prentiss reminded him.

"I know. I just hope it doesn't get too rough. I forgot about McLafferty."

CHAPTER FIVE
August 24, 1977

Dollars Dome—6 P.M. (C.S.T.)

They had buckled her into the comfortable safeness of the couch, and she had swallowed a pill, and then vaguely felt the faint prick in her arm.

There had been dreams and dreamy times and maybe dreams which were hard to sort out, but as she came more awake, she decided the truly-half-awake times had been only the ones where she swallowed what someone told her to, and float-walked to the toilet and back again.

She was very hungry. Somebody came and unstrapped her arms, and left her to free herself after that from the rest of the fastenings. She sat up stiffly, stood up on prickling feet, and stepped into the corridor. A white-coated young man looked horrified, came running at her.

"Sorry, Miss, I didn't think you'd be up so quick."

Vaguely, she recognized him—or his jacket?—as the one who'd unfastened her. Then, with a rush of clarity, she saw it was Johnny he'd been standing with down the corridor. She stepped forward and whitejacket caught her arm.

"Steady—"

"I'm all right." She took another step, and the prickling began to ease. Johnny didn't look any better than she felt.

"Home was never like this," she muttered.

"Huh? Feeling rocky, babe?" His face was gray but he was a lot steadier on his feet. "Takes getting used to," he said, but he didn't sound as if it made much difference. He wasn't even looking at her. He kept staring at the couch behind him.

She stood still. *Getting my Moon legs,* she thought nervously, and wished the damn whitejacket character would go away, or Johnny would kiss her, or preferably both.

"Hello?" she said, small-voiced, and put her hand on his arm.

"Hi, babe." He turned and really looked at her this time, and closed his other hand over hers. "Better yet? I was just looking at this setup—didn't get a chance when we boarded. It's changed some since—They've improved it a lot, but it seems to me there should be something better than all this belt-and-buckle junk. There must be some kind of synthetic fabric that would do the job," he said thoughtfully. "See, if you had—"

If I had half a brain, she thought, turning the mounting irritation back on herself, *I'd have stopped to think I'm not the one who needs coddling this time!*

"—made up into a net—soft enough for comfort, but rigid—"

He *was* keeping his brain busy. *Fine. But what happens next?*

"—enough to hold shape on a frame, you could work the whole thing with a pushbutton—"

The whitejacket type looked as impatient as she felt.

"—Give it a kind of dead man's brake," Johnny rattled on, impervious, "so it won't work during blast—"

Whitejacket gave her a pleading look. She took a deep breath. "Hey," she said. "Mister! You know which way to the Dome? I'm a stranger here myself—"

He grinned, shook his head as if to wake himself up. "Sure. Right down this aisle, lady. Step right through the double doorway to your right...ea-ea-ea-zee does it. You are now breathing the fresh pure air of Kansas City, imported direct to the Moon for the benefit of Dr. Christensen's walking talking researching exiles. Siberia was never like this either. Well, how do you like it?"

I don't know, she thought. *I'm too busy liking you.* She made herself stand still, not look around. If she looked, if she seemed to notice anything different, it would go away. *Oh, Johnny!* she thought, remembering suddenly, sharply, the man who had gone to Mars.

But he's still that way, lots of times, she defended automatically, even to herself; and told herself right back, *Sure he is—on Earth!* But they weren't on Earth: they were on the Moon, and Johnny hadn't even been able to listen to *talk* about space for a year and a half now without flipping his lid...

Never mind, she stopped herself. She didn't have to understand it; she could just be grateful for it.

"All right, snotty, *be* blasé," she said aloud. "Me, I'm a greenhorn. I'm impressed." And she was, too. Startling, how anything could be so much like what you expected, but so much—what—so much more *real.* Like seeing art-book reproductions of Degas' dancers, and suddenly finding yourself in front of a full-scale canvas, alive with the breath and brush of the artist. And even now, all she was seeing was through the protective refraction of the great air dome. She wondered if visitors could ever get outside...

"Hey, babe, stop staring and come say hello to the nice man."

She turned and smiled at Chris, with what she meant to be only a sideways glance at Johnny. His face was open and relaxed and easy...a face she remembered from long long ago, and saw now only for fleeting moments in great privacy and dim light. But even while she watched, it disappeared under the familiar mask.

"You'll have to excuse the lady," he was saying to Chris. "It's her first experience as visiting firelady off the planet of her birth, and..."

"I'm just Moon-struck," she broke in. "Hello, Chris. I...it...well, *thanks* for asking us."

"Believe me, it's a pleasure to see you." He reached out a big hand, and took hers in it, then released her to shake hands with Johnny. "Having any trouble walking? Good. Those shoe plates are supposed to make just enough difference, but gravity and magnetism aren't exactly the same. Some people have trouble at first. Come on.

Got some chow waiting for you. Even the Moon has traditions. Banquet in the dining room every time a ship comes in."

They were walking across a curious concrete flooring, flecked with sparkling bits of silvery stuff, away from the dome and wall, the great air-lock "gate" through which they had entered, leaving the two tall ships and the Moon-vista behind them as they approached the center of the base.

The shiny bits in the floor must be the magnetizing element, she decided, and became pleasantly aware of the difference Chris had mentioned. She felt light, buoyant, fluidly effortless in all her movements—but still her feet behaved as they were accustomed to behaving under normal gravity.

"I guess the people who feel uncomfortable walking must be the ones with feet out of proportion to their bodies," she said thoughtfully, remembering how the plates had been carefully trimmed to size and attached to her shoes at the spaceport on Earth. "I mean, if your feet were a little small, the surface wouldn't give you quite as much attraction as you needed to make it feel the same...?"

Chris nodded. "We have special plates made up with thicker soles for overweight people, if they're staying on. Although, once you get used to the idea, it's kind of fun not to use them at all." He smiled. "You see what kind of solitary pleasures a man is reduced to in a setup like this? But I can't very well go floating around the place where the hired hands can see me, so I only do it when I'm alone in the executive suite," he added, to Johnny, and went on:

"Listen, if you folks would rather skip the love-feast today, we can have something sent up to my place. Whatever you'd rather—?"

"Makes no difference," Johnny said curtly. "Whatever you want. They'll be expecting you, won't they?"

She heard the tightness in his voice, shot a quick unnecessary look at his face, and did her duty: "Frankly, I would appreciate it if it's not too much trouble," she lied. "I'm...kind of dazed." *That* was no lie.

"Sure thing. Wait here a minute, will you?" Chris stepped off more briskly in the direction they had been going, caught up with a group a little way ahead, and spoke quickly to a tall gangling redhead in shorts and a violent patterned shirt. The redhead glanced back at them, nodded, and rejoined his group. Chris came back, smiling, and they turned off the wide main "street," down a side corridor, heading "out" again now, toward a different part of the dome wall. A little later they turned again, and lost sight of the outside, walking up a ramp that led to another corridor, this one lined with doors. Chris paused in front of the last door along the row, and pushed it open.

Lisa took one step inside and gasped. Her first impressions of the room itself were vague. That didn't matter. She was facing a full wall section of the dome. From floor to ceiling, and perhaps eighteen feet along the side, the clear plastic brought the incredible outside right in with them.

She heard Chris laugh, and Johnny said, "Hey, babe, you're obstructing traffic." She stepped forward to let them in, but never moved her eyes. The only thing she thought about at all in that brief time of pure perception was to wish that Chris would go away, so she could know if Johnny was sharing her delight. Then Chris went away.

"'Scuse me. Check messages 'noffice,'" he said. Or something like that. He vanished through a side door, and she took her eyes off the outside long enough to look to Johnny and reach out her hand. He stepped closer, took her hand in his own, and stood next to her, seeing it with her—but just for an instant; then he stepped away.

Awareness of his movements around the room intruded gradually on her preoccupation. She turned, and found him studying the titles in a bookshelf; looked around herself, and took in a low couch, table, comfortable looking sling chair. Another table, writing height, in the far side of the room, with a straight chair in front of it. Everything else was built in: shelves, drawers, cupboards.

No pictures. She was beginning to approve of Pete Christensen. Anyone who'd hang a picture on a wall in the same room with what she'd just been looking at...

Dinner was the biggest surprise yet, because it was so normal— normal for Earthside luxury, that is. It arrived, scant minutes after Chris had mixed and served cocktails, on a hotel-type wheeled table, which came up in a sort of oversized dumbwaiter. On a plastic cloth, plastic dishes and earthenware containers held what was literally the banquet Chris had promised: appetizer to mints, with all stops in between, and roast beef featured in the middle. Plus a wine she could not identify, but found delightful.

"Our own brand," Chris chuckled. "So was the 'gin.' For that matter, damn near everything on the table is. I'm not sure offhand whether the dishes were made here or not, but the ceramic stuff was. And the plastic cloth. And the roast beef."

She had known about the hydroponics farm, and there was really nothing startling, if you thought about it, at the idea that where man can grow starch, he can, and will, also distill spirits. "Which tank do you grow your beef in?" She asked skeptically.

"No tank," he said, beaming. "That pink slice represents one of our biggest scores to date, gal. Experiment in transporting animals *in utero*. First viable one we got was a pig—wouldn't you know it? But we have practically a complete livestock farm here now, and we've got the process down to where we—" He stopped, as if checking himself, and then finished smoothly. "—we think we can pack up any kind of stock a space traveler orders and ship it to him—anywhere, any time. Not bad, hey? We're fooling around with deep-freeze now—the embryos, I mean. No luck so far; but—?"

His shrug, Lee thought, was magnificently eloquent: all around her, in front of her, even being ingested inside her, was evidence of the stubborn, determined, bull-headed damn dumb optimism of that shrug. Pete Christensen had *made* this station—fought for it, worked at it, schemed on its behalf—*made* it almost as literally as though he'd built it with his hands, unaided.

"You still headin' for the wild blue yonder, man?"

Johnny. Lisa looked once at his tight sardonic withdrawal and thought with a shiver:

He made that, *too.*

Dollars Dome—7:30 P.M. (C.S.T.)

Half an hour, Phil thought. He'd give it another half-hour, then he'd have to go up.

"You get so it seems normal," he said in answer to the comment from one of the three new all-alike young biochemists. *How do they turn 'em out so same-all-over?* Once upon a time, scientists at least had been odd ducks, individualists—Okay, escapists; but *individuals.* Now...? "It's morning now, Moonwise. Just dawned yesterday. But at Moon-night, all the difference is the blinds are down—that's the effect. The dome lights actually give you the same color and quality of light. You just can't see out, very far. You have to make your own day-and-night for living purposes. That's one of the tests you'll be getting this week. Find out what kind of routine or schedule looks best for each one of you, and after a while 'night' is the time you go to your room to sleep." *You'll get used to it before I will, I bet,* he thought, amused at the knowledgeable confidence he managed to convey.

Half an hour, at the most. God only knows which bit of fur Chris was rubbing backwards now. *Or which way Lightning Boy will strike when ole Doc Kutler shows! Well, might as well live dangerously—if there was no safe way to do the job...*

He confirmed the opinion of another of the triplet fledglings that the day-night bit might be behind some of the psychogenic systemic malfunctions he'd been warned about.

"Damnedest industrial hazards popping up these days," the third one said. "Used to be in our line all you worried about was catching malaria or getting too much roentgen. Now you sign a release about asthma and psychosomatic hypertension before they'll hire you."

"Well, that's really my job here," Phil said. "I'm the chief headshrinker in charge of eustachian tubes. The day-night thing makes trouble, but nothing like what that inner ear of yours will try to do. Not to mention all the things your involuntary reflex system has to learn all over, and—"

"You know, I never thought of just how *many* things low gravity and rhythm disruption could do to a man!" Biochem No. 1 broke in, "Man, *that* could be fascinating!"

Well, all right. Phil started to feel better. At least one out of three was not Cool Cat straight to the core. The lad had spoken out of turn, and out of character. Phil made a mental approving note and fixed the still-nameless face in his mind. Then he stood up.

"I'm going to have to run out on you for a while," he apologized. "Boss-man has super-visitors upstairs." No. 1 grinned; the others looked politely baffled. *Carrera*—that was his name.

"Scuttlebutt around St. Thom wasn't so far off, I guess," No. 2 said to No. 3.

"Everyone was saying *Johnny Wendt* would be on board," No. 3 explained. "Who is it anyhow? Or do we get Classified Personnel up here?"

Johnny Wendt. In emphasis. Even from this jerk...

"Everyone was right," Phil said flatly. "He's up with Dr. Christensen now."

"Oh?"

"Dammit!" said No. 2. "I *know* I'd have recognized him. I'll swear he wasn't on the *Messenger.*"

Phil shrugged. "Maybe they have private luxury compartments?" he said with a suggestion of a leer. "He brought Lisa Trovi with him." And turned and went, knowing he had penetrated the professional boredom of No.'s 1 and 2.

Johnny Wendt!

Maybe the boys back at the table were more jazzed up about Lee being there—but they didn't say her name in caps or italics. Well, he thought, it was nice to know you weren't the *only* sucker in town. And Christensen's bulldoggish efforts for the first time to get Wendt's name back on the rolls made full *objective* sense to Phil.

He tossed a mental apology at Chris. Amendment, rather. He'd actually begun to think the director *cared* about Wendt.

Or maybe he did; it wouldn't matter *if* he did. He didn't care enough about *himself* to make a centimeter's difference if the blueprint was the plan for space. Whether he cared or not, he *needed* Wendt.

Phil started up the stairs to see the immovable object visiting the irresistible force.

Plus, of course, Lisa.

Dollars Dome—8 P.M. (C.S.T.)

The big wheel drifted in a sunlit void. Cargo ships snuggled cozily into the vast hub hold. Tiny toy-robots and toy-men who looked, in outspace gear, more like the robots than the robots did, clung to the outer shell, making their way in spiraling circuits around the great rim and the hub, checking, repairing, resealing the scars of cosmic dust and ultra-high-velocity pinpoint pebbles.

Inside the ion tubes, geiger-suited crews cleaned and inspected. Fuel shuttles took their turns at the maw of the tanks. In the rim living quarters, crew couches were stripped and sprayed, deodorized, sanitized, and u-vee'd, covered with fresh plastic sheets. A team of two went through inspecting straps and webbing, and buckles.

All the routine of the *Messenger's* two-day Moonside orbit went on as it always did. Shuttles came and went from and to the three domes. And as routinely as all the rest, magnetic tweezers plucked a thin strip of microfilm from a minute wall hole; a piece of candy offered and accepted was sucked till the candycoat came off the hard center—a pellet precisely shaped and sized to tonguing into the cavity of a false tooth; two men conversed about supplies and schedules, talking fluently meanwhile with their hands.

The shuttles went in and out, and before most of the residents of Dollars Dome knew who their guests were—or that they *had* special guests—the top man in every national delegation at World Dome, plus Dr. Chen and his aides in Plato Crater, knew that *John Wendt* had come back.

They also knew that Wendt had refused to go back into space since his first return from Mars—or that that was what the American government *said*. Now he was brought up, with absolute secrecy—kept in his bunk the whole way—as a prisoner? or for Security reasons? by choice? *why?*—and that a "woman friend" had accompanied him: presumably the American tri-di dancer, Trovi.

Why?

In at least sixteen different rooms in the three man-made Moon oases, men sat silently asking themselves the same questions, or conferring worriedly with other men about it.

In Dollars Dome, the word gradually spread too. And in Dr. Peter Andrew Christensen's living room, Trovi and Wendt sat sipping wine and coffee, while the Director made small talk and speculated about those sixteen—or more—rooms, and what was going on inside them all.

"...still headin' into the wild blue yonder?" It didn't come out light, the way he'd meant it to. He avoided Lee's quick look.

"You seen any leopards change spots lately, John?" The bastard laughed as if the joke was on himself. Sure.

Yeah. This cat over here, man. Flyin' tiger turned to pussycat. Yeh-man!

The self-made leopard looked like licking cream, rambling on to Lisa about food again. "Food gets ridiculously important to us here," he said. "But the psych boys had that taped ahead of time. Found it in the World War Two, with the sub service, and then they doubled it in spades on the nuclear jobs. I guess they figure all of us for—what do they call it?—oral regressives—anybody who'll get into this kind of spot at all. Anyhow, that's one thing I never had to fight for. Johnny can tell you, even at the beginning, before we really had the farm going, we used to get beef and turkey sent up, even when there was no shipping space for lab supplies! Lord, how that used to gripe me!" He stopped a minute, to empty his wineglass. "Coffee?"

"Let me do it," Lee said.

Busy little bee, ain't you just, baby?

"Of course that was before we had the *Messenger*," Chris was going again. "Every ounce counted, ten times over then."

"Yeah," Johnny heard himself saying, his voice coming from somewhere outside his volition, but inside himself: "We had pretty good chow on The *Colombo*, too." That was how it came out. But how was unimportant. From where? *Why?*

He tried to remember when he had last so much as completed a conscious *thought* about that travesty—let alone said a word about it—Except *No* or *Go to Hell!* Or like that. He tried to see Lee's face without her noticing. Tried to find something else to say, while they sat waiting. Tried to think of some way for them to be on the shuttle tomorrow when it took off again.

Eight days, he thought. Eight whole long twenty-four-hours-to-the-each old-fashioned Earth-type days. *My God!*

It had been a mistake to come. But he'd known that. *Old Johnny-can't-turn-down-a-dare,* he thought, with small amusement.

That wasn't quite right, either. It took *three* dares: Chris; then Lisa; then that damfool McLafferty with his idiot committees. Good ole Solidarity Wendt, all-out for ole buddy Chris. Yeah.

There was a little wine still in the bottle. He picked it up.

"Lee?"

"No thanks," she said. "I'm on coffee now."

"Chris?"

"Just a drop—no, never mind," Chris said. "I've got some brandy someplace around—" But he made no move to get it. "I've got to get some work done tonight yet. Always busy as hell around here when the *Messenger's* up," he added, to Lee.

"How long does she stay in orbit?" Johnny asked, hoping it sounded idle.

"Two days. Starts back Friday morning, but for our purposes, it's Thursday night. Anything out of here has to get off the ground by ten tomorrow at the latest, to make orbit. Then she's back by next Wednesday. One thing, at least, you don't have to worry about late trains when they run on orbit!"

And when did I hear that joke the first time? Johnny thought, while Lisa gave her nicest duty-laugh. *This party's sure getting dead,* he thought. *And guess who killed it? Hell!*

Eight days. Okay.
Eight days?
He finished the wine.

"By the way," Chris said, leaning back, "I've been catching up on that ESP stuff since I saw you that time, Lee. You know, I used to fool around with it quite a bit back in school—the Rhine cards and all that. But I lost touch."

"Decided you couldn't push rockets with wishes?" Johnny bit in.

"That's about it," said Chris equably. "Now I think maybe I should have stood with it. I'm sure as hell not pushing 'em any *other* way."

"If spaceships were wishes," Johnny said, and stood up. "It's in there, isn't it?" He pointed to the bedroom door.

"Huh?" Chris double-took. "Oh, yeah, right through the bedroom."

"Excuse me." He went out and left the other two in brief uncomfortable silence.

"You know," Chris said after a moment. "Telepathy would be damn useful sometimes, when you think of it."

"It's okay, Chris." Lee smiled, with obvious effort, and stood up. No matter where she sat or what she did, her eyes kept turning back to the stark lithographic contrasts of the weird lunar landscape on the other side of the curved wall. "It's—"

...a lot better than I was afraid of... Well, you didn't say a thing like that: not even to a beaming-father-type like Chris. *He's not married,* she realized suddenly. That was too bad; he was a man who ought to have children. *Children!*

The landscape blurred, and she blinked hard and fast.

"...matter of fact," he was saying, "your man Potter seems to be getting a lot of respect. Maybe we *will* push ships with PK someday, if he's right. Telepathy would be a lot more help just now, though—I'd give a pretty to know what they're up to at Red Dome, and Intelligence doesn't come up with much. His idea on telepathy is that it amounts to a semantic translation of a total set of somatic conditions, right?"

"That's how I get it." Outside, a shimmering blue-tailed beetle skimmed in a long parabola through the sky. Somebody's shuttle-ship. *That's how we looked, coming in!* "Doesn't sound too likely, though—I mean, how many people would get the right message ever, if it depended first on one of them being able to—well, *project* his own nerve and muscle sets to another, and then the other one having the right frame of reference, semantically, to 'read' the somatic set? Like, it won't do us any good when we meet up with Jovians or the bug-eyed types from Arcturus Three, will it?" *Keep it light that's all. Just keep it light.*

"Oh, I'm willing to let the Arcturians wait," he laughed. "I just want to know what the boys in Red Dome are dreaming up. Now if you just fill me in on how to make your muscles feel like my muscles—come to think of it—that's up Kutler's alley, isn't it? Wonder if he's up on this at all?"

"Talking dirty again?" Johnny stood in the bedroom doorway looking from her to Chris to her. "Kindly keep y'all's muscles in different parts of the room," he said, with a grin that was not a grin at all. "Or," he went on, facing Chris, still with the smile that made the words an official joke, "you will start feeling *my* muscles."

Oh, Lord! Stop it, Johnny! please stop!

"How in hell did you two get around to the Phys Ed department?" he went on. "I thought I left you up on thought-steam rocket ships?"

"Too rarefied," Chris said. "They forgot to think us up some atmosphere."

"Oh? Oh, yes, when did Young Doctor Kutler join the party?"

"Well, he hasn't yet. Matter of fact, I thought he'd be up here by now. He took over as official greeter for me with the new people who came up with you."

"You mean," Johnny said slowly. "Kutler is up here too?"

"Sure. Didn't you know? Lee, you knew...?"

Yes. Yes, I did. "Hmmm?" She made a great thing out of tearing herself from the view. "Oh, is he here *now*? I knew he *had* been up, but—?"

Chris swallowed it. Not Johnny. Damn him, damn his eyes! He had no right to know so much about her and so stupid-silly little about *him*.

"Sure, he's on the payroll now. First time I ever did anything the Security boys loved me for. We've had this problem of sending people on leave one month out of every four. Plays hell with our schedules and personnel problem, which didn't bother them downstairs—but when they started tightening up on Security, they got *damn* bothered about all these classified project people being Earthside on their own so much. But if they stay up here, without that relief, they don't last a year, most of 'em. Every psychogenic trouble in the books—plus some Phil can write his own book about it when he's done. They—there he is. Come in. Hi—we were talking about you."

Phil came in, smiled quietly, nodded to Lisa, and crossed to where Johnny stood, hand held out.

"It's good to see you again," he said.

"Is it?"

Phil dropped the hand Johnny had ignored.

She knew exactly what would happen next, and could not even start to think how to avoid it. She was appalled, but in a way almost relieved, to find she was not even going to *try.*

The two men stood two feet apart, face to face, for a hovering moment. Then Phil turned, with a faint shrug. "How do you pick these guys you hire, Chris? I swear, when you talk to a bunch of them, you'd think they were all manufactured in the same—"

"*I* hire?" Christensen started. "Hell of a lot *I* have to do with..."

"I asked you something, Doc," Johnny said at the same time, and reached out and put his hand on Kutler's shoulder, turning him back. "Are you so damn sure it's so good to see me?"

Kutler shook his shoulder sharply; Johnny's grip tightened.

Lisa stood watching.

"For krissake, Wendt!" Chris stepped forward. "What did *he* do?"

"Nothing," Johnny said through almost clenched teeth. "Not a goddam thing!" He didn't look at Chris; just at Phil. He dropped his hand. Neither one moved.

"So *you're* the bright boy who's been making plans?" Johnny laughed, a short ugly bark. "I should of known. Okay, boy, here I am. Still in my head, more or less. You proved your point. Lightning didn't strike. I made the trip, and so what? What's next on your list of magic tricks?"

"Oh, Christ, Wendt, forget it, will you?" Kutler said. "*I* didn't ask to get you here. I only work here." He turned to Chris. "I'll see you later, I guess?" He turned to Lee. "I'm sorry."

That was the cue, of course. Johnny took two steps forward and his arm drew back. "Leave. Her. Out. Of. It," he said. "You. Son. Of. A. Bitch."

For one quick instant, the script almost went through to the end. Something exploded in Phil Kutler's eyes that Lisa had known must be in the man—because he *was* a man, but had never seen or heard in any way. Then the doctor reached out again and drew back the male response.

"Okay," he told Johnny mildly. "Have it *your* way." He turned and left.

The silence he left was like the death of sound after a thunderclap. Johnny stood tense, his arm still half-set for a blow, until the door closed. Then he dropped into the nearest chair, went loose all over, and looked down at the floor.

"I guess I figured things a little wrong, Chris," he said tiredly. "I shouldn't have come. I'm sorry as all hell." After a moment he looked up at Lisa, and then away. He said nothing to her. Dimly she knew that—for the first time?—maybe not?—she had had nothing to offer him.

Damn it, oh damn, damn, damn, oh damn it all!

"Maybe it would be better if we went back down this trip," Johnny said, still to the floor.

"I'll see if I can work it," Chris said. Something in his voice made her look closer. It was incredible, but it was true: Chris wasn't angry; not even disappointed, specially; he just knew it was no good. Maybe he also knew it hurt Johnny even more than it did him to know it; but he no longer cared. It wouldn't work: that finished it. He went to the cabinet, set a full bottle of Earthside brandy on the table, and two glasses.

"Why don't you two take this along to your place?" he said, casually as though nothing had ended, nothing had even begun. "I'll see what I can do about shifting some schedules. We might have to try and get you onto a UN ship, okay?"

Johnny nodded. "Thanks." He stood up, started to pass the bottle up, and couldn't do it. Lee followed. *Damn it,* she thought, *this time he wasn't even drunk!*

He made up for it. He was drunk *and* asleep when Chris phoned to the room two hours later. "He's sleeping," Lee said softly.

"Oh? Well, listen, we've got a problem here. I can get *one* bunk. *Only* one. UN ship's full up, a bunch of VIP's who won't wait. And I can't squeeze out more than one here, this trip."

She was silent. She looked at the square solid face in the screen, and wished...well, what was there *to* wish?

"The only way I could do it, Lee, would be as Priority Emergency, and I think that might make some—well, some unpleasant publicity."

"It's all right, Chris," she said clearly. "Suppose Johnny takes this one, and I'll go next week, the way we planned."

"Do you think that's—a good idea?"

She smiled. Johnny was not going to think it was a good idea at all. "It looks like the only thing we can do, doesn't it?" Well, Johnny could think what he liked. "I—frankly, I'd just as lief stay the week, if it won't—Well, you're the boss. Just, if you think that's best, it's perfectly all right with me."

She waited breathlessly. "Sure," he said. "I just didn't think you'd want—I thought you might be uncomfortable staying by yourself."

"No. I'll tell Johnny when he wakes up," she said.

"You send him to me," Chris said. "I'll tell him." She did not contradict.

After she hung up, she went to the outside wall and pulled back the drapes that Johnny had drawn. Light flooded the room. She closed the drapes again, and stood outside them, nose to the window like a kid at a candy store.

Instead of being worried, or upset, or angry, or nervous, or anything she *ought* to be, she kept looking and wondering if people ever got tired of a scene like that.

CHAPTER SIX
August 25-September 2, 1977

Dollars Dome—Thursday, August 25

"Yeah. Sure. If it's all right with Lee, it's okay." *Sure, what the Hell? Why shouldn't I leave my girl behind? Give the other boys a chance...* That was idiocy. Or was it? You couldn't say Chris had failed to *notice* Lee. *Well, who does? You want a babe nobody else wants, find yourself some old bag. Plenty of girls who'll be overjoyed to marry the great Wendt.* Plenty of 'em. Sure. For all he knew, this time might have torn it with Lee anyhow. He stood up. "I'll go see if I can round her up and see what she thinks, okay?"

"Right. See you in half an hour? I've got to get the changes cleared through soon as possible."

"Right." He went out of Admin and across the mall to the guest residence. The place had changed since—well, sure it had, he was thinking four years back and more. He hadn't really *seen* it when he came through on the way back from—

All right, leave it lay... Forget it!

She wasn't in the room. He found her finally in the dining room, drinking a glass of milk with a tableful of awed young scientists. If he could laugh today, it would be funny—the way their eyes swiveled after her when she got up to come to him. *Plus* the double take when the whispered word went round the table about who it was she'd gone to. *The great Wendt!*

Well, the great Wendt was getting sent home for being bad. And he couldn't have mama's hand to hold, this trip.

"Chris says he can swing one berth, but that's all," he said. "The way I see it, I'm a heel no matter what I do. You rather stay alone till next trip, or what?"

"Well—what do you think?"

"I think—never mind, babe, you don't want to know that. I guess there's nothing to do but go along with it? Unless you think you'd be—"

"What?"

"I don't know. It's that ole sou'then gennulman training coming out. You know what I mean."

"*Here?* Don't be an idiot, darling. I'll keep my chastity."

Damnedest part of it was; she would, too.

"Okay, babe. I'll go let him know." But he stayed where he was. "Babe?"

"Hmmm?"

"Hell, I—I'm sorry, that's all. I don't know what the Hell...!"

"It's okay, Johnny. Let it ride, huh?"

"Sure."

But there was something missing. After he talked to Chris, he wandered out, thinking he'd find her and see if there was anything he could do, in the three hours he had, to help things. Then he knew what he really meant by "help things," and made sure he *didn't* find her.

She wouldn't stop him. But it wasn't what she wanted. Or what he had any right to ask.

Be a good thing if she did find someone else, he thought. He swallowed the fury in his throat, and found the bar.

TRIP TO MOON FOR PROCESS SERVER?
DOME DIRECTOR SUBPOENAED
McLafferty Demands Christensen
Testify at Special Hearing For
Space Security Next Week

Mexcity, Aug. 25: Dr. Peter A. Christensen, Director of the All-Americas Laboratory for The Investigation of Extra-Territorial Phenomena, has been summoned to testify at a Special Hearing of the Security Subcommittee of the Joint Congressional Space Affairs Committee (SAC).

The Subcommittee convened in special session yesterday to study evidence previously announced by Chairman Ramon E. McLafferty (I.E.Ch.) as "seriously questioning the efficacy of Space Research Security." The nature of the evidence has not yet been revealed.

Special Hearings on the matter, which Rep. McLafferty describes as "most urgent," will commence next week, in advance of the convening of Congress. Dr. Christensen was called upon by the Committee today to appear voluntarily for questioning in regard to Security measures in the Moon Dome.

Queried on the procedure of the Subcommittee if the Moon Research Director should fail to comply with the request for voluntary appearance, Rep. McLafferty said that a subpoena definitely would be issued.

"The Moon Dome is a territorial part of the Americas," stated the East Chilean Industrialist, who is a candidate for Senator from Chile this fall. "If it is necessary to send a subpoena there," he told a press conference this morning, "we will do so." He added that he did not believe Dr. Christensen would fail to comply with the Subcommittee's request.

Dollars Dome—Sunday, August 28

The Biochem labs occupied a complete "building"—a structural unit shaped like a pie-slice with the first forkful already gone—a pumpkin pie, possibly, or any fallen custard filling that would provide for greater height at the outside than in the center. Eight such buildings extended from the central Mall to the crater walls, rising by stepped-back stories till the top two levels in each were single rows of rooms facing the transparent dome wall above the crater. These were, for the most part, living quarters, but in Bio even the top stories were taken over for lab space by now.

Still, there was not room enough in the one building. The "Mars-bugs," which had occupied perhaps one cubic meter in their sample boxes on the *Colombo* twenty months earlier had been so carefully, prudently, frequently, and multi-experimentally proliferated in the meantime that a department which had once shared the single building with two other sections had now—and recently, nearly half of the growth having occurred in the past three months—overflowed into corners and corridors all through the Dome.

There was a batch of cultures in Metallurgy being studied for "evolution-mutation" response to various mineral environments. With the assays and testing of (non-self-reproducing) Mars samples long finished in that department, and its original function in connection with rocket construction and propulsion become an economic dodo, the once-proudly-inorganic chemists turned eagerly to working with bugs.

The hydroponics farm had suffered no such financial blight as had Metals and Fuels and other non-maintenance projects; but efficiency in the building known as the Farm had so minimized space requirements during eleven years of steadily increased personnel *and* improved living standards, that one whole tank room was available—and thus put to use—for "farming" experiments with bugs.

A section of Electronics was currently being cleared and remodeled for the cybernetic approach to a theoretical understanding of "controlled evolution" by construction of analog computers which might "act out" the mathematics that had to date eluded all other efforts at analytical understanding.

As a matter of fact, the bugs had already, in one sense, overflowed the Dome itself. One farm-tank full had been "planted" in an open pavilion outside the walls, roofed against meteors, but incompletely enclosed: "The Shack" was the simplest way to conduct Moon-environment tests.

Lisa followed Thad Bourgnese down ramp after ramp in the Bio building, listening with half an ear as she was trailed through the upper levels where the Earth-normal atmosphere work was done, down to the glassed-off pressurized chambers near the crater floor where experiments were conducted by space-suited scientists in Mars-normal, or at least a half-dozen variant approximations of Mars-normal, atmosphere.

This was the only building she had not previously toured at least superficially; and Thad was seeing to it that her tour here was *not* superficial at all. But by this time she was chronically half a day behind herself, still absorbing mentally what she had seen in the morning, while she tried to retain what *was* shown her in the afternoon long enough to digest it that evening.

She hadn't realized; she hadn't even *begun* to realize before she came: she had known everything there was to know about Johnny Wendt—except what mattered.

She knew the public hero, the lover, and the tortured man. From very far and very near, especially from near—from inside-out almost—she knew him better than, perhaps, she knew herself: certainly better than *he* knew himself. But now, in his absence, she *was* learning for the first time in concrete specific terms just *who* Johnny was—what he had done—and *why* so many people *gave* a damn.

Nine-tenths of the research inside the Dome was directly connected with what Johnny had brought back from Mars. Half of the total stemmed directly from investigations initiated by either Wendt or Laughlin on Mars, or by Johnny on the trip home.

The popular tag, *astronauts,* was misleadingly limited, and Johnny had never done or said anything to correct the misconception for Lee. The fact was, he and Doug had not been sent just to pilot a ship, collect specimens, and carry them safely home. That job could have been accomplished with robots; the justification for risking human life was the requirement of trained human judgment. The two men had not just picked samples: they had decided *what* to pick; had run the first tests and experiments on the spot; initiated whole lines of research; and judged on the basis of their findings what was worth carrying home and what was not.

They had worked hard for a year and more on Mars; and harder, perhaps, training for ten long years before. Between them, they had contained a practicing knowledge of the whole spectrum of analytical and investigative sciences. Doug was the "biologist"—which, in that team, meant doctor, farmer, organic chemist, cook, as well as the branches of the life sciences; Johnny was "physicist," which meant, in particular, the whole range of cybernetics, from its application to neurology and linguistics, to its most abstruse "big-brain" computing techniques. As such, he was pilot and navigator, engineering crew, construction and repairman, inorganic chemist, civil, mechanical, and electrical engineer, nuclear physicist, and mathematician.

It had taken ten years of Academy and post-grad work, and then special training on the Moon, to prepare these two, and a score of others for the complex job. In the end, Johnny and Doug had seemed the best team for the trip.

Lisa had known all this, but known it as one knows, for instance, that the diameter of Earth is 7928 miles; now she was learning it firsthand, as one knows the diameter of a plum is small enough to be held inside one's hand.

And it was awkward, always, because everyone—bar Chris and Phil—took it for granted that she knew already.

Naturally, Johnny would have told her everything; naturally, she'd have seen the slides and films, read the records, heard the stories over and again.

But—naturally—she knew nothing, except what she had read in public print, heard from Phil Kutler, or pieced together from Johnny's infrequent, oblique, and most often uncompleted references. If he even owned any slides or pictures, Lisa did not know about it; she finally had to ask to see the stereos of the Martian "city"—the crumbling ruins of whatever civilization had once existed there. Then, when they found out that she really never *had* seen anything, they brought the whole works out for her. Marscapes and space shots and all the "Mars-bug" micro-shots that were not too classified to show.

And all the time, wherever she went, whatever she did, right outside and visible every time you crossed the mall, was the Beyond, the still-unborn world of the Moon, and Space itself, the stuff of dreams that ruled the whole life of a man like Peter Christensen—that *had* ruled, guided, channeled Johnny's life, until—

Till what? Till he went out too far? Till he woke up? Until the big dream turned to a steady nightmare for some reason no one, Phil or Chris, Johnny, or she herself, quite knew.

The strange thing was, the more she learned, the more she understood, about the John Wendt she had never met, the harder it was to think of going home to the sad travesty of the whole man who waited for her back on Earth.

Well, not yet quite on Earth: it was now Sunday afternoon, and he would be en route along the Belt from Perigee—or even spiraling downward in the Earth bird by now. Since Thursday night, he would have been in the same state of drugged calm in which they had both awakened just enough to take nourishment and eliminate wastes, still half-unaware, all the way up.

"Well, that's about it…"

Lisa pulled herself out of her private world of worry and wonderment, and followed Thad back up the ramps. "About the only thing you haven't seen yet is the Shack," he was saying.

"Shack?"

"Outside," he explained. "We figured the easiest way to study these babies at Moon conditions was right out there on the Moon. You've probably seen the Shack from your window. You're in North Hall, aren't you?"

"Yesss…oh, of course, I thought—" She giggled, realizing for the first time how absurd the immediate assumption had been. "I thought it was some kind of *guard* house."

Thad laughed and pushed the lounge room door open for her, leaned past to hold it as she went through. He nodded to two men deep in discussion near the door, waved to a group across the room. It was cheerful and late-afternoon feeling inside. A handsome redhaired girl detached herself from a knot of white-coated technicians at the tea table and approached them.

"Hi, Lee." His voice held a special warmth that made Lisa look again, more closely, at the girl. It was astonishing, really, how many of these girl scientists were lovely women as well…

Well! How quaint! Shades of great-granddad! …but it was true, all the same, she thought stubbornly. You just *didn't* see this particular kind of—well, loved-loveliness—in most busy-brain career types on Earth. But here, even the plain ones seemed to have that sort of *glow*...

So? There were at least as many men as women here, she reminded herself—and no fluffy chicks to grab off the men from the brainy types. So why shouldn't they look loved-and lovely? They *were*, that's all. As to wit, Thad's voice just now...

Oh, Johnny! Johnny, come back! Wherever you are, all the rest of you, darling—come back!

The three of them sat together, drinking hot tea and talking: the dance, and biology, McLafferty and psychosomatic cures, the current topics of gossip and news in the Dome—all but one, Lisa thought. None of them mentioned John Wendt.

He's down by now, I guess...

"What time does the rocket get down to Earth usually?" she asked.

"Oh, six, seven, eight, maybe nine—depends on the Belt and ionosphere conditions, mostly."

She nodded, sipped tea. It was nearly six now; he'd be on Relay, or on the way down. What was he thinking? What had he been thinking?

Nothing, of course. He'd been asleep all this time. Four days in her life that had simply *not-been* for him: it was a strange thought, and an unpleasant one.

She was up in her room, just done changing for dinner, when Chris phoned, to tell her he'd received clearance on the Earth landing. "I just wanted to let you know," he said a bit awkwardly. "Everything's fine..."

"Johnny—?" She took a firm grip on the words this time: "Johnny was all right? He wasn't upset, or—anything?"

"He's fine. Tell you the truth, Lee, I asked for a special call on it. He came out of it fine. Calm, sent word he'd meet you at Baja next week."

"Oh thank *God!*"

She had not meant that to be said aloud; she was not even certain that she had. But the words stayed in her brain like a refrain for hours afterward: *thank God, oh, thank God!*

"...told them I'd ask you, and see what you..."

"I'm sorry, Chris. I was wandering. I missed something."

"The World Dome call."

"Which World Dome call?"

"You were wandering, gal. I was telling you, I had a call from the UN Dome right after the one from Relay. They heard you were staying on this week, and wanted to know if there was any chance of getting you to give an evening performance before you go?"

"Performance? Here? On the *Moon?*"

"Well, I said I didn't know—Why not? I should think this place would be a dancer's dream?"

He was dead right, of course. And she was shocked that in five days here she'd never even *thought* of the things you could do dancing at one-sixth gravity!

"I'd *love* to, Chris, but—listen, I'll try some stuff tonight and see how it goes, okay? Can you let them know tomorrow morning?"

"Sure. It would be all rush-rush, anyhow. Not much difference tonight or tomorrow. You had dinner yet?"

"I was just going. I told Thad I'd eat with him and that lovely girl—Rita?"

"Rita Donovan?"

"That's right. But if I'm going to practice, I think I'll eat later. Are you going down now?"

"I suppose so. Why?"

"Well, would you tell Thad? Or what's his room? I'll call—"

"I'll let him know. Now can *I* ask a favor?"

"Any time, Chris." He was such a *nice* man.

"Frankly, I feel kind of foolish," he said, with his slow smile, "but Kutler's been up here sounding off about your dancing, and tell you the truth, I don't usually take much time for that kind of thing on tri-di. I—"

She let out a peal of delighted laughter. "*Doctor* Christensen, are you asking for a stage-door pass to watch rehearsal?"

"I guess that's the size of it." He actually looked sheepish...!

"Okay, but on one condition—"

"Yes?"

"Where's the stage?"

He started to answer, and she interrupted. "I didn't mean the stage. I meant a place for practice. All I need is floor and something to play tapes on. Oh—can I get some stuff from the library now?"

"All the time," he said. "Like the dining room. Library has to stay open, around here. Everyone's on such whacky schedules."

"Well, good, I'll change and go see what they've got. Suppose—how about meeting me there? Then you can show me where to set up shop?"

"Great. Twenty minutes. I'll see Thad on the way."

"You're a doll." She switched off, humming the tune that had started to run through her head as soon as she thought at all seriously about dancing here. But how could she not have thought of it once all this time?

She shook her head, smiling, still humming, and changed to dance leotards, added a full skirt, and slipped on soft dance shoes.

Before she left the room, she stood for a long moment looking through the dome wall at the brilliant mid-day moonscape outside.

If I ask to see the Shack, they'll let me go out, she thought; and thought afterwards, it was silly to *want* to so much. But she would ask.

Mexcity—Monday, August 29, 9:30 A.M. (C.S.T.)

The General refolded his morning paper, and set it neatly in its accustomed upper left-hand corner of his desk. He was pleased. By now the gossip columnists would be in full cry; the afternoon papers would be worth seeing.

From his briefcase, he took a flat envelope, and excerpted three microfilms. He threw the first one on the desk reader, and glanced through it again: Chris was too damn involved with Wendt, he thought worriedly. The message was somehow, almost intangibly, *fuzzy;* not Chris' usual clear-stated summary, anyhow. And somehow the man had completely missed seeing the obvious newspaper advantages.

Prentiss had just about bust a gut getting the press release ready when word came from Relay—and Chris hadn't even thought to call him during the week on it, so they could get set ahead.

Nobody (but nobody, the General thought chuckling reminiscently) was going to believe that Johnny Wendt had gone up to the Moon, in the company of a beautiful dancer, both under strictest security to the point of full-trip sedation, and come back the same way, the same *Messenger* orbit, leaving the gal behind, for purely personal, non-significant reasons.

He found it hard to believe himself. The more he thought about it, the more the overtones—or undertones?—of the courier-message from Christensen bothered him.

Hell, he decided: *It's good copy. That's all.*

And what *could* Chris be pulling?

It didn't make sense enough to worry over.

So he stopped worrying.

The next film he had also seen at home the night before, but he studied it carefully again. It was long: five single-spaced typed pages, compactly written; and it contained the life history of Ramon E. McLafferty, Congressman from East Chile, white hope of the Industrialist Party, Chairman of the Space Security Subcommittee of the Joint House Senate Space Affairs Committee—former ranch hand, bookie, stock yard "insurance"-protection boss, newspaper owner, fighting union smasher, contractor for nearly 20% of the work on construction of the *Messenger*, minority holder of Undersea Corp. stock, and probable next junior Chilean Senator.

The General spent some time rereading, and reading again, the story of Ray McLafferty's rags-to-riches rise—plus an abstract of a psychoanalytic report, and some dirty-edges peripheral track-trailing. When he felt quite sure he had all the pertinent facts in his mind, he took the film and placed it immediately in the special miniature safe at the back of his bottom desk drawer.

The third film was a standard form from M. I., stamped across the top with block-lettered TOP SECRET's. This one Harbridge had gotten on his way to work. It was, as it turned out, the most interesting document of the three.

In one unsensationally worded paragraph, it stated conclusively that definite evidence had finally been obtained regarding the Palisades Query. There had been a physical transferal of subjects (ref. PQ 1579J-2z) on several occasions, first known being 9/12/76; most recent, 3/14/77; two known dates in between, and three suspected. Transferal in small quantity, but sufficient for purpose of investigation by instigators.

Which meant simply that on at least four occasions, small, but significant, samples of Mars-bugs had been successfully turned over to agents of Red Dome, where said samples might now be assumed to have flourished and multiplied, and to be under study at least as intensive as that at Playfair?

The General pursed his lips thoughtfully. He removed the film, and held a match to the edge, dropped it into a metal bowl set with precision at the right front edge of the desktop, watched it dissolve into smoke and a small residue of chemical matter.

He repeated the procedure with Chris's report, smiling as he thought about Ray McLafferty:

Lordy, what he'd give to see that *damn paper!*

The smile was because there *was no* possibility that any such information could get to the Congressman's hands.

Dollars Dome—Tuesday, August 30, 1977

"I hate to stop and eat, even," she said. Her cheeks were pink, and her smile was one of pure sensual pleasure. You could see in the way she walked that she was still feeling the wild pleasures of leaps and pirouettes to soaring music, free from the weight of a lifetime on Earth. "You know, I just can't figure out why I never even *thought* of it till they asked!"

Phil smiled, and manufactured a leer. "Come let me show you my couch," he said. "We'll find out why."

"Darling," she said. "But I'm *hungry.*"

"Well—okay," he said. *"After* dinner."

They laughed at each other, and impulsively, she reached for his hand as they walked into the dining room. Damn if it wasn't catching, he thought with amusement, and yet with a sharpening edge of concern—because it just didn't *fit.* But when you looked at the tables in here, the groups of two, four, five, six, eating and talking and smiling...

It reminded him of something dim, in the background of memory...

He caught it: photographs, in his childhood, of Israeli and Russian co-ops. Propaganda shots, of happy smiling healthy "free workers."

But the scene here was not posed. It was for real. And it went on all the time, all the hell over the slaphappy Dome. And it was getting more pronounced. He noticed it more than he had at first, in spite of getting used to it. *And* he thought it had started to show up in the clinical picture too. Nothing conclusive yet, but—

"Hey?" She'd said something he missed.

"Just—I wish I was going to have time to *do* that show."

"Well, why not? Chris said something about them calling again today. If you gave the word now, I'll bet they'd get it set for tomorrow night?"

"*Tomorrow?* Don't be silly, dear. I'd need at *least* four more—well, maybe three days. But I'm just *starting* to get an idea what I can do. Phil, it's like—like starting all over, say to learn ballet, *after* you've been an expert in, say, African dance. It's *that* different!"

"Yeah? Well you could fool me, kid. I'm just ignorant enough to think you looked damn good back there."

They took their dinners to a table where Thad Bourgnese and the Donovan girl and a couple of others were already seated. Thad jumped up to move a chair for Lee next to his own. Phil pulled up his own chair alongside Rita, watching her.

By every damn bit of experience he had with anyone he'd ever known, this particular girl ought to flip her lid this time. Instead, she turned and smiled and said, "She is just too beautiful to believe, isn't she?"

"Yeah." Phil ate his soup, and kept his thoughts to himself. When Chris joined them a few minutes later, and took Lisa's other side, engaging her in intense quiet-voiced conversation, he watched Thad from out of the edge of his vision.

Bourgnese turned to Rita again. That was all. You'd have sworn no one anywhere around the table had felt the least ruffle of irritation at any point.

Phil was beginning to believe they *hadn't;* for the first time, he started mentally reviewing, *seriously,* some of the startling improvements he'd seen in his hypertension cases. *It figures,* he thought, reluctantly. *Dammit, if it don't figure...*

"Phil!"

"Hmmm?" He looked past Rita and Thad to Lee's rosy face.

"Remember what we were saying before?"

"Yeah?" *Which what? Which before?*

"Well," she said, brimming with laughter, "Chris wants to know if I'd be willing to give up my berth this week, so he can take it!"

"I got the official bit just now," Chris told them all. "They want me to testify next Tuesday. But, Lee, we can switch someone else, if you think—"

"Oh, *no*. I mean, thanks, but—well, frankly, I was just telling Phil when we came in, I wished I could have some more time for practicing. Now I've got started, I'm just *flabbergasted...*"

Later, he got her alone long enough to make sure she had not spoken spur-of-the-moment, before she thought about Johnny.
She hadn't.
"Chris said I could radiowire him this evening, and if he wants, he'll be able to call me, tonight or tomorrow. So we're not announcing anything about the performance yet. But he got a report that Johnny was fine when he landed, and—oh, dammit, Phil, one week won't *kill* him. One *more* week, I mean. And when do you think I'll ever get a chance to do this stuff again?"
"Honey—*I'm* not saying No."
"I know." She looked at him with such affection it almost hurt. "I'm not arguing with you, either, dear—just with me. But you know—I'm beginning to think maybe Johnny's a lot tougher than we give him credit for. *I* think he'll be okay." She stepped away, turned back for a moment. "Or maybe I want to find out if he is," she added, and vanished down the ramp to her practice room.

St. Croix, U.S.A.A.—Friday, September 2, 1977

The bar was cool and dim in the daytime, a good place to sit and look, without the added haze and heat and too-bright light, into the anyhow doubtful mirror of your mind. But as dusk dropped on the island, the bar conversely brightened. With the evening's coolness, it grew warmer inside. At midnight, it had become a gaudy splotch of brilliance a-burst with noise, fragrance and stench, sweat and promises.
Light and color, odors and entreating bodies, these could be shut out, he had learned quickly, simply by keeping his eyes on his glass, and his glass full enough. But the noises—shrieking and murmuring, laughter and shouts, the sound of glasses, of cards and rolling dice and clicking wheels, of shuffling feet, pounding heels, of silver coins and golden rum in swift exchange—the blood-beating rhythm of the calypso band in back of the thousand sounds of passion and delight, despair, forgetfulness, lust and seduction in the tropic night—these

could not be shut out, nor would he do so if he could. They built a barrier over the darkness that shrouded the mirror of his soul.

Johnny sat where he had been since noon, in the carved wooden booth, and the girl's voice for some reason emerged by itself, separately, from the sound of the room, drawing him back from the dazed withdrawal with which he had countered the bar's evening dawn.

He looked at her apprehensively: lovely kid. He shook his head: "No thanks, doll. Thanks, but no thanks. Siddown. Have a drink."

She sat.

She was young, very young. Her shoulders were bare, and the white ruffles of her blouse on breast and arms gave her an oddly pure look in the cacophony of color in the midnight-bar. When she sat, the cerise skirt and black lace ruffle of her petticoat were hidden; all he could see was the blouse and bare skin above. Light spilled on golden skin; the crimson of her lips was all the impact of color she made; all the rest was black (hair and eyes), and white (blouse, teeth, eyes), and glowing tan-gold. She might have been anything from a grown-up twelve to well-preserved twenty-two—well preserved, that is, for an island girl of her trade. Johnny guessed seventeen.

While she drank rum-and-coke, and he sipped a fresh bourbon, he gave the whole idea some serious thought. A lovely girl, certainly. Clean looking, too. He could check with Jake. Jake would know; Jake was his buddy. Jake said, don't take any babes up without checkin' first. Half of 'em's sick, and most of the rest is thieves. Jest check with me first. That's what Jake said.

Jake was at the bar now. Johnny toyed with the thought of taking the girl to the bar, and then maybe upstairs. The room upstairs was big and dim, cool, quiet now at midnight as it had been in the bar when he came in at noon. At noon the room was hot, and even through the blinds the whiteness of high sun crept in.

The room was cool now: cool and quiet and all alone.

Lisa...

"What's your name, doll?"

She told him, and it was hilariously funny, because it was Dolly, and he'd called her *doll* so she'd thought he knew all along, and the band came and played *Dolly Dawn*. When they went to the bar, Jake nodded and said Dolly was fine, Dolly be good for him. So he gave Dolly five dollars, for being a good girl, and shook hands with Jake, and went up alone to the dim cool aloneness where nobody knew or cared anything anyhow he could sleep deep and no dreams.

But he remembered before he was all the way asleep that it was Friday—*had been* Friday—and tomorrow—today—he would have to leave...back to where the world was and people who knew all about it...about everything.

When he woke up, the newspaper was under the door for him: he'd told them when he came: no papers, no tri-di, no nothin', till Saturday. Bring me a paper on Saturday. And here it was.

They were all right. Jake, all of them, they were okay.

The headline was right on page one.

MOON LAB DIRECTOR WILL TESTIFY
Christensen To Appear
At SAC Hearing Tuesday

Mexcity, Sep. 2: Dr. Peter A. Christensen, Research Director of the U.S.A.A. Moon Laboratory, is en route to Earth today, to testify voluntarily for the McLafferty Committee, at a hearing next Tuesday, Aug. 23.

The announcement of Dr. Christensen's compliance with the request of the S.A.C. Security Subcommittee Chairman, Rep. Ramon E. McLafferty (I., E. Ch.) was made today by Brigadier General "Jed" Harbridge, Decagon Science and Space chief. The Moon Lab program, although under Congressional control primarily, is sponsored in part by the U.S.A.A. Space Academy, and associated Decagon Space Research units.

There was no comment from Gen. Harbridge on the "evidence" McLafferty claims to have regarding Security leaks, and general laxity, at the Moon Dome. The official Decagon statement said only that Dr. Christensen boarded the *Messenger* satellite last night, and will appear, of his own volition, at the Tuesday hearing.

Dr. Christensen's decision followed an official request from the Subcommittee radioed out to the Moon on Tuesday. Acknowledgement of the message and compliance with the request was then received on Wednesday by Representative McLafferty, it was learned at his office here today. Dr. Christensen will arrive on Earth Sunday, Aug. 21, at approximately 8:00 P.M., at St. Thom Spaceport. The rocket, previously announced to land at Baja Spaceport, was rescheduled for St. Thom after receipt of Dr. Christensen's message to the Decagon.

Johnny smiled wryly. Poor Chris—everything had looked so rosy to him five years ago. They were really ganging up on the guy now. *Yeah—poor Chris! Poor benighted bastard! Damn good thing*...but you couldn't help feeling sorry for the man. He meant well; he was a Hell of a good guy.

Just stupid, that's all!

Johnny shrugged, dropped the paper, picked it up and rimed through for other news, feeling luxurious because he didn't have to leave today after all. The ship was coming to St. Thom. Twenty minutes away, was all. Plenty of time, if he left on the six o'clock jitney tomorrow. "About 8 P.M." usually wound up to mean about midnight...

TROVI TO DANCE ON MOON

Well, well, we're getting around, aren't we?

It was a good picture of her, one of the batch they had taken out at the edge of the pool last September: Lee in Peter Pan costume, poised on one toe, it seemed, right on the edge of the pool—about to take off, you'd swear it.

A brand new art form will be born this coming Saturday night [this is what it said underneath] when Lisa Trovi, the world-renowned tri-di dancer, will give a precedent-making performance at the Moon's World Dome. Miss Trovi has been staying on the Moon, at the U.S.A.A. Dome, since August 24, practicing for her appearance this Saturday.

"It's a completely new kind of dance," Miss Trovi says. "I'm just beginning to realize what can be done in light gravity. It's like changing from swimming in treacle to swimming in water."

The performance, scheduled for 8.30 P.M. (G.S.T.—3.30 P.M. C.S.T.) will be broadcast live if conditions permit. Tri-di tapes will be aired from New York at a later date.

Saturday...

But *this* was Saturday. She wasn't on the wheel. She wasn't coming.

He realized only slowly that he was not surprised.

"Stands to reason," he thought. He showered and went down for a big breakfast of ham and eggs, pineapple juice, and good native rum at the bar.

CHAPTER SEVEN
September 5-18, 1977

Acapulco—Monday evening, September 5.

"Still no dice?"

"Nothing. God knows where the dam fool is." Chris came back from the telephone, sat down in the webbed chair, and stared without seeing at an expanse of mountain, sun, water, and forest that would have demanded the full attention of any man who did not live in daily view of heaven itself.

"How bad was it?" Harbridge asked.

"Not too. He had sense enough to suggest going back himself, before it got worse. I just wish to hell *I* hadn't been such a fool. I should have known—I'll tell you, the one I feel sorry for is the girl. Lisa. He doesn't know what he's—Hell, sure he does!" *I keep forgetting,* he thought, ashamed. *Johnny's entitled to anything he can get!*

"I don't know what's going to happen now," he said thoughtfully. "If he's not home, he might not have gotten her wire either. Hell to pay if he finds out from the papers, or—Well, let's hope he took off on a bat after he did get the message. But I hope she's heard from him."

Harbridge was smiling with a sort of tolerant amusement. "Must be quite a girl," he said.

"Go to Hell," said Chris amiably. Both men laughed, and turned their attention to the less entertaining but more urgent business of the next day's testimony.

Chris was astonished, as always, at a glimpse into the workings of a Harbridge operation. Jed had a list of the questions that he would be asked. Jed also knew that McLafferty planned on parlaying the week's hearings into a trip to the Moon for himself. And he knew which reporters would cover the day with what biases.

"Reporters?" Chris was surprised. "Isn't it on the air?"

"Nope." Jed's mouth wrinkled briefly in half-smile. "The Honorable Congressman from East Chile says that he will not further endanger the Security of the Americas by utilizing a hearing chamber in which matters of utmost secrecy must be discussed as an open-air forum for personal publicity. I quote," he added, "from a rather extensive article in the current *Time.*"

"Well, well. Whaddya know? This boy is not stupid."

"Not even a little. Bear it in mind. Now; suppose we run through the questions. Take the stand, Doctor."

They went down the list. Occasionally, Jed would stop listening to make a suggestion. Once he proposed a complete change of treatment. Mostly, he nodded with satisfaction. "You're really doing a job up there, Chris," he said when they finished. "Damn! It's a pleasure to see someone once in a while who knows what goes on in his own bailiwick." He went to the bar. "What'll you have? Scotch?" He poured, shaking his head. "Sometimes, lately, it gets to seem as if everyone has his eye on the ball so hard that you'd swear they don't know what team they're playing for. Or what game it is. I don't think I know more than a dozen men in Mexcity who actually do their jobs—that's not true, either," he stopped himself. "I know plenty of them—but they work for somebody. I meant men at the top. They're so busy staying there, somebody else has to 'handle the details.' Which means, do their work for them, while they keep a weather-eye out on the lookout post. Anyhow," he said briskly, "Ray McLafferty *knows* what he's doing. He's no pushover, Chris." He drank deeply, and walked over to where his comrade-in-arms of twenty years' battles sat.

"Listen, Chris, what I'm saying is: watch out for this guy. He's dangerous. Frankly, I think I might just have outsmarted myself this time."

"That's not how you sounded an hour ago." Chris twirled his glass in his hand. He did not look up. He knew Jed Harbridge pretty well. There was more coming. "I thought we had it made?"

"Here's how I see it—as of right now. Ray'll shoot the works on this thing. It's a sure ticket into the Senate for him, if he plays it right. And he wants that seat *bad.* He's aiming high. Frankly, I'm with him. He's smart and he works hard, and he's got enough imagination to see what that ass in Americas House couldn't see if you painted it out for him color by color. The day Ray gets in there—and I think he'll make it in twelve years, with any luck—we'll *have* a Space program and we won't ever have to go through this kind of friggin corruption to get what we need again."

"So? This is bad?" Chris put his glass down. He was beginning to understand, and he did not like the way it felt, somewhere around the middle of his belly.

"Maybe. For you. Play it tough tomorrow, Chris. But when he comes to the Dome—I'd play it soft if I were you. He wants a Space program—but he wants it under his thumb. If you're *too* tough— Well, he'll probably be head of SAC next year."

"I think I follow you, but I don't know if I like the looks of the terrain. I take it you mean, *we're* going to win, but I just might lose?"

"I didn't figure it that way, Chris—Well, hell, you know that. This McLafferty is new; I underestimated him at first...I still think we can handle him. I just don't want to see you go in there without knowing everything."

"Yeah. I know." Chris stood up. "Guess I'll try Johnny once more, before I quit. Say—wasn't there something about a subpoena for him? Maybe he's ducking—"

"Or maybe they're keeping him tanked up and happy until the right day. That's one thing that does worry me, Chris. I hope you find the guy."

"Yeah. Well, there's nothing that he can say, really. Christ, he didn't even *see* anything but the Dome. Had him kept under sedation the whole way." He stopped in the doorway and turned back. "Here's how I figure it, Jed. Like, I dragged Johnny up there because his name would help, and I guess after I met the girl, I knew she'd push too, right with us. She wants him back on his feet. She's a smart chick. She knows he can't make it from flat on his fanny; he needs a job to do. So: I get the guy up there. But I keep him knocked out all the way up. Why? Because I knew damn well he'd flip sooner or later, and I wanted to be on hand myself when he did. Hell, I don't mean I thought it out that way, in so many words—but I can see it easily enough from here.

"So Johnny's my old buddy. Like you and me. Blood and sweat. And tears. The whole routine. I didn't give much of a damn what it did to *him*. I got my newspaper story. If he'd cracked some other way from how he did, I might even have got to him and got him back to work. Snake pit. You know? But I wasn't thinking about *him*.

"So if Johnny's expendable, who gives a damn about me? Tell you the truth, I'm getting old enough so I should maybe get back to Earth anyhow." *And get married...?*

The unbidden thought stopped him cold. "Don't rush anything," Jed said drily. "You're not quite fired yet." His mouth wrinkled again in the not-quite smile. "Why don't you give this dish a job up there, man, instead of trailing her back here?"

That sonofabitch knows too damn much!

"Okay," he said. "Why don't you talk the boys up on the hill into setting up an institute of the dance upstairs? Maybe a whole Art Academy? They might go that a lot quicker than a manned flight again."

When he got the operator again, he was surprised, and obscurely annoyed with himself, to find he had to clear an adolescent lump from his throat before he could give Johnny's number.

And there was no answer, still.

Dollars Dome—Monday, September 5, 5 P.M. (C.S.T.)

The job itself was proving unexpectedly satisfying. Dr. Kutler brought his last patient's card up to date and sat back, swiveled his chair around and pulled aside the shutters that closed off the Dome wall during consultations. For the victims of the variety of ailments that constituted what they had started to call "loony-sickness," even the sight of the alien land could interfere with the effort at therapy— no matter how eager the patient was to be there, or how idealistically or aesthetically pleased by the sight. When a man's body is in rebellion against the disruptive effects of just-too-much-difference in his environment, it helps to minimize those differences—as much as possible—while trying to cure the bodily disorder.

The basic cause of the internal "dyscommunication" which caused hearts to pump overtime and reaching fingers to tremble and muscles to twitch could not be shut out or turned off or even disguised. Low gravity was the devil man had to fight—and conquer—on the Moon; and if he could have turned it off for his patients, Phil would not have done so.

That was what quarterly leaves did. His job was to help them teach their bodies to live *with* the difference.

Some people could do it. To the doctor, that meant that most, if not all, could *learn*. Chris had stayed healthy for eleven years of almost-solid Moon residence. Johnny had no psychosomatic troubles through two and a half years of low-grav and no-grav on the Mars trip. There were at least a dozen others on the Dome staff who had always regarded the required leaves as a nuisance, and had volunteered eagerly for experimental work—more eagerly than usefully. The valuable patients were those who *got* sick.

The valuable doctor, however, stayed healthy. It was too soon to tell, of course, about himself. Kutler knew his own weaknesses better than most men do; but how predict strength or weakness against an unknown assailant?

That didn't hold all the way either—He knew he could predict Lisa's immunity. The woman was so incredibly *in control* of her own body. He remembered her at World Dome, soaring like a new—better?—kind of human...a free creature...

He tried to dispose entirely of the idea gnawing him. It was so absurd he should never, he thought, have allowed himself to think the idea through verbally. But he had; and it sure as hell *wasn't* absurd from his own point of view. *She* was a teacher who could be trusted to put her words in to practice, to teach by doing.

Okay, so it's a great notion. Get yourself somebody... Plenty of dancers and physical therapists would love the chance.

He went to the intercom, dialed, and waited. No answer. He had almost switched off when the screen suddenly lit.

"Oh, Phil—Hi!" She was breathless. "I just got in, heard the thing buzzing. What's up? Have you heard...?"

She stopped as he shook his head. "No. I called to see if you had. Got in from *where?*"

"Thad Bourgnese took me out to the Shack. Phil, it's so silly, but you know I'm halfway in love with this place? I feel like a stinker, I mean, I ought to be chewing my fingernails to get home, but I—well, damn it, I'm glad I couldn't take the last trip down!"

Defiant, she was rather more lovely than usual, he decided. "Well, fine," he smiled. "I was just thinking about a job for you here."

"*Here?* Dancer-in-residence?" But before she laughed, a look of surprised delight had fled across her face, and an expression of chagrin had followed it so quickly it was unlikely anyone but a trained observer would have noticed the change from the first flush of reaction to the laugh.

"Why not?" He did not follow it up; he was more than a little annoyed with himself for having said anything to begin with. "Okay, kid," he said. "I was just checking in on you.

"Right. I'll see you, Phil, thanks for the call...hey!" She reached to the side of the screen, toward where the tube slot must be. "There's a message. I didn't notice." She tore open the radioletter, glanced at the bottom, and nodded: "Johnny." Then her face went white, and her mouth started to open as if she'd been slapped in the face.

The screen went dead. "I'm sorry, Phil. 'Scuse me." The audio clicked off too.

The bastard! The lousy lushin' whining wailing nasty minded bastard!

Phil went to the couch, knelt in front of it, and beat clenched fists against the padding till he felt his rage subside.

He got up, went to his desk, pulled out his own old-fashioned typewriter, without which he could not think, and started typing. When he got up, half an hour later, he was Dr. Kutler again—and even Phil, plain Phil, had recognized that whatever Johnny wrote, it was in response to the knowledge that his wife did not want to come home.

Because she *was* his wife—whatever *she* thought about it.

And she did *not* want to leave, whether *she* knew it or not.

And it was a hundred to one, at least, that Johnny had picked the nastiest, hurtingest, angriest *way* to respond; but that was just foolish—not vicious.

A man has a right to react when his girl—or his wife—stands him up.

CHRISTY TOPS McLFTY
Moon Man Takes Decision Over Congress
Quizzer at SAC Subcommittee Hearing

Mexcity, Sep. 6: "Chris" Christensen, Research Director at U.S.A.A.'s Moon Dome, swapped questions and answers here today with Ray McLafferty, East Chile Congressman, whose chances of election to the Senate may hang on the outcome of the special hearings now being conducted by his SAC subcommittee on Space Security.

Reporters present at the closed hearing agreed generally that the scientist won this round. In answer to Committee queries, he outlined a solid Security plan in operation now, and invited the whole committee to come and see for themselves what conditions were.

Confronted with the till now mysterious "evidence" which initiated Rep. McLafferty's interest in Moon Security—a news item on new research with "Mars-bugs," which violated Top-Secret classification, according to Rep. McLafferty—Dr. Christensen said that the contents of the article had not been classified, due to laxity in the SAC offices.

The material, he explained—in spite of the obvious lack of interest of some Committee members—had been contained in a Special Report submitted by him to SAC for approval and financing on June 19 of this year. Dr. Christensen's proposal at that time concerned the newly enlarged Biological Section, in charge of research on the Martian micro-organisms ("Mars-bugs") brought back in the ill-starred *Colombo* by Col. Johnny Wendt. The Moon Research Director requested permission to move the Department, bugs and all, to an Earth laboratory where Security would be maintained more effectively, and the expansions then under consideration might be effected with a great deal less expense.

His report was "not accepted," said Dr. Christensen. Instead, he was granted additional sums for personnel on the Moon. Apparently the original report was never "processed" officially in the SAC office at all, but Dr. Christensen testified that copies were made there, and that he saw one himself which had been typed in that office.

The scientist added that some of the personnel funds had been applied to expansion of the psychiatric staff of the Dome, in an effort to solve the psychogenic problems that have made extended quarterly Earth leaves mandatory for Dome personnel. The statement anticipated queries from the Subcommittee regarding Security provisions during such leaves. Dr. Christensen said there was no way to insure strict Security while the leave system was in operation.

Rockland—Tuesday, September 6, 10 P.M. (E.D.S.T.)

Johnny set the heli down on the lawn gently, feeling his way almost by touch, without the field lights. He switched off the ignition, and got his bag out of the trunk space behind the seat. Picked up the pile of newspapers, climbed to the ground.

Half way to the house, he heard the noise in the trees and stopped.

"Who's there?"

"Colonel Wendt?"

"Who are you?"

A man, middle-sized, middle-aged, middle-anything, as far as the moonlight revealed him, came from the trees.

"Colonel Wendt?" he said again.

"You're on private property, mister."

"You are Colonel John Wendt?"

"What's it to you? I said you're trespassing. Now—*get out!*"

"Colonel Wendt, I am a duly sworn deputy of..."

That was as much as he managed. Johnny dropped the bag and papers, and swung with the same motion. The middling man went down like a ripped sack of flour.

Johnny grinned. He rubbed his fist, pleased. *First damn time I've felt half-alive,* he thought, *since...*

It was just as well not to think back that far.

He picked up the papers, grabbed the suitcase again, and let himself into the house. He turned lights on, prowled through the rooms, looking for—what? He wasn't sure. Whatever it was, it wasn't there. Everything normal, just as they left it. Lee's things still in the closet. *Well, what did you think? That she'd teleport them out?*

He switched on the field lights, went back outside. The man was gone. Johnny turned back sharply, went in and got the key, locked up behind him this time when he came out. Went five steps and turned back, unlocked the door, went into his den, and came out a few minutes later with a gun full of birdshot. He held it conspicuously in plain sight while he locked up again. Then he paced off the distance to the heli, watching the trees to the right and left of the path closely.

"Don't mind shooting anybody trespassing on my property," he remarked aloud.

He was out on the field when he heard the crackling twigs of the man's retreat. He smiled. Maybe instead of putting the ship up, he ought to take off and...

A brawl wouldn't solve anything.

But it sure as Hell would *feel* good.

He flexed his shoulders, felt muscles tighten, and decided regretfully that he'd better get back in the house and stay there.

He hangared the heli, locked the garage, and went back indoors. Then he took the stack of newspapers and spread them on the coffee table in the living room. They were full of it, all right.

CHRISTY TOPS McLFTY.
WENDT TO BE CALLED.
McLAFFERTY WILL GO TO MOON DOME
SCIENTIST LAYS BLAME FOR 'LEAKS' TO SAC

He read with particular interest one headed, DR. C. SAYS WENDT SEDATION WAS S.O.P. SECURITY MEASURE, where he learned for the first time that sedation for the trip was ordinarily limited to the self-powered shuttle trips at each end: all other passengers on the shuttle that carried him and Lisa to the Moon had been awake in the *Messenger,* and all but himself, coming down. According to Chris, the precaution was taken in his case to avert possible efforts by "any agents of other powers" to get information they thought Col. Wendt might possess.

Chris also explained that his trip had been "only a visit," but it sounded so phony, no one would ever believe it.   Again Johnny grinned; Chris was always a scrapper, when they got him mad.

Damn, but a good old-fashioned street fight would make a new man out of him...

And get him subpoenaed.   He figured to stay in the house for a while.

One paper had pictures of Lisa's appearance at World Dome on Saturday, and a review, which mentioned the presence of Dr. Kutler among the U.S.A.A. party at the performance.   "Miss Trovi was escorted by Dr. Thaddeus Borgnese, Chief Biochemist at U.S.A.A. Dome," it said right afterwards.

Well, whaddya know? We're makin' time, hey?

He was startled at how calm he felt about it all.

When he found the wire from her in the facs chute, with last Tuesday's date on it, he did not want to open it.   He almost threw it out.   *Leave well enough alone. It's done, it's over. Forget it.* He had already told her so.   His own wire would be in her hands by now.

He wound up putting the envelope, unopened, in his desk drawer. Tomorrow, he could decide what to do with it.

He did not drink. He went to bed at midnight, cold sober. To his surprise, he fell asleep without trouble, and slept well all night.

Dollars Dome—Monday, September 5, 9:30 P.M. (C.S.T.)

Okay babe if that's how you want it. It was fun while it lasted, I guess. My least sincere congratulations to whoever—whoops, whomever—the lucky man may be.

Easy come, easy go, babe.
Better luck next round.
                    Johnny

She must have read it through fifty times, looking for something, some clue, somewhere in it, that would explain what it meant. Because it couldn't mean what it said. That didn't make sense.

She knew there were thirty-nine words in it. There'd been a movie or book once called *Thirty-nine Steps*. A movie—she saw it at the Museum. Thirty-nine steps to where? Out. Right out, obviously. But...

Why? Because it was *Johnny*, that's why! There just wasn't any other reason to find.

The phone buzzed. Phil. She'd promised to call him back, hadn't she?

"Hey, kid, you hungry yet?" he asked.

"N'nnoo. Thanks, Phil."

"Well, how about a drink? A walk in the Mall? The way I feel tonight, gal, I'll even go dancing with you..."

She kept shaking her head, but she smiled.

"Phil, you're sweet, but I think I better..."

"I think you better listen to Doctor. Turn on your screen?"

"Phil, honestly, I—"

"Let's put it this way. *I'll* go have a drink. Then I'll come pick you up. We'll do whatever you want to do. Or just sit and talk. But be ready in fifteen minutes, or you'll find out—" He made that improbable leer of his. "—I ain't like no lily myself. Hate to go banging doors down, but—" he shrugged fatalistically "—sometimes, you know...? See you. Fifteen minutes." And he switched off before the seed of laughter turned to tears or gave her voice enough to answer.

She tried to call back, but he wasn't in, or didn't answer. She washed her face, and got dressed. She was just putting lipstick on when he knocked.

She nodded casually at the envelope on the bed.

"May I?"

"Go ahead."

She watched in the mirror while he read, saw pain flush his face and retire, and the doctor face take over.

For a moment, she was certain that his pain was for her, and felt an answering surge of—gratitude? Then she told herself not to be foolish; Phil had plenty of reason for pain of his own when Johnny pulled one like this.

They wound up in his office. Two days before lunar sundown, the view from this side of the Dome was a sharp contrast in near light and far dark; but even the still-lit portion of the Moon's surface was without glare, since the shadowless Dome itself filtered the rays of the low-lying sun to give the moonscape from this window almost the look of atmosphered land.

They sat in front of the window, with the inside lights off, and talked.

They talked all around it, brushing it lightly just once in a while. She knew he would not push; but she also knew that she *had* to talk to him, now. He wanted to give her reassurance and friendship; but this time she really needed advice.

He was rambling on about a theory of heart disease he had seen in a journal of psychosomatic medicine, when the right moment came.

"Phil?" she broke in.

He stopped talking. That was all. No question, no look her way, even. He knew she was ready.

"Phil, listen, this mess is—well, I don't know if I mean it's worse than you think, or better? If I could just tell for sure what he really wants—I mean—Phil, does he mean it? Or is he going to change his mind next week, and come yell for mama?"

"You probably know the answer to that one better than. I do."

"I guess I already answered it," she admitted.

Silence. Then:

"So I guess *I* have to decide what I'll do when he does?"

"Or you could just decide what to do *now.*"

"How do you mean—? Well, yes, I hadn't thought of that." She heard her own short laugh, like that of a stranger. "I'll have to have someplace to go. And my things are all well, that doesn't matter. There's plenty of *money,*" she said angrily. "That helps, doesn't it?"

"Where were you thinking of going?"

"Well, I *wasn't.* I wasn't *thinking.* And I kind of resent you making me start now."

Nothing. She looked at him. He was looking at her, smiling. An old friend. He *knew.*

He didn't know everything, though.

"Phil?"

"Hmmm?"

"Remember that time I had lunch with you, right about when Chris was down?"

"Yes."

"Remember I said Johnny might have to—to face up to something he wouldn't like?"

"Yes?"

"Well—I—I'm pregnant, Phil. I thought so then, but I wasn't sure."

Well, she thought gleefully, *I did it at last!* Phil Kutler had jumped forward in his chair, just like any *normal man.*

"You thought so in *June?*" He was absolutely *staring!* "How far along are you then?"

"Well—four and a half months or so, around there, I guess."

"Stand up." She did.

"Yeah. I guess so," he said, and sat back again. "It *could* be—at four-and-a-half—with you. I'll be damned!" He was watching her closely, and, she realized, with a warmth of affection that made all the rest of the mess *much* easier. "So?" he said. "For heaven's sake, sit down, Lee. I've had my look." She sat. "Now: I guess that means you—"

"It doesn't mean anything one way or the other, Phil. It just means that whatever the rest means is *more* so, that's all." Here she was on solid ground. *This* part she'd thought out beforehand, and carefully. "The thing is, Phil, that other time even, when I first *thought*

I might be pregnant, I realized I couldn't go through with it the way things were."

She saw his slight start, and smiled. "I don't mean *that*. I meant *marrying* him. I—"

She had kept herself beautifully under control up to then, but suddenly everything inside was clogging up. "I—" She stood up. She walked around the room, sat down at last on the couch, behind his back. "I decided," she said carefully, "that unless things changed a lot at home, if it turned out I was, I would just leave, and not—I mean, not even *tell* him."

"But you didn't. Hold up! *Does he know or not?*"

She shook her head. "No." She looked up at him, feeling awfully foolish for some reason. But it made *sense*, it all made sense, this part of it. She'd thought it all through, and through again. "Look, Phil, I wasn't just being—well, emotional. I really meant it that way. But then, right at that time, Chris came down; and Johnny agreed to the trip—and then he kept putting it off, all summer long, and every time I thought, 'He won't do it after all,' he'd set a date, and every time it got close—well, you *know*." She had to stop, and get the clogged-up stuff clear inside again.

Phil just stood there. He put a hand on her shoulder, and she groped for it with her hand, held on to it *hard*, and found she could talk again.

"Don't you *see*, Phil?" Her voice was a wail, but she didn't care. Her face was streaked with tears; it didn't matter. "Don't you *see*? I— I couldn't let *Johnny's* child grow up with—*oh Hell!*—with *Johnny* for a father. The way he's been. *Could I?*"

"Oh, you poor kid!"

Lisa was silent a moment. Then: "This won't stop me dancing, I think?"

"No...no reason it should, for a while."

She took a deep breath. "All night. I want the job, Phil...and the sooner I get started the better. Lisa Trovi, Famed Tri-Di Star, will give an impromptu recital in just one hour..."

Dollars Dome—Monday, September 5, 11 P.M. (C.S.T.)

Mounting with the beat of the bongos, she climbed to the pinnacle in step with the quickening pulse of the piano; then poised, spread-winged, against the high-flying clarinet's sharp sweetness.

The big wings rustled, swayed, started to move slowly back and forth to the pounding measure of the muffled bass. Back on the drum thump—forward on the twinkle of the cymbal—arms pumping faster, stronger, with each beat, while the bass jumped the tempo and the cymbals turned from tinkles to a crash.

The clarinet slid up and off the top of a final run; the piano faded slowly to a hush; the bongos fell in line behind the bass and cymbals. Then they stopped.

For one measure there was silence from them all. The single sound in the crowded room was the flapping beat of the great gauze wings.

Drums crashed—like the surf, like thunder, like an earthquake, like a bursting dam. With a final sweep of wing-width, Lisa leaped forward, beating and fluttering, beating with the arm-wings, a-flutter in a mist of multi-hued chiffon—leaped out and downward, turning and twisting with the slowing slant of the widespread wings.

From the midstage high riser down to the floor, she floated like a dragonfly, drifted like a leaf.

She landed like a bright bird fallen to earth, in a deep crouch. Then with the final cymbal-clang she thrust upward, outstretched on toetips, arms back and open, head proud and lifted, her whole face brilliant with the afterglow of music, of dancing, of climbing, of flight down to earth.

They clustered around her, smiling and cheering. Somebody stayed at the bongos, tapping out a light-mood intricate rhythm. Someone else went to the piano, and began to mesh trills with the bongo jokes.

Two of the men lifted the dancer—veils, wings, and radiance—onto their shoulders and paraded her around the practice room.

In the deep armchairs shoved back to the wall, three couples sat in intertwined delight, watching, clapping, cheering the impromptu, cakewalk-conga-line that followed the accolade around the room.

Two women went out quietly and returned with a wheeled cart of sandwiches, cool bottles, frosted glasses, coffee and cakes. The men put down the dancer and claimed their own girls from the cart. One pair took over an armchair vacated by a dreamy couple who left the party, holding each other's waists with secret smiles.

Other pairs settled down, or wandered off. A crowd around the cart sorted out into more couples, and at last left a mixed group, six or eight, perhaps, standing and laughing and eating, drinking, unpaired yet.

Lee gobbled shamelessly, suddenly famished. She sat alone in the midst of the small group, watching, delighted, as the joy of her climb and fall spread to all the rest.

The dark-haired doctor stood a pace apart, just outside the laughing group, watching *her*. The hunger in his eyes found no matching thirst in hers; it flickered, and died.

The group remaining settled down to shop talk. Lisa left; Phil went with her. At the door of her room she turned and smiled that marvelous marveling radiance. "They felt it, Phil," she said. "They felt it *with* me!"

He nodded and smiled back and watched her go in.

Acapulco—Wednesday, September 7, 8 P.M. (C.S.T.)

"Kutler? Sure... Hi, Phil, what's up?"

"How private is this wire?"

"Hardly at all."

"Well— Did you call my friend?"

Kutler's friend—Johnny? Chris couldn't think who else it would be. "Tried to. Been trying. Jerk doesn't answer."

"Figures. He wired. Yesterday, very negative," Phil said. "Got his information mixed up, I'm afraid."

"Yeah. I can see how that would work. Well, he'll get the source material Sunday."

"I don't know. That's what I wanted to talk to you about. I'm not sure about sending it now?"

"Oh." *Damn this open beam anyhow!* "I don't see," he started thoughtfully, and Phil added: "I'm not the only one. In fact, it wasn't my idea originally."

"Oh?" *Oh!* The fat was *really* in now, then? "Well, whatever you think," he said reluctantly. "Damn, I wish I was up there!"

"Yeah. Look, there's one other thing. That therapist I asked you to get me...I've got an application from—"

"Which therap—?"

"Good. I hoped you hadn't done anything yet. I've got a hell of a good applicant. *She's worked with me before.* I just wondered if I could hire on my own, or if it had to be done through Mexcity?"

"Well—I don't know—" Then it all fell into place. "Look, Phil, I'll have to check on that," he said. "I gather you want a fast answer?"

"I'm afraid we might lose this girl if it goes through channels; I don't know how long she can wait."

"Will she wait till I get back up?"

"I'm sure she could do that much."

"Right. I'll check on it here, and we'll get it worked out when I get home."

Chris talked a few more minutes with Bourgnese, about routine lab affairs, and switched off. Across the room, Jed was waiting with raised eyebrows. "What was *that* bit?"

"Damn that open beam! I wish I could have had two minutes with Kutler alone. Sounds like Wendt heard the news on his own—or didn't like her wire—or anything. I gather he flipped, anyhow, and either she doesn't want to go home, or Phil doesn't think she should, or Johnny's threatened something, or—I don't know. But that bit about the girl who used to work for Phil—that's how Johnny met Lee. She was doing some kind of dance therapy with a group of Kutler's. So I assume he's thinking of using her now. Up there. I don't know...?"

"You *don't?*" Jed was clearly amused.

"Okay, so you were kidding about a job for her up there, but how's it going to look—?"

"You're slippin', fella," the General said. "Think it through, man, think it through."

Inside-Outside: Like it's a meteor shower of secrets from space all over town this week...not to say out-of-town... Those stories you heard about ex-Astronaut (Col.) Johnny Wendt chasing the subpoena server off the family acres with a ray gun might be slightly exaggerated... Seems all Johnny did was pop him one, but the SAC boys are takin' it hard anyhoo... Be a leetle charitable, fellas: they tell me Johnny's had a hard time lately. Not even one dancing girl left to his name... And speaking of dancing girls, yummy Lisa Trovi, whose name has been linked with Wendt's off and on, is still Mooning over us. Her name came off the down-bound *Messenger* passenger list at the last moment on Thursday for the second week in a row... Kid just can't get herself down to Earth, I guess, after the way she wowed 'em in World Dome... Or it could be like "Chris" Christensen figures he needs a good hostess for Ray McLafferty's visit next week? ...Ragin' Ray takes off Sunday week to make the Moon scene for a one-night stand, but he's taking a bunch of the boys along to stay a week and have a good look at the Security plumbing... Somebody complained about leaks... Christensen goes up tomorrow. We put our dough on this boy, after hearing him softsell the subcommittee on Tuesday, to get things set up for Ray's party in a week easy...

> *from the syndicated capitol gossip column,*
> *"Phlip Asides From Inside," by Lenny Phlip,*
> *Mexcity, September 10, 1977*

Moon Dome
September 15, 1977

Johnny dear—
("Dear John," I guess, in reverse?)

I've taken this much time to decide what to do, after getting your wire, partly because I had to wait for Chris to get back, to know if the suggestion Phil made would be all right—partly because I just couldn't think too clearly at first, after your wire came—and partly, I have to admit, because I kept hoping I'd hear from you again.

There doesn't seem to be much point in hassling over anything. I know you're capable of sending a message like that in anger, and then withdrawing it. But that's the point—I know you're also capable of withdrawing it, which is saying quite a—

I said there was no point in hassling, didn't I? All that matters now is that I've finally decided you really meant it. You don't want me to come back. I could hardly argue with that anyhow, but it's also possible you're right—so I've decided, for the time being, anyhow, to stay on up here. Phil needs an assistant to do the kind of dance and music work I used to do with his therapy group in N.Y. And—well, I like it here. As long as Chris is willing, I'll stay put for the time being.

If you want to get my stuff out, let me know and I'll write Jeannie or Edna to come take care of it.

Damn, I'm sorry it had to be this way. It's not what I wanted, Johnny—

Love (still)
Lisa.

P.S. Only damn it, if you do change your mind, or have changed it, you idiot—don't wire—*call!*

TO: J. A. Harbridge
FROM: P. A. Christensen
DATE: September 15, 1977
BY SPECIAL COURIER

Attached regular news release will give you dope on Lee Trovi; also attaching copy her letter to J., and much good may it do you. Suggest you plant one of your own boys up here for this kind of job. I'm too old to learn bitch games.

No more word from J. on this end. Any news? Please. fastest whenever. K. wants to go downstairs, some notion in hand about personnel here makes him think maybe has new approach for J. I tend negative: only account probable subpoena if down. ?????

Check-thru for visitors satisfactory. Place clean as a whistle. One problem: Shack outside Dome where Moon-normal work done last two months. *Wide* open, actually. Alarms, etc., but—???

Better leave up, posted guard, etc.? Or take down, risk mention by someone? Damfino. Advise—

Earth news sounds like last week added up okay. Keep 'em crossed—

PAC

P.S. Kutler just buzzed me to ask could I get some confidential authoritative opinion on medical aspects of pregnancy, childbirth, here. That's all he said. Draw own conclusions. I don't want to. Couldn't allow anyhow, I guess. Add: if subj married, why shd K. clam up? *Ouch!* Please rush answer. pac

TO: I. K. Trozhikov
FROM: Chen L-T RE: Bio Project
DATE: September 15, 1977
TOP SECRET INFORMATION—FOR THE PARTY
EXECUTIVE COMMITTEE ONLY

Tests Alpha and Beta, Schedule Nine, concluded Sep. 13 and 15, with results as predicted (4.5% average margin of error). Test Gamma in progress; indications point to predicted results; expect terminate Sep. 18.

Schedule Ten follows immediately, unless countermanded.

Test results attached. Please rush computer results. Med. Off. C.N. Gregoriev suggests possible correlation with effects here noted in Para. 5-G, his report, Sep. 1. Computer data on tests to date may provide basis for broad theoretical approach.

Chen

(Attached)

Dear Ilya,

I trust the implications of this report will stagger you as they do me. Wish we had some better notion of how far they have gotten in this line. (If anywhere; pragmatism has its drawbacks.) Also, how controllable is the effect—if it does exist? Suspicion here (mine and Gregori's, especially) is, if correct, they must soon know what we do and v.v. Or perhaps retroactively? (Think that through!)

Also: will you handle the Maria Harounian matter yourself? I feel some obligation, as she will not name the father, and symptoms have progressed to where Maria can not be held responsible for her own care immediately. Keep the quiz boys off her if you can, for a bit? She comes down next trip, I hope.

Lian

...Johnny's been hittin' the bistros just like in the old days before he began goin' steady with his favorite dancing girl—who practically vanished from tri-di as well as the nite spots while they were makin' it together... Let that be a lesson, kids: don't hide your light o' love behind a bushel, or even a bushel of high-priced acres. If you don't take her out to shine every once in a while, she'll take off the first time some guy offers her the Moon...

from the syndicated capitol gossip column,
"Phlip Asides From Inside," by Lenny Phlip,
Mexcity, September 18, 1977.

Dollars Dome—4 P.M. (C.S.T.)

He watched her face through the clear plastic of the pressure suit helmet, and tried to identify the "waiting" look. She was too absorbed to see him staring, but she wasn't just thinking, or daydreaming. Listening? That was how it looked, but not *quite…*

He touched helmets. "What do you hear that I don't?" he asked.

Lee started slightly, like someone snapped out of daydream. "Hear?" she asked. *Well, it was worth a try*, he thought. Maybe just plain fantasizing, after all?

"*See* is more like it," she said. "I was looking at the design they make. I guess I got half-hypnotized, following the lines."

He looked. When he first looked, before he began watching her instead, he had noticed only a small marble interweaving of ganglion-like ropes of cells. Now the randomness of the arrangement was less apparent; it could hypnotize if you tried to follow the branchings-off and connections between rope-colonies. There was a sense of *almost-order—*

He shook his head and looked away.

"Damn! You know I never really *looked* at them before. They *do* get you…"

"Oh, they're not all like that," she said quickly. "Just the ones out here. Every time you change the soil or air, *they* change. One of the tanks in Earth-normal, you'd think it was full of just *dirt*—they're just scattered through like regular Earth soil microorganisms. But this Moon-type mutation links up this way, and Thad says—" That was at least the twelfth time on the trip he had heard *Thad says*. "—says the things that look kind of like nerves are actually linked up that way—I don't mean, they're really like *nerves*, but each rope is a separate colony, and he thinks they might have some kind of communication even, where two ropes connect. Either that or some kind of symbiosis or *syzygy* or—"

"Thad say all *that?*" Phil broke in, laughing at the earnest student manner of her recitation.

"And *more,*" she retorted. "But now *you'll* never know—We better get back, I guess. I'm supposed to make like respectable for tonight."

She started laughing, and took a step away so helmet contact was broken. He saw the laughter continue, but the sound broke off in the middle. Inside the pressurized half-track, she opened the face-plate, still chuckling. "It gets tougher to get dressed every day," she said. "I mean, work clothes are fine, but when I have to get *dressed*... "

"Well, take plenty of time," he said, soberly. "I don't know what the honorable investigators would make of it if they knew, but it's a sure bet they'd smell headlines in it."

"I'll try to worry about it," she said. "Phil, you know, it's the *damnedest* thing—I suppose I'm in a jam. Or something. I mean, when I think about it, it's practically classic—the unwed mother bit, and my man is sick-sick-sick—and probably half stoned besides—and here I am taken in by the men in the Moon—maybe that's what makes it seem like lovely nonsense instead of Something Awful?"

"You've been pretty happy the last couple of weeks, kid?"

"Yes," she said quietly. "Yes, I have, Phil. And I mean what I was saying—It seems like I *ought* to be worried and troubled, but—I'm *not.*" She looked away, and back again.

"Phil, I'm not even worried about Johnny. I don't know what's gotten into me. I don't mean I don't *care*. I do. Just—it doesn't *feel* like anything's wrong. We're just apart for a while, that's all. I don't mean that's what I *think*, Phil, just what I—Oh, *you* understand! You know, Thad says..."

"Does he?" Phil said meaningfully.

"Phil! You don't think I—? Oh *no!*"

And he actually believed her. She seemed not *too* startled, but just enough—not *too* scornful, just the right amount. And her laughter was free.

"Okay," he said. "I retract. But quit saying it or I'm just as likely to start sulking." He managed what he thought was a creditable smile.

Dollars Dome—7 P.M. (C.S.T.)

The dining room on arrival days always wore a bloom of festivity. The only decorative extras available were the glowing white onion-lilies provided, one for each table, by the farm section each week (carefully cultivated in defiant evasion of the ubiquitous regulating in quintuplicate official schedules of production and supplies). But the bright plastic tabletops were somehow gayer, the lighting more luminous, even the clatter of dishes and cutlery in some way more cheerfully hungry, at Wednesday dinners.

The big difference of course was not in the place but the people: and not just that they tended to dress a bit more than usual, laugh a bit oftener, talk a bit freer, but that they were *there*, all together.

"Days" in the Dome were marked off by Mexcity's Central Time; but without external dark-and-light cycles to pattern the twenty-four hours, the Dome worked round the clock, each person fitting his own preferred schedule into the complex of work-to-be-done. Ordinarily, only one section of the dining room was in use; and it was in use at all hours, as groups came and went to and from their elected shifts. But on Wednesdays, anyone not absolutely required at his job was fairly sure to attend seven P.M. dinner, after the shuttles came in.

This Wednesday night, in particular, the Dome was out in full force—in party mood, party dress, party manners—to welcome Congressman Ramon McLafferty and his picked crew of super-snoopers.

Dr. Kutler was seated with four of the congressional investigators and three higher-echelon Dome scientists at a round table so close to the speakers' table that he was literally back-to-back with Lisa Trovi. He confined his own part in the dinner talk to polite replies and concentrated on his uneasy appraisal of the behavior of the Dome people at large, and an amused, but equally uneasy, eavesdropping on the exchanges between Lee and the visiting congressman.

Lisa's attitude seemed to be in keeping with the peculiar response of the Dome as a whole to the invasion: a sort of high faith that warm welcome and willing liking were enough to absorb anything from outright ill will to malicious fancy to simple self-interest.

That McLafferty fell short of sharing this feeling was evident. He *knew* the dinner, the gaiety, the enthusiasm that greeted him, were put-up jobs; he accepted them gracefully as his due. And he maintained this knowledge, based on experience, at least half the way through the meal. By that time he was so thoroughly conscious of the deep sincerity of Lee Trovi's empathetic interest that the stanchions of isolation supporting his cynicism were sorely shaken. And when he rose to say the expected few words after dinner, he was much too practiced an orator to misinterpret the swell of applause that surrounded him for either the patter of polite boredom, or the too-regular thumping of planned demonstration.

Chris used the moment to lean across and say a single word in Lisa's ear. From where Phil sat, turned around right behind her, the word looked like, "Thanks."

She turned to Chris, eyebrows, raised, baffled.

He nodded toward McLafferty.

She cocked her head, shrugged bare shoulders: *What?*

He shook his head slightly. "Later," he murmured, and sat back, watching her and the speaker, his face carefully neutral. But Phil thought he saw an echo of the same unease he felt himself.

Later, in one of the larger conference rooms, twenty-odd of the banquet elite drank coffee and brandy and listened to newly-arrived music tapes. McLafferty's crew was staying a week, till the next orbit down; but the congressman himself would leave tomorrow. Conscientiously using his time, he made a point of speaking with everyone in the room, taking notes occasionally with an air of apologetic industry. His manner was briskly efficient, but leisurely— yet somehow it took hardly half an hour's time to cover the group, and permit him to drift over casually to the circle of chairs where Lee and Phil sat together with Chris and Thad Bourgnese.

"You know, you fellows really have got something here," McLafferty's smile should have been engaging; somehow it was not. "One thing," he said, with a nod at Lee, and a sweep of the arm around the room, "you certainly have the best-looking lady scientists *I've* ever seen!"

Thad grinned. "I can see it now," he said. "Headline: Congressman Gives Lunar Ladies Blanket Clearance. Or: Selenite Scien*tistes*—hmmm—need a verb with an *S* and something about Security. Well—" He rose, made a mock bow to Lisa, who was laughing helplessly. "Beggin' yer pardon, mum, you bein' Medic in any case, and not Lab Staff, present comp'ny excepted an' all that."

It could have been nasty. It wasn't...perhaps because Lisa's laughter *included* McLafferty? Or just that comment and reaction were both so spontaneous? Phil couldn't tell for sure.

Bourgnese excused himself, and went off in the general direction of the redheaded Donovan girl, leaving the seat next to Lisa for the congressman, who had passed with astonishing speed through startlement, chagrin, mild amusement, and suspicion to sudden hilarious delight.

"One thing," he said, regarding Lee with warm approval. "You folks don't scare easy."

She blinked. "What are we supposed to be scared of?"

"Nothing," he said. "*Absolutely* nothing."

And damn if it didn't sound just like he meant it!

Rio de Janeiro—12 A.M. (S.W.A.T.)

It was the fourth club that night, and he was positive he had said hello to all the same people at each one. He sat at a single table, watching red and black and orange and blue-green female rumps writhe to rhumba beat and wondered how they contrived to stock each joint with The Crowd between the time he left one and arrived at the next.

No more pub stops, he told himself firmly. Next time he'd go direct, maybe to *Los Gringos,* yes, that was a good bet—tourist trap kind of place The Crowd wouldn't be caught dead in. Go *straight* there, find out. If they were there anyhow, he'd *know...*

He could swear those jazzy bottoms out on the dance, floor were *exactly* the same ones he'd watched all night.

He finished his drink, thought about another... Hell with it, make the move *now,* catch 'em off balance. He got up and started to weave his way through the full tables. The band had stopped. People were coming off the floor.

Behind him, a voice he knew said high and clear, snide and cruel, "Well, she always had a yen for Phil Kutler—"

Gentlemen don't slug lady bitches, he told himself, carefully unbunching the muscles in shoulder and upper arm. *Leave it lay, lad. Don't even look.* He knew he knew the voice, but he did not know *whose* it was; best to leave it that way.

He dodged past a couple of strangers, got blocked at the next table by a crowd of six sitting down. The high vicious clearness followed him.

"But I'm not so sure that's it. I can't say *who* told me, but it's someone I *usually listen* to, and the way *he* heard it, the reason *Ray* let that Moon scientist off so easily—"

It died away. Another voice, lower and less clear, urgent in undertone, blocked it off. Johnny's way was still stopped. He turned, not meaning to; walked back past the table between without wanting to, went up to the red-gown bitch who owned that voice.

The deeper, lower, one, the man at her side had been saying *his* name.

He smiled, and he knew just how damned unpleasant that smile was.

"Pardon me," he said. "I believe you were saying something about a friend of mine?"

"Excuse me," she said coldly. "I don't believe—" She turned to the white-jacketed man. "Darling, do you—?"

"Yes," he said wearily. "Johnny Wendt, Linda Har—"

"Forget it," Johnny said, suddenly sick of the whole thing. Why pick a fight with a perfectly nice guy over a bitch, or a pair of them? "Skip it. I'm sorry. I don't want to know your friend. Should've cut out like I started to. Teach her some manners, hey?"

He turned and started to edge his way past the table again.

"Bob!" The high clear vicious voice. *Yeah?*

He grinned. Nobody could say *he* started this one. He tensed himself for the hand that would touch his shoulder.

Okay! He wheeled back, driving from the shoulder as he turned, with great satisfaction.

Dollars Dome—11:30 P.M. (C.S.T.)

"Oh, I'm sure you *could!*" Lisa turned to Chris. "Where did Thad take off to before? He usually works this shift, doesn't he?"

"Usually," Chris said—a little reluctantly? Phil wondered if the same thought that had crossed his was in the Director's mind? Thad had left with Rita Donovan; hadn't Lee noticed? It wasn't like her to be so tactless, if she had. And, he thought a bit grimly, it was unlikely she had *not* noticed. *Checking up?* He felt almost ashamed of thinking it.

"I was just telling Ray I didn't see why he couldn't tour some of the labs *now*, if he really wanted to. Thad would probably be in Bio anyhow, and—"

"I imagine Dr. Christensen has a more formal tour ready for tomorrow," McLafferty broke in smoothly.

"Sort of," Chris said easily. "But it wouldn't make any difference that I can see. I'm not sure Bourgnese is working tonight, but I'd be glad to take you around myself any time. We don't go much by the clock around here."

"That's what I was telling him," Lee said. "Ray was so startled when we came up to daylight again, he asked how we were able to stay on a regular schedule, and I was explaining how it worked." She stopped and laughed, a rippling silver sound that Phil recognized quickly as the trainee professional one. *'He* said a place like this would suit him fine, because as soon as he saw the sun, he thought it was morning, and he was all ready to start a day's work. So *I* said, 'Why not?' and—there you are."

Chris shook his head admiringly. "You Mexcity types always flabbergast me. If it was really dawn, and he'd been at an all-night brawl, I'll bet he'd feel just the same way."

"Company helps," said the congressman. "Depends whom you've been with all night."

McLafferty didn't see it. Probably even Chris didn't. But Lee winced under the import of the heavy compliment, and threw the briefest pleading sort of glance at Phil.

Well, he thought. *Here we go on the white charger again.* He turned to Chris.

"Why don't you take Mr. McLafferty to see the farm?" he suggested. "You know *that's* got to be working now—" All the Maintenance sections would be. "He could see that stuff now, and the labs tomorrow." To the congressman he explained: "Wednesday night's the one time the labs run on skeleton staff. The big dinner throws everything out of whack when the ship's in." With considerable satisfaction, and at pontifical length, he made clear to the impatient visitor that the obviously special-festive character of the earlier banquet was not quite as special as he'd undoubtedly thought, but a weekly, normal, occurrence.

"This is Saturday night in the Dome," he wound up. "About the only thing you'd see in the labs now would be tapes and cameras and people tending them. But Maintenance runs all the time, of course. And I'd think from your viewpoint, that part of the routine—that part of the staff, for that matter—would be most—" He hesitated. "What would you call it? Fruitful? Suggestive? Whatever it is, I'll bet they've got the most of it." He turned to Lee, glanced up at the chrono above the Mall fountain. "About time for us to get back to work—hey, kid?"

She took it smoothly. *And* gratefully. "I guess so." The gratitude showed only in her look at him, not in her voice, which held just the *right* reluctance. "I don't suppose—?" she said.

"I think the way they're coming along, by next week they'll be able to handle the one session on their own," he said. "Or with me. I blow a mean tape, myself; I just don't look as good as you tapping my foot to the beat."

McLafferty, without actually moving a foot, had somehow edged forward, silently questioning.

"Jam session thing we've been trying for a group that's had trouble with schedule adjustment," Phil explained, marveling at the inventive capacity of the knight-errant. "Idea is to create a regular emotional rhythm each day. Seems to be working out pretty well... Oh, look, Lee, if you want to cut out this once, I don't suppose it would—"

"Don't be silly," she said firmly. Her smile was snakey-demure. "We wouldn't want the Investigating Committee to think I don't earn my pay, would we?"

"She thinks of everything, don't she?" McLafferty said, smooth as ever. "Tell you what, Chris—why don't we have a look at your farm while they get organized, and maybe stop in at this session afterwards—If you don't mind, Doc?"

Phil thought it over. "Don't see why not. Sure. There's no actual therapy at this. I don't think the group would mind. Come on, gal. We've got about two minutes now. See you folks later—"

The two of them hurried off, not-hearing Chris calling after them: "Hey, where *is* this thing?"

"Let you know soon as we do," Phil muttered.

It was really no problem. They rounded up ten eager listeners in the dining room, and got set up in Lee's practice room a good ten minutes before the touring party found them.

And Lisa had no trouble getting two theoretical dormitory-mates to go off with her afterwards. "You know," she said sleepily, "I think this works more for me than for you folks."

"Night, kids," Phil said. "Well, Mr. Mc..."

"Call me Mac," he said grudgingly. It sounded just like, *Your round, man! But don't walk down any dark alleys...*

CHAPTER NINE
September 25-October 3, 1977

Acapulco, Sunday, Sep, 25

Dear Lee:

The General says he can get this to you with comparative privacy, which seems like a good idea. Apparently I don't mind broadcasting my nastier moods; it's just if an unaccustomed brief spell of humility comes over me, I can't stand to have anyone know I occasionally behave like a civilized human.

If I do, or am, which is probably open to doubt. Particularly after my last radiowire to you.

Your reply caught up with me the first time the facs company had an address for me, which was during a couple of refreshingly sober days in the Rio jail—great place, by the way, clean, spartan, healthy as all hell. Might have done better to have done worse (I took a poke at a foul-mouthed ass in a night club) and been kept longer.

Anyhow, it seemed a bit late, and hardly the place, from which to answer your PS. Hoppen Harbridge also located me there; he'd been concerned because of the subpoena for me being withdrawn. Thought maybe it had been served instead and I was being maybe too royally entertained somewhere in private until T (for testimony) Day came. Man seems as uneager for me to take the stand as I am, which gets *me* a bit concerned. (It will be no news to him when he reads this; I've already told him so. I suppose I'd rather have him read it than him *and* every other damn snoop or spy from how many? countries, which is what I gather already happened to our previous by-radiowire exchanges.)

I seem to be rambling on, just possibly in an effort to avoid coming to the point. Which is as follows:

I'd very much like to take you up on your implied invitation. I have only recently learned how much I need you. I learned it, babe, from Toronto down to Rio, with many stops in between. Or amend that: I started in St. Croix, worked my way up to Toronto via home, and etc. But in the process I learned a couple of other things, most important of which is that there seems to be remarkably little of Johnny at home these days—barring some mixed crap and fury, a bit of which I got rid of in that Rio ginmill. Some more of which

136

probably is creeping into this letter, no matter which words I reach for.

So I need you; so what the hell do you need me for?

And is it just what a guy wants most, to *need* a dame? You *don't* need me. You've made it damn clear, and I, belatedly, bless you and thank you for doing just that, doll. God help me, I do think you *love* me. Or loved, as the case may be. It occurs to me that with effort and application I might learn to do likewise in return. If I can't I can at least *stop needing.*

So tell ole Chris thanks from me—or Kutler, whoever *did* mastermind getting us up there. I might have gone on leeching on you the rest of my life, or yours (which might have been shorter; how long could you stand it anyhow?) if *something* hadn't happened to blast us apart long enough for me to back off and get a good look at J. Wendt. The veritas in vino is stronger proof in night clubs, maybe? Or were you watering the stuff at home, babe?

The Gen. says 10 minutes, if I want to get this into the package. (10 minutes with or without time for him to read?) So—

I understand there is about to be a new subpoena for me. I'd enjoy slugging the next guy, too, but am temporarily convinced it is better not to do so off home property, and also better to stay off home property myself for a bit, for many reasons, not all of them tactical.

(Speaking of tactics, it's only fair to warn Harbridge, which I haven't directly, as yet, but will, that I am still on the other side of the fence. My distaste for McL. happens to be stronger than my preference for throwing spokes in space wheels. But Gen., if you think you are harboring anything less than a viper in your bosom, be disillusioned.)

Anyhow, this is to let you know that my immediate future plans consist of a knapsack, a couple of books which, if I bother to read them, might bring me up to date in my supposed profession, and probably a jug of honest tequila under a bough. The last is not part of the Grand Reformation Plan, but should be mentioned as still the great likelihood.

In any case, I will have no address for a bit, so tell Kutler not to try looking. Even Harbridge won't know where I am. (The Gen's mysterious sources show that Kutler's subpoena is already signed—like my own—and will be going up same orbit as this.) As for you, babe, stay put a while if you can. You'll hear from me, soon as I know what to say. Thanks for the chance to say anything. Apologies for what's been said—for a lot of things, for me, I guess. Convey same to Chris, will you?

Listen, babe, I am one crazy-mixed-up bastard, as you have better cause even than most to know—but for what it's worth, I do—Hell, I can't even say that. Let me say, I do *want to love* you. If I make the grade, I'll let you know. Meantime—

Hell, Johnny

FROM: Christensen
TO: Harbridge
DATE: Sep. 29, 1977
VIA SPECIAL COURIER

Seems I missed a few bits, while McL was here. Phil says I have gone soft in the head like the rest of the Dome people. That's not what he says, but how I read it. He'll undoubtedly explain his notions to you, and to you they might even make sense. You two boys should have a ball come to think of it. But I don't know what I'll do here on my own, so don't keep him away; I seem to need a headshrinker for chief aide up here. At least, it's been working that way.

With that off my chest: McL's boys have behaved themselves here. In fact, they've been too damn nice (which is part of Phil's theory), probably. To hear them talk today, butter wouldn't melt and all that, but we'll find out, I guess, when they hit dirt again. Can't give you anything to build specific suspicions on, because what investigating they did seemed pretty damn routine and unenthusiastic to me. Mostly, they goofed off seeing how far they could get with the female personnel. Hope they got sent home happy, and appearances would indicate as much. (But it worries Phil; I'm getting an education, man. Always thought psychers were supposed to be *less* puritanical than us plain folks.)

Thanks for getting that letter to L. Big help. Phil will fill you in on her too; he finally let me in on it. Hope you didn't—sorry. Was about to hope you didn't really let Wendt out of sight, but I ought to know better by now.

As you can see, I am confused by a lot of what's going on. Will try to get clearer by next week. Or am I missing some data?

PAC

LUNA LAB LOVE NEST
SAYS McLAFFERTY

Mexcity, Oct. 2: Scientific research is losing out to research in the art of love among the elite inhabitants of the U.S. Moon Dome, according to Rep. Ramon E. McLafferty, Chairman of the SAC Security Subcommittee.

The Subcommittee, which has been conducting Special Hearings probing Security leaks in the Space program, will turn its attention next week to a serious "impairment of efficiency and morale prevalent in the Research Center" at the U.S.A.A Moon Dome, according to a statement issued after Chairman McLafferty conferred with members of an investigating team which returned from Moon Dome on today's shuttles. The Representative went to Baja California Spaceport earlier this afternoon to meet with the investigators immediately on their arrival.

In a press release issued after the conference, the nature of the alleged "impairment of efficiency and morale" was not specified, but another paragraph stated that "the findings of the investigators are such as to suggest a thoroughgoing congressional probe into the personnel of the Moon Dome and the moral attitudes and practices prevailing there."

Questioned by reporters, Mr. McLafferty added that the testimony he hoped to produce at the new hearings would be of such an "intimate and personal" nature in "many cases" that not only will the hearings not be live-televised (as was true for the Security hearings a few weeks back), but may be closed to the press as well. If this should be true, the Representative assured reporters that the entire proceedings would be filmed, for subsequent release to the public, after editing to "protect any innocent persons whose names may be brought in either unintentionally or with malicious intent."

Usually authoritative sources close to the congressman said, off the record, that there was definite evidence in McLafferty's hands of "certain instances of loose living and certain unconventional sexual arrangements" at the Moon Dome. Rep. McLafferty's comment on this was: "We certainly do not plan to level any specific charges at this time." He referred to "unbelievable" conditions reported by his investigators, and added: "We certainly will probe the matter thoroughly, and put an end to this sort of corruption, if it does exist, before it can become a national disgrace."

Queried as to whether hearings on the alleged immorality would be conducted by his Security Subcommittee, or by the SAC itself, Rep. McLafferty indicated that he felt the security leaks originally under investigation by his team, and the new findings, were definitely related to each other, and that the hearings would continue under the aegis of the Subcommittee.

One witness scheduled to testify during the coming week should be able to shed considerable light on "immoral practices" such as those alleged. That is Dr. Philip Kutler, Staff Psychiatrist for the Moon Dome, who was subpoenaed by the Subcommittee last week, and arrived today on the same shuttle with the investigating team.

Reporters present at the shuttle landing at Baja California Spaceport saw no signs of unfriendliness between Subcommittee investigators and Dr. Kutler, but were unable to obtain any statement from the doctor.

Subpoenas for a number of other members of the Dome staff were issued today, and shipped via Moon shuttle in the hands of a Dome staffer returning from Earth leave who was sworn in as process server just before takeoff time. An official list of those named in the subpoenas will not be issued until after service on Wednesday evening (when the shuttle arrives at Moon Dome), but among those named in authoritative circles as probable witnesses were Research Director P. A. Christensen, who testified two weeks ago on Security control; Dr. T.L. Bourgnese, Biochem Chief at the Dome; Leonard Lakeland, Hydroponics Technician; Dr. David Chernik, Medical Staff; a number of female staffers, whose names were withheld, and quite possibly the newest female staff member, tri-di dancer Lisa Trovi, whose appointment as Psychiatric Assistant made headlines a short time ago. It was not known whether Miss Trovi would be questioned about her own experiences at the Moon Dome or in connection with Col. John Wendt, whom she accompanied to the Dome on the mysterious visit six weeks ago about which the Subcommittee has been eager to question him.

A new subpoena for Col. Wendt has also been issued, but since his release last Saturday from Rio Detention House, where he served two days of a twenty-day drunk-and-disorderly charge, Col. Wendt has disappeared.

Acapulco—Sunday, October 2, 11:30 P.M. (C.S.T.)

Under grizzled hair, the General's face was still strikingly young: the tight-skinned smooth-jawed face of a man whose energies are never at the ebb. A man capable of restraint and of control, conscious of power, continually on the advance. A dangerous man, thought Kutler—a man almost without weaknesses himself, and entirely without empathy for weakness in others.

"Frankly, I think it's damned important," Phil said crisply. "You know better than I do what shape he's in right now. But I wouldn't want to be responsible for what he'll do when he sees *this* bloody foolishness." He rattled the folded newspaper in his hand.

"I'll be just as frank," Harbridge answered after a moment's thoughtful silence. "Of course Chris was right. I know where Wendt is, and I *could* reach him for you. But it's a risk I don't think is warranted. We're in a position to—let me say, *prevent* any wild behavior on his part. Meantime, I'd as lief not—draw enemy fire?— by contacting him."

That would be final. Phil had hoped for the admission of knowledge, worked for it. Now he had it, and realized he had gained nothing.

"All right," he said tiredly. "You're the tactician." He was suddenly not so much angry as disgusted.

"Jed," he said, and didn't even realize till he was halfway through his speech that the General's first name had come naturally. "I understand your hesitation about contacting Johnny." *You don't dare talk to him. It would mess up all your thinking, wouldn't it?* "But in the event that you should be in touch with him in the next few days—or have some means of sending him a message—I think you might do him a favor to let him know Lisa is pregnant."

Harbridge had to repress a faint grin. So he had known all along. Phil had counted on shock value in that one.

"I had the impression the lady did not want him to know?"

"The lady is of several minds in the matter. But I think it would be easier if Johnny felt that she sent him the message before he reads or hears it from some public source."

The General thought that one over. He shook his head. "I can't see it, Phil. It don't fit. What you said about Ray McLafferty and this whole new pitch fits fine. But not throwing the girl to the wolves. What would he get out of it?"

"Revenge?" Phil said, testing.

"Revenge?" Harbridge smiled indulgently. "This is politics, Kutler, not couch games." He thought a moment more. "And let's say Ray isn't the man I think he is—Why take it out on *her?* You or Chris, I could *maybe* see. Why *her?*"

The man was good. Damn good. But from the outside only. Damn fine analysis; no understanding...no, that was wrong too...no compassion? ...no *insight,* no intuition.

We'd make a great team—if we could stand each other.

Phil shrugged. "He's not the only one to think about."

"He's the important one. He puts out the releases." Harbridge looked up sharply. "One thing maybe you left out? Ray's not the guy to take *no* for an answer. Not very easily. He'll damn well *see* to it Trovi's protected. For now."

"It may not be up to him."

"What the hell are you driving at, Kutler?"

"He's got a mess of subpoenas out. Including for her. People talk. *She's* not much of a liar either. Or take me." *And take special note of the fine set of rattles while you're at it.* "It may sound quaint, but I have an aversion to perjury. So do some other people—non-political types. Scientists. Like that."

"You don't think *he's* overlooked that? Why in hell do you suppose he sacrificed coverage? *He* gives the press conferences."

I'm damned if I'll spell it out for you. I warned you. That's I enough.

Phil shrugged again and let it drop.

Acapulco—Monday, October 3, 7:30 A.M. (C.S.T.)

The General had been awake for fifteen minutes when the call came. He was still in his pajamas, sipping his second coffee and reading through Chris' message again, reviewing the talk with Dr. Kutler in his mind; he had just realized that he had never gotten around to hearing Kutler's pet theories, when the call came. He took it where he was, in the bedroom.

Wendt's face was taut as his voice, but he was in control. He looked surprisingly young, tanned, and healthy. Could be quite a guy, Jed decided, if he stayed sober long enough.

"Saw this thing in the paper," Wendt said, without preliminaries. "What's the scoop?"

"I can't say for sure," Jed told him. "And if I could, I wouldn't on the phone."

"Anything to it?"

Harbridge shrugged. "You know more than I do. Last time I was up was to pin eagles on you."

"That's right—*sir.* I damn near forgot, didn't I—*sir?*"

"Come off it, Wendt. It was stupid enough, calling me. Don't let's play games now."

"No, *sir.* Sorry to have bothered you."

Jed saw his arm tense; he'd be reaching for the switch. "Hold on, John," he said sharply. The damn fool call was made. Might as well get some use out of it.

"Yes sir?"

Harbridge sighed. All right, two could play that, if necessary. "I take it you have decided to accept the subpoena?" he asked acidly.

"I have my heli right here—sir—to go get it with."

Jed grinned. "At ease, will you, Wendt?" He saw the other man relax imperceptibly, unwillingly. "Okay, as long as I know you're a law-abiding citizen, and not calling to ask for assistance in this absurd evasive maneuver—" He allowed just the corners of his mouth to twitch slightly. "—I can tell you this much. My own opinion is it's a personal spite feud. I think he's got it in for Chris or Kutler or both of them. I had a talk with Kutler last night and—"

"Excuse me, sir. Are these Dr. Kutler's opinions you're giving me, or your own?"

"Both. Why?"

"I'm not sure I'd put my faith in his explanations."

"They're the only explanations I've had so far," Jed said crisply. "Maybe next week I'll know more."

"That's what I actually called about," Wendt said, dropping the mocking-game altogether. "Do you, or will you, know which witnesses will be subpoenaed for next week?"

"I don't know now. You'll probably see it in the papers same time I do."

"I see." His eyes made sure he didn't believe a word of it. "I was hoping there might be some way to have a word with one of the people whose names I saw mentioned."

"Sure. Any time you get tired of hiding out, just drop by and I'll arrange a call for you. Glad to do anything I can. Stop by this evening." He glanced at the wall clock, visible in Wendt's screen, trying to remind him that by now they knew where he was. He thought he got an answering flicker.

"Well, I'm taking up too much of your time, General. Suppose I give you a buzz tonight, anyhow?"

"If there's anything *important* on your mind, sure. But, John—"

"Yes?"

"I—wouldn't pay too much attention to the news stories. You understand?"

"I think so. I'll buzz you. So long."

Balsas, Mexico—7:45 A.M. (C.S.T.)

He left the phone booth, stepped into the hovering ground car, and took off on a cushion of air, silently. Inside fifteen minutes, he entered the outskirts of Teloloapan, without incident. He parked the rented car neatly on a residential sidestreet, and grabbed an airbus downtown. His clothing would be least conspicuous in a working-class place. He found a ginmill open for the go-to-work quickie trade, and settled down.

After a week of water and coke, the Mexican beer was biting and strong. He drank slowly; he had a lot of thinking to do first, and over that bridge there had to be room for some action still.

Meanwhile, there was plenty of time to think; and to drink— slowly. It was too early to do anything else.

At nine o'clock, he began on the phone, trying to locate Phil Kutler. Anyone else would have been better. But like the man said, his was the only game in town.

By eleven, the operator had him convinced that the doctor was not registered at any hotel in Mexcity; the only forwarding address at his New York apartment was Moon Dome.

"Have you tried Decagon Information?" And why in Hell hadn't he thought of that *first?*

"Just one *mommmmment...*" And she was back—with Jed Harbridge's Acapulco phone. *Great!*

He went back to his booth, drank one more bottle of beer, and decided to be logical this time. He walked down the length of the bar, toward the sleepy-looking middle-aged Mexican who had perched on the barstool all morning.

"Listen, chum," he said, without preamble, "I have to talk to the boss, and it irritates him when I make public calls."

The sleepy man looked at him sleepily. "Senor?"

"Oh come off it. Look, how about we take a walk? Get acquainted a little?"

The sleepy man thought it over. A faint glint showed in his eyes. He shrugged fatalistically, climbed down off the stool, threw a coin on the bar, and followed Johnny into the street.

"I owe you congratulations anyhow," Johnny said. "I sure as hell thought I'd throw you this morning."

The man, no longer sleepy, smiled. "It was nothing," he said proudly. "I have long experience."

"Damn glad you do," Johnny said, and meant it. "Look, I wasn't kiddin'. I want to call your boss. I tried this morning, and he didn't like me using a public phone, so we couldn't say much. If you'll just..."

"But *Senor*—" The man was clearly pained. "If I *could*, I would help you gladly, but I have no means..."

"I'm not asking you to give me your junior G-man kit or wrist radiophone or anything," Johnny said patiently. "Hell, I don't *want* to know what kind of setup you've got. Put it this way. I'll go back in the bar. You get in touch. See what the man says. Tell him I want some private talk that's all. Okay?"

The man opened his month. "But *Senor*—"

Johnny said, "Fine!" and slapped him briskly on the back. Walked back into the bar, sat down, got one more bottle, and nursed it, like the first three. He would make it last as long as he could. It was the last one, either way. There was too much to do.

Just *what* was to do, he wasn't sure yet. The first step was Kutler. After that he'd know. But for Kutler, he needed his wits.

If the sleepy man didn't show by the time the bottle was gone, he'd have to find some other way to get hold of Phil. Or make up his own mind, without Phil.

But he was goddam tired of sitting around waiting—for nothing. It was just about time to go get—

What? What you goin' to get, boy? What's to get?

145

Good question. But it didn't matter much. Just so long you could sit on your ass, that's all.

Rather get knocked onto it, hey, boy?

Not very damn likely!

Tough guy! ????

Maybe.

Yeh. I remember. Did some fancy gettin' and goin' before, hey man?

He stood up. Carried his bottle to the bar. Stood a moment indecisive. Put the bottle down, waved to the barman and walked out. Find the sleepy man...find Harbridge...find Kutler...find Lee.

And there you were. Simple, when you came right down to it.

Let 'em have their spaceships and cootie-bugs and truth drugs and politics and screw 'em all. Including the pallbearers. Let 'em play their games. Johnny Wendt didn't care. Let 'em have anything they wanted, except *one* thing...

The one thing is you, Lee. Lisa, Love, Lee, I want you...

He strode out of the dim bar into the sunlight, arms swinging, teeth white in laughter against the tan of his face. A sad-faced woman in black gown and mantle scurried out of his way, crossing herself fervently.

Drunk or devil or what? he wondered. *What does she think I'll do? Damn fool dames don't even know a crazy man from—*

From what—?

His laughter shouted in the street.

—from a crazy-in-love man. That's what!

The woman peeked back around the edge of her veil, and her face looked a little less sad.

If I had a damn rose I'd throw it at her!

He felt clean all over. Only *where* in Hell was Sleepy keeping himself?

Mexcity—Monday, October 3, 1:45 P.M. (C.S.T.)

"For you—"

The congressman handed the desk phone to the doctor with as much flourish as if it were a saber or pistol. Phil took it as cautiously.

"Yes?"

"Kutler? This is Jed Harbridge."

"Oh?"

Then he realized there was no point in playing mum; McLafferty would be recording it all, anyhow.

"Just wanted to let you know: I've got an urgent call for you here."

There was still nothing to say but "Oh?" The more so, knowing Mac *must* be recording. Let Harbridge decide how much to say; he *knew* his way around this rat race.

"If you're not tied up for lunch, maybe you could get over now?"

Phil wished he knew his own way around better; which of these two had sharper teeth? And which was more likely to stick in a fight? And how do you decipher what a man tells you in the presence of the enemy? And was it the enemy, anyhow? It was hard to see any real difference of attitude between the general and the congressman, when you sat in between them, as he literally was doing now.

"You say 'urgent,'" he formulated carefully. "Does that mean immediate? Or very important?"

"Some of both. It *can* wait a little. Frankly, I think the immediacy is more on your end. Oh, look, I hate to sound cloak-and-dagger; it's nothing like that. A personal matter—what you were asking me last night. I'll be more specific if you like, but I assumed—"

"That's all right, Jed," he broke in. At this point, there was just one thing he had to know. And he saw no reason not to ask. "I take it it's not from the Dome? You said 'personal'."

"That's right." Jed sounded relieved: presumably he, Phil, now knew what it was all about. He saw no good reason to let Harbridge know that he knew less than ever now. All the personal matters he could think of, right now, were 250,000 miles away...

Except one. But he *knew* Harbridge wasn't about to let him talk to John. And if he *was*, why call him *here* to let him know? That wasn't it; and it wasn't from Lisa. So it could wait.

"What time do you go out?" he asked.

"Twelve, twelve-thirty..."

"I'll try to make it," Phil said. "I think I can wind things up here pretty soon?" He looked across the desk at McLafferty, who nodded, shrugged, mouthed, *Any time...*

"Right. As soon as you can?"

"Right."

He handed the phone back. "Seems something's come up," he said briskly. "I want to catch Harbridge if I can before he goes out for lunch. So let me jump in with both feet." He smiled. "I'm not much good at the ringaroundrosy you boys play, anyhow."

"You do all right," the congressman said ruefully.

"Thanks. I think. Look, is there still anything you want to ask me? Before we do it in public, I mean?"

"Nothing awfully important. We've about covered the ground."

"Okay. Then there's something *I* want to *tell* you." He saw the other man brace himself almost imperceptibly, and smiled again. "Relax, man. I didn't say *tell you off.* I said *tell.* Like, information. What you're after. Pay dirt, man."

McLafferty was mentally balancing on the balls of his feet, with both arms up, guarding. *Change of pace,* Phil thought approvingly. *Always works.* Reluctantly, he admitted he could probably get pretty good at this kind of bull if he had to.

"Okay," Mac said, on balance again. "This is the sure-enough assay office. Let's see what color your dirt is."

"I assume anything I tell you here is confidential—I mean as far as the press is concerned?"

"Well, I can't give you a blanket yes on that. Anything you tell me that bears on the investigation, I can't keep concealed…"

"I'm not asking that. Put it this way: I have a piece of information I think will be of use to you, and certainly of interest at least. It has nothing to do with anything that's happened at the Dome—or in connection with the Dome—except that the person it concerns happens to be there." He stood up, walked to the window. He wasn't sure enough of his ability to use his face. His voice he could play with skill; but usually people weren't watching him when he talked. "Frankly," he said to the window, "I'm telling you this because I believe you'll feel, as I do, that making it public would do no particular good to anyone, and might do great damage to the person involved. It's something that could come out easily in the official inquiry, but—"

He had to turn back because this way *he* couldn't see the other man.

"—Look, I assume you record conversations here?"

Mac looked pleasantly neutral; made no reply.

"So I know I'm putting myself on a limb when I say this. But I'm hoping that what I tell you will help you decide what questions to ask me tomorrow—or which ones not to ask." He laughed, a bit nervously and it took no effort to sound that way either. "I guess I better put it on record, after that, that I'm not asking for preferential treatment for myself or anyone else, but merely attempting to provide you with certain background extraneous information which I believe will help you to frame your questions in such a way as to protect innocent persons from unnecessary publicity. Does that cover me?" He tried the laugh again.

"Beautifully. Ever think of going into the law?" McLafferty's manner was warm, inviting.

"Often. I'll return the compliment. You ever think about headshrinking?"

There was no perceptible difference in the warmth or sincerity of the laugh. "As a matter of fact—often. From the other end of the couch."

This man was much more his own type, as a matter of fact, than Jed Harbridge was. But Jed's type, too—Phil became aware of an unfamiliar sensation of grave respect. The bland-looking man across the desk had *both* kinds of awareness. *Talk about dangerous men...*

"All right," Phil said. "I've wasted enough time."

"Just one thing," Mac broke in.

"Yes?"

"You understand I have made no pledges of silence or secrecy?"

"I do."

"Okay. Shoot."

"What I wanted to tell you is simply that Lisa Trovi is pregnant."

It was heart warming to see it register. *Bland*, hey? About as bland, behind the meringue face, as baked hot peppers... "Man, you don't think I can—?"

"About *six months* pregnant," Phil said. He waited for the meaning to sink in, and added, "Well, five and a half." McLafferty smiled, but it was weak. "Wendt, I suppose?"

Phil shrugged. "The lady won't say," He managed to make it quite lewd. Mac's eyebrows shot up briefly.

"Well," said the congressman, "I see what you mean. I'm not sure—"

Busy brain whirring away, thought Phil admiringly.

"—You understand, I'll have to give this some careful thought. Offhand, I don't see how it really concerns this investigation, but—"

But you see all that lovely black ink, don't you, man?

149

"—I'll tell you one thing. I wish to Christ I could talk to Wendt. This damfool hiding-out doesn't accomplish anything."

Oh, no, Mac! Really! How much do you think you can do me for? And then, startled, he thought: *Well, whaddya know? Ole doc's ego acting up! At this stage yet...* And finally, amused: *Got to see my psychiatrist about that!*

"Wish I could help you," he said smoothly. "Frankly, I'd like to get my hands on that boy myself." He reached out his hand. "Well, I hope you'll see this thing the way I do, when you've thought it out. I better haul out of here now. Can't hold up the whole Decagon."

The only thing that bothered him when he left was that he might have underestimated Lisa's effect—again. McLafferty ought to be arrow-proof; but so should a lot of others. Who weren't.

Mexcity—Monday, October 3, 1:45 P.M. (C.S.T.)

He parked right inside the Decagon lot, and to hell with them all. If they tapped him now, they would, and that was that.

But he knew it was damned unlikely they'd have a paper waiting for him here.

He had no trouble getting to Harbridge either. He showed the guards and the secretaries the same thing: his face and a five-dollar bill. He was upstairs in ten minutes flat, with the private secretary.

She was new. He said patiently, "Please just buzz and say, *Johnny's* here.' That's all."

"I'm sorry, sir. I'll have to have your full name."

"Let's say I'm his long-lost son. Johnny Harbridge, okay?" Why not just *tell* her? He didn't know.

"Oh, Mr. Prentiss—I wonder if you could—"

Johnny looked at the smooth-young-man who had just entered. The smooth-young-man looked at him, got noticeably ruffled around the edges, and said, "Just a minute, Glory. You—er—What can I do for you, Colonel? I'm Al Prentiss, the General's Press Secretary."

"Pleased to meet you, Al. I was trying to persuade the young lady that the General would want to see me—since I'm here, I mean."

"I imagine he would," Prentiss said, deadpan. "If you'll wait just a *moment,* I'll let him know..."

He went through a door across the room.

Johnny waited.

He got tired of waiting, and followed through the door.

Prentiss. Harbridge. Kutler.

"Well," he said. "Old Home Day. All we need now is Chris."

"All right, John," Harbridge said wearily. "What are you trying to do?"

"Brace yourself," Johnny said. "Especially you, Doc. Sit down. It'll be a shock." He strode to the desk and looked straight at Harbridge, "I'm trying to find out how I can get to the Moon."

The General shook his head. "You do need Chris then. I can't authorize it."

You're full of bull. "Oh?" He turned to Phil. "All right. Who authorizes trips down? You or Chris? I don't think the environment up there is quite right for Lee."

Phil shrugged. He was good at it. "Tell *her,*" he said.

Johnny looked from the doctor to the general and back again. No point in crawling. Both men were set. He felt the inviting ache in his shoulder, and set it aside. If he was sure Prentiss would stay out of it. He could clean up the other two without getting winded...

Good thing Prentiss was there. Just as well.

"Okay," he said. "I'll do that."

He started out.

"Colonel Wendt?"

He turned, halfway. Bully-boy Prentiss. "Yeah?"

"I just thought I'd mention—the backroom boys think it's pretty sure she's subpoenaed. That would mean she'd be down next trip anyhow."

Pacifier? He didn't think so, somehow. The guy almost seemed human.

"Thanks," he said. "I didn't think of that."

New York—Monday, October 3, 7 P.M. (E.D.S.T.)

The city hadn't changed; it was he who had.

Such a short time—and actually, very little had happened. *Very little. Sure. You just went right out of this world.*

So: two years later—damn near—the doctor gets around to knowing what the man meant. Phil marveled, not for the first time, at the ease with which we assume communication; fool ourselves into the oddly arrogant delusion that we have heard, that we know, understand, even share, the consciousness of our fellowman.

Phil Kutler walked the streets of the city he loved, and felt *bruised.* Everywhere were barriers. Walls: not only of brick and stone and wood, but walls of tougher, harder, more hurtful, flesh and blood and emotion.

He wished, wished with all his heart, fervently, that someone in all the millions of his city, *could hear him now—as he, finally, heard Johnny Wendt...*

"Mars is heaven, that's what..."

As he had *heard* Lisa—what was it? Four weeks—One month ago? It seemed hardly possible—and *understood* that her need was not his own desire. Understood it, and still desired—hell, still *loved!*

It was, looking back on it, highly improbable. *I am not that big a man,* he told himself soberly. And it was true. But he *had* been. Then. There.

Maybe Johnny was right. Maybe men ought to stay where they acted like men...

No!

No, damn it, Johnny was wrong! As wrong as a man CAN be. "Something up there makes us love," he paraphrased nervously, and admitted it frightened him, and stopped fearing it.

If anyone was right, Doug was!

He laughed. It was that simple. *Just that simple.* No one would ever believe it, but he was deeply sure. He knew, because he was certain it was exactly what *he* would have done.

A stiff-backed, powder-caked claw-fingered female, rushing on tight-toed stilt heels, miscalculated; a bony shoulder knifed his bicep; a sharp elbow rose reflexively, caught him in the chest.

"Whyncha look wareyagone?" she shrieked.

"I beg your pardon," he said. And wondered what Moon-change would happen to *her,* if she could go too?

Wondered, more practically, if that odd feeling of kinship with McLafferty meant the other man had felt it too? Smiled, thinking: *All that work and sweat. And suppose the big oaf has turned into a gentleman?*

It wouldn't matter much. Actually, all the sweat had not been needed. Johnny was already on his way.

Damned rude of him not to wait for me to push, Phil thought, delighted.

CHAPTER TEN
October 5-9, 1977

The Shack—Wednesday, October 5, 4 P.M. (C.S.T.)

She switched off the half-track engine, and as the spotlight faded, the world directly ahead of her blinked out.

She opened the cab door and stepped out into heaven. Above her, the gorgeous enormous full Earth, gleaming blue-greenly against the black velvet star-diamonded backdrop of everywhere—always out there.

And right ahead, now, the muted twin glows of the Shack itself and the Shack guardhouse.

She flashed on her helmet lamp, picked her way over Moon crust to the guardhouse. Looked in, exchanged smiles, and went on to the Shack.

She sat down in front of the tank, where the greyish-white ganglions had long since ceased to show discrete patterns. Now they crowded together, piled on each other, multiplied, multiplying. The daily "watering" of a month ago would have been hopelessly inadequate now; a steady trickle of nutrient fed the tank from a storage drum—and even the daily ten gallons hardly seemed to account for the burgeoning of the white cells.

Lisa looked. Watched. Stared. And *listened.*

A nagging thought stopped her. She switched on her radio. "Jim?"

"That you, Miss Trovi?" From the guardhouse.

"Yes. I meant to ask—will you call me at six? I want to get back for dinner tonight."

"Sure thing."

"Thanks."

She switched off, and let herself drift into—what? where?—

Far out. Or far in? That used to be a joke, *so far out you're in, so far in you're out, but it's no joke, it's not funny, it's fun.*

Swing on a star...climb up a moonbeam...feather-light, fearfree, far sands of home...Hello!...Hello, I know you, don't I?...Don't know your name, but...funny-fun!...the soul is familiar...

Foolish to want a name. Baby has no name. What name for baby? *Doug, we'll call him Doug...Hello, Doug...*and the well opened up again, great valentine lake of lovely, good, lace-edged, beating heart, two hearts in three-quarter phase...

Where are you? Hello? Hello?

Oh!

"Oh. Oh, hi. Six *already?*"

"No," Jim, the guard, was leaning over her, helmet to helmet. "They been trying to call you from Dome, Miss Trovi. We kept gettin' the call on our sets, but you didn't answer, so I figure your radio's off, and come in to tell you."

"Oh. Thanks, Jim."

She switched on the helmet set.

"Hello?"

"Lee! Thank God! You had us worried. Been trying to get you the last twenty minutes!"

"Who's that? Thad?"

"Yuh. Listen, we've a call for you. Earthside. Better hurry. We can't hold the frequency much longer."

Earthside?

"Johnny!" She jumped up. "Hold it, Thad," she said. "I'm on my way."

Mexcity—Wednesday, October 5, 5:35 P.M. (C.S.T.)

"I'm sorry, Johnny. We've been doing our damnedest. She's on her way back now, but Relay will cut out in two minutes."

The distant voice was Chris', but yet not Chris. He couldn't get *through,* somehow.

"Okay," he said. "Look, I don't have to talk to her. Will you send her down?"

"I'll tell her you called. I'll tell her you asked her to come. I can't *send* her, Johnny."

"Okay." *Bastard! You'll tell her—yeah! But what? What can you tell her to be so sure she won't want to come?* "Okay. If that's it, that's it."

"I'll tell her," the voice named Chris said again.

"Hey! Chris! Listen!" He felt his throat tighten up, but the words squeezed past. "Chris! If she—never mind if—Chris, can you make room for me to come up Sunday? Maybe she ought to stay—"

"I don't know—"

"We-are-sorry-to-interrupt-this-call-but-Relay-Station–has-passed-out-of-range-This-is-a-recorded-message-We-are-sorry-to-interrupt—"

The sound cut out. Johnny turned from the mike, and saw Jed's hand on the switch.

"Well," he said. "Thanks. I—appreciate everything."

Harbridge took a single step forward. "All right, Johnny. I'm glad we could get you through. Wish you'd connected better. But I imagine she'll be down Sunday. She *is* on the subpoena list, you know, so—"

"She *is?*" He hadn't even read that. He'd forgotten about it. The headline was all he saw, really. "You—wouldn't care to tell me where Phil Kutler is?" he asked, feeling the ice in his gut again, just like he felt it when he saw the paper, her name, and Phil's picture.

DANCER PREGNANT, SAYS MOON DOC

"No. No, I don't think I'd care to tell you that, John. In fact—Al, I think I hear your phone." He looked meaningfully at the young man, who undraped himself from the corner of the desk, mock-saluted, and left. "Now let's get something straight, John," Harbridge said. "I got your call through. That's as far as I go. You had no damn business coming in here again. If you had half a brain, you'd realize what it means if they get you into that hearing room *now*. If you care about Lisa at all—Well, that's your affair. But you busting in here is my business. This is the last time you do it. Try it again, and you'll find yourself in the jug before you're halfway in the main door. You follow me?"

"*All* the way," Johnny said. "Sir."

"All right. I'm going to do one more thing for you, and then I'm through. I wouldn't do it for you, but it happens to be more convenient for me this way. I'm going to get you the hell out of here without any of the process servers who are outside by now getting hold of you. After that, will you please, kindly, *get lost?*"

"I hear you talking," Johnny said tightly. "I'm not sure I follow you though."

"You follow me all right. Come on."

Johnny followed. There was nothing else he could do. What counted now was Lisa, Lisa and nothing else. No one else. If he had to eat Jed Harbridge's crud, he could do that too. *And remember it too—*

but for now, he followed. He followed the General up to the private parking roof, and accepted the loan of a heli, and took off.

For where?

Home seemed less unlikely than most other places.

Dollars Dome—Thursday, October 6, 2 P.M.

The woman was positively glowing at him.

"You *do* understand, Lee? I can't take a chance on letting him come up. Not now. Maybe in a month or so, if things quiet down. But one more mess now—I'm sorry to put it that way, Lisa—"

"I *do* understand, Chris." She smiled impishly. "Anyhow, you wanted publicity, didn't you?"

"God help me, I did." He looked at her suspiciously. "You know, I keep feeling as if you're just sitting there waiting for me to do a reverse switch and tell you I've changed my mind and sure he can come."

"Well, it would be nice. Do you think it would help if I *concentrated?*"

"Concentrate any harder, and—I don't know. I know I won't change my mind. If I *could*, I *would* have, by now."

"All right, then." But she still sat, smiling.

"You sure you don't want to go, after all?"

She shook her head. "I don't *want* to. And even if I did, it wouldn't be a good idea." Her laughter poured out. "I can just see myself on that witness stand!"

He winced. She stood up.

"It's all right, dear. I'm not *going* down. Tell them to come get me, if they want me that much."

He tried visualizing that one, and liked it. "I might just do that," he said, and then reluctantly: "About Johnny, Lee. What do you want me to do?"

"Let him come up."

Damn you, woman! You know what I mean. "Short of that," he said gruffly.

"Give him my love. Tell him I want him to come."

"You don't want to—well, send a letter or anything? I could deliver it myself. Privacy—"

She hesitated. "No. No, I don't think that's the way. Oh, Chris, don't *worry* so! If *I'm* not worried, why should you be? It's going to be all right. *I know it.*"

The worst part was: he believed her. You couldn't not believe, when she was there with you. But—

"Have a good trip," she said.

"Thanks. Take care of yourself, Lee." She moved to the door with that fantastic grace she seemed to have developed lately. "Oh, Lee—"

She turned back, smiling.

"If you don't mind—I'd just as lief you stayed in Dome while I'm gone. I'd hate to think of you out at the Shack—Well, like yesterday. It bothers—"

"Oh, stop *worrying*, dear." She turned, and was gone.

Baja California Spaceport—Sunday, October 9, 5 P.M. (P.S.T.)

"No, she didn't come this trip."

"Well, what do you suggest, Dr. Christensen? Will you accept delivery, or should we return to sender?"

"Can you tell me the name of the sender?"

"I suppose—I don't see why not. Colonel Wendt."

"I'll take it," he said decisively.

The Port Manager handed it over with relief. "All right. Will you see the reporters now? They've been waiting…"

Rockland—Sunday, October 9, 10 P.M. (E.D.S.T.)

He couldn't see why he'd never thought of it before.

All the times he'd sat in this room and stared at that damn impregnable glass wall, and never realized he had something so simple that could—if not damage it, then at least—make an impression on it.

He got up from the couch and picked up the five darts from the floor. Two others stuck to the curved surface of the giant window, both from previous tries. He had been leaving them there, timing himself to see how long it took to get them all up. But that didn't work, because he didn't stick with the game. Now he got an absurd satisfaction out of wrenching the two suction cups loose. He'd keep score the other way instead—see how many *turns* it took to get them all up.

At least it wouldn't be too quick.

Not that it mattered; it was ten now; if she didn't call soon, she wasn't going to. Unless the landings were *really* late this time?

He dialed for the news, and sat back, not listening to all the headline part. Landing times would come at the end.

The first shuttle had been scheduled for five-thirty, Central time. That was two and a half hours now he'd sat waiting for the phone chime; dialing for no-news; pacing the room up and down; opening the liquor cabinet and closing it again; getting—and forgetting—five cups of hot coffee from the bleak kitchen.

Somewhere along the way, he'd thought of the darts.

Given a near-impossible combination of luck and skill, you could make a suction dart stick on curved glass one time in—how many? That's what was wrong with the first scoring system; this way he'd find out.

He threw all seven, one after another, as fast as he could.

One caught, clung, dropped. The others just bounced. The phone chimed.

The phone!

He reached for the switch, and the screen lit up, and—*damn it to Hell, you fat bastard, where's Lee?*—it was Chris!

"She didn't come," Johnny said.

Chris shook his head. "She asked me to give you a message."

"Yeah? Okay, give it."

"She *couldn't* come."

"No?"

"The doctor says..."

"*Which* doctor? Ole buddy Phil?"

"No, the Medic. She's not supposed to take the trip till—"

"You always were a bum liar, Chris. So she didn't come. So?"

"All right, I'm a bum liar. If you want to know, I wouldn't let her. And you ought to have your head examined, for wanting her to. She's been subpoenaed."

"Me too. If they get around to serving it."

"Yeah, but her left isn't as good as yours. Do you want to hear the message or not?"

"Sure. Why not? What is it? Love and kisses?"

158

"As a matter of fact, that's *exactly* it."

"Okay." But he had seen Chris hesitate. There was more. He waited.

Chris waited.

"All right, spill it, will you? What's the rest?"

"You turning mind-reader too?" Chris said nastily.

"Leave it lay, man," Johnny growled. *"What else did she say?"*

"She said for you to come up."

"Okay. Got room next trip?"

Chris shook his head.

"The one after?"

Same bit.

"No room, huh? She stays up, I stay down, right?"

Chris never said a word.

Johnny switched off and got out the bottle and picked up the darts, and started keeping score by how many belts it took to get a dart up.

Damn things wouldn't stick at all.

CHAPTER ELEVEN
October 13-18, 1977

Dollars Dome—Thursday, October 13, 3:30 P.M.

"It bothered Chris too," she said.

"I'll bet. And you can't see why?" He watched her face with every bit of intelligence and knowledge at his command. He found nothing there but serenity—and some tenderness and amusement.

"Phil, what on Earth—well, all right, what in Space could *happen?* Am I supposed to be afraid of the dark?"

"Everything spooky spooks worse in the dark," he said. "And kid, this bit with you and the Shack has got spooky."

"Well, I don't know what I can say to that." She stood up, smiling, but a little impatient now.

"Lee—suppose I say you *can't* go?"

She did not seem to understand.

"Suppose I *forbid* you to?"

"Phil!"

It was complete in itself. The one word said it all. *By whose authority? With what right? For what reason? Darling—you're fooling, aren't you?*

"Suppose I said *Chris* forbade it?"

"You mean you want to know what I'd do if I were actually made to believe I *couldn't* go?"

He nodded. She thought a moment.

"I'd try anyhow. Then if I *couldn't*—I mean, *really* couldn't—" She grinned. "—I wouldn't."

What does she want me to do? Throw my arms around her and hold her here? Maybe she did: it was a nice thought, anyhow.

Her smile changed, and he remembered, sharply, too vividly, that one kiss the day she told him about—

The baby. *Johnny's* baby.

"Phil, I suppose this is the time to say it. You are the kindest, most decent, most *loving* human being I've ever known. Sometimes I wish it was you who needed me."

That was all. And it was enough. Of course that was the difference, and he had, really, always understood, just as well as he did now.

But it mattered that she had told him. It mattered a great deal.

"Thank you, Lisa. I do love you very much." The words tasted good. Fresh. *Pure.* He was glad he had said them. "I—almost wish I needed you too." *But I'd rather love you.*

When she was gone, he sat and studied that one out. He didn't get very far. It was easy to analyze—simple masochistic crap. And/or false superiority: *Better to love and not have than to be needful and get?* Feed that to the pigs—or the bugs. It wasn't for Kutler. Except it was. So?

So nothing. So live with it. Someday you go back to Earth and get analyzed, lad. Till then, don't try to understand. Relax and enjoy it.

Which was the damnedest part. He *did* enjoy it.

He got that settled in his mind; then he tried conscientiously to worry about Lee. She had gone to the Shack again, of course. She was out there now, dreaming whatever she dreamed when she stared at the wild growth there. It was *dangerous*—

He laughed. What in hell could be dangerous about it?

Spooky things...scared of the dark... And of course: *scared of bugs.* Just that simple.

He stopped trying to worry.

But what made her think he and Doug Laughlin were so much alike?

He was curious; he dug Laughlin's pre-trip psych profile out of the files.

She wasn't so wrong.

Rockland—Friday, October 14, 5 A.M. (E.D.S.T)

He wouldn't be able to do it until all the darts stuck. He knew he wouldn't. But he knew when the darts stuck, he could. Easy. No sweat. He knew just how, but...

Won' work till they stick, gotta all stick. .

He kept throwing. Took a lot of drinks to make one stick. Got to do it soon, run out of drinks otherwise.

Damn bottle was empty. More in cellar, but cellar Hell of a ways, besides he didn't want. *Lousy stuff. Gets you nowhere.*

He laughed.

Man; I wen' nowhe'...This boy did that job...Yessir, Johnny Wendt went, went nowheah atall...

Stupid business, two darts won't stick. *All the other ones stick, what's matter with two?*

Maybe no-good darts?

He picked them up again and took them to the wall. Stuck one on, then the other. *See? Stick fine. See?*

He almost cheated, but it was no good, it wouldn't work unless he *threw* them all and *made* 'em stick.

He took the two off again and went back to the couch.

Threw and picked up and threw and picked up and threw and picked up and had to get another bottle after all and threw and picked up and threw, and *there you are.*

You wouldn't believe it, both 'fem stick 'tonce!

He got up and went out the back door, feeling in his pocket for keys. Somebody came up and asked him if he was Wendt, but he fooled 'm, just said, "Man, I ain't even come yet," and kept going to the garage.

He got in the car and *it* Wendt. *Jus' fine.*

Wendt, went, when it went, Wendt went straight into the damn glass wall.

161

Tricky going for Wendt, but this man used to be crack pilot. Nerves of steel—all that. Slambang into window-wall, crrr-aaa-ck, and slam on brake, and *there you are...*

He climbed out and walked into the living room, feeling fine.

Not many guys could do that. *Not damn few very many.*

Crack-smash that damn wall and not touch a thing inside. Car right outside where it ought to be. Johnny inside. Good. But no damn curved glass wall. Seven damn darts and a couple of jugs, or a few maybe, and the ole car, and there you are: no damn glass wall!

He was tired. He lay down to sleep.

Red Dome—Friday, October 14, 4:30 A.M. (S.S.T.)

They sat in a group around the woman, Maria. Nobody talked.

They sat for a long time in silence. Perhaps an hour, perhaps more. Then Maria began to murmur. Nobody moved. The tape recorder ran, as it had run, since they started. Only two of them in the group knew English well, but all of them listened with the same deep attention.

From time to time, someone came in and took over a seat from one of the circled sitters. Maria stayed where she was, quite content.

Rockland—Saturday, October 15

Someone was screaming. It wasn't Doug, because Doug wasn't Doug now, just a million little Dougs and his leg itched where the Dougs kept biting, *damn! damn Lisa, Lisa wouldn't scream, ice cream, whipped cream, Lisa whip cream, lovely Lee, Lee, Lee...*

"*Leeeee!*"

He opened his eyes for one moment, saw the ceiling of the living room, felt floor rug underneath, and heard his own voice screaming, "*Leeeee!*"

He closed his eyes, shut his mouth tight, moved convulsively, rolled over, and lay on the floor a long time, sobbing without sound, dry angry sobs that shook his frame and jarred his guts—but brought no release, so after whatever time, long time, it was, he stood up, got his balance, and walked steadily through the house into the kitchen.

Turned, went back through the living room and bedroom to the shower. Shower first. He had a sour smell that sickened him.

He came out of the shower and blower and stood in the bedroom and thought it would be nice to sleep. *One drink and go to sleep...?*

He put his shorts on, and a shirt, socks, shoes. Cup of coffee, maybe...*might wake up.* He didn't *want* to sleep again. *Okay—coffee.* He started back through the living room to the kitchen. The house was a wreck, and the floor was full of broken glass, but that...

He saw the car outside, and remembered...

There it was. *The damn window was busted!*

How in Hell had he managed *that?*

He could figure that out later. And clean things up later. Right now, no time—first things first.

First thing was Lee. *Quick!* before he was too late. *Too late already, anyhow: too late for Doug, for ever, too late.*

Too late for lots of things, too late for Johnny? Maybe, but if not too late for Lee, then maybe...?

He remembered some more. He couldn't go.

Couldn't go.

Couldn't?

He took the word out, out of his aching head, and looked at it. Studied it, turned it over, tried to turn it inside out, but there it was, all the time, like a neon light:

c-o-u-l-d-n-apostrophe-t

Couldn't.

He shook his head tiredly, but the letters danced behind his eyelids even when he closed his eyes. He was very very tired. He took off his jacket and went into the bedroom and took off his trousers and lay down.

When he awoke again, it was dusk. He knew exactly what he had to do. He was cold sober, not hung over, fiercely hungry too. But he was afraid it might already be too late to get things done today.

Which day? Friday? Saturday? *Sunday?* Eating could wait.

He went to the phone, and flicked the switch, the operator thought he was kidding, but she finally told him: Saturday. And almost eight o'clock.

He went to the kitchen and made himself a sandwich with two thick slabs of rye bread and a stack of old dried-looking boiled ham slices from the refrigerator. He was too hungry to care if it was dry or tasteless.

He took one large bite, wrapped the rest in a napkin, and shoved it in his jacket pocket. He started out, then remembered seeing a quart of milk when he got the ham. He went back, and drank all but an inch or so of the milk, right from the wax container. *Then* he went out, a little worried, wondering if he'd done something to the heli too, that he didn't recall.

The funny thing was, he was so set on getting to someone from the Committee, to tell them he'd take the subpoena now, that when the little man in the brown suit stepped out from behind the hangar, and served it on him he didn't even think to be surprised. The only thing that startled him was the big bass voice asking his name; it came from such a *medium* guy.

Afterwards, a hundred feet up and building speed, he was astonished at the man still being there. He shook his head and grinned. "Guts!" he said out loud to nobody, admiringly.

Later yet, over Philadelphia, he had to decide which way to go, and realized he didn't know where they were firing from this trip. It occurred to him, hovering there, that he was not quite as clear-headed as he felt he was. The sandwich was still in his pocket, for instance, and he didn't know where to go. Also, belatedly, he wondered if he'd have any trouble with *this* bunch about going up.

He kept on south. It would be either Andes or St. Thom, that much he was sure of. Just beyond Wilmington he saw a field with service stations and no traffic to speak of. He dropped, left the machine for servicing whatever slipshod way the station did it, and went inside to the phones.

Senor McLafferty was not at home. He was in Mexcity, at a verrree imporrrtant conferrrence.

"Can you tell me where to reach him?" Johnny asked urgently.

She was most sorrreee, but the number was one she was not allowed to give.

"Can you reach him?" There was no time for arguing.

Reluctantly: Yes, she could.

"All right, now listen. Call him *right away*. I'm at a pay phone, and I haven't got much time, and believe me, he wants to hear from me. My name is John Wendt, you understand? The number here is Wilmington Five-seven nine oh-eight jay six. Please ask him to call me as *quickly as possible*. You got the name, now, John—"

"Yes, *Senor.* I *know* the name." He relaxed. He could see the difference. She did know the name, and she would call McLafferty. He flicked off, bought a soda, and sat down in the old metal chair out front to wait for the call back.

It was midnight here. Ten, Central time. The rocket would blast at eight ack emma Central, *latest*—seven, more likely—from wherever they were shooting from. If the idiot congressman called back but *fast*, and if it was St. Thom, he could make it. Andes was probably impossible even now.

Dollars Dome—Sunday, October 16, 4:35 P.M. (C.S.T.)

Thad Bourgnese pursed his lips in a silent whistle, and passed the news wire across the desk to Kutler. "Here we go again," he said.

Phil glanced down the sheet rapidly. "Could be," he said. "But I wouldn't put any money on *where* we go. Or he goes. Or—"

"She goes? Obviously, friend: whither he goes. I mean, you're the doctor; you've noticed, I'm sure?"

"Only thing I'm not sure of," Phil laughed, "is what you mean. Was it the belly or the heart I was supposed to diagnose? On second thought, that's not the only thing I'm not sure of. It's practically lost in the multitude."

"All right. Here's another one for you. How in the name of all that's holy did he get *on* that ship? Last time I heard Chris on the subject, J. Wendt wasn't going to hit Moondirt again till death did them."

"One of the many uncertainties I mentioned," Phil said noncommittally. "You never know. A lot can happen in a week Earthside. Or maybe Chris was willing to take the risk if he was on the same trip..."

"The *trip* wasn't the problem. They could keep him under, like last time. I dunno—the old man's gettin' soft, maybe—" He broke off.

"Hi, gorgeous," he said, as Lisa pushed the door open. "What brings you back from the Great Unknown so early and all of a glow?"

She gave him a smile-in-passing, but her question was for Phil. "Is he coming *with Chris?*"

"Dunno, honey. They're both coming. Hard to say whose idea it was or who's talking to whom." Thad was right about that *all-of-a-glow* bit. *Pregnant women get that way,* he told himself, and now with Johnny coming...

"Hold on, beautiful. Didn't anybody ever tell you it's bad manners to listen through keyholes? If we had a keyhole, I mean."

"But I *wasn't—*"

"They're still running radiowire service, chum," Phil stepped in. "Or were, last I heard." Odd, now it came time to accept the idea, admit it, quit nibbling around the edges, how easy it was. Damn sight easier than querying and wondering about things that just didn't *fit,* any other way. "Glad you stopped by, kid," he said to Lee. "We've got to get moving with the new program. Never catch you any more when you're not working or sleeping or out visiting your buggy buddies."

"All right. But did you get the news report yet?" He nodded. "May I—?" He passed it over.

She looked it through quickly and handed it back.

"Nothing you didn't already know, hey?" Phil stood up, trying to look brisk and efficient. "The more I think of it, the more I think we better get that new program set up now. I have a feeling," he said in Thad's direction, "I may be losing my chief assistant headshrinker a little sooner than I expected."

He hustled Lee out of the room ahead of him, and set a fast pace for his office. He needed a little time to think, before he verbalized into his conscious intellectual Gestalt the reality that so far existed for him only in awareness.

And before the verbalizing, he had to determine—if he could—how much *she* knew.

He closed his office door, and switched on the Busy-light. No approach like the obvious, he decided.

"Lee, how *did* you know about Johnny?" he asked as soon as she was settled in a chair.

"How—? Oh. I thought you really thought I got a wire." She looked at him almost warily. "I told you before, Phil, I *knew* he'd come. When it was time."

"Just feminine intuition?"

He had intended the remark to be neutral and light. It came out harshly sardonic.

Lisa sat forward, startled. "What do—" she started. She searched Phil's face for—what? He didn't know. Then she withdrew: her eyes turned inward; she sat back, not relaxed as before, but erect, spring-coiled for some as-yet-undetermined action.

"No," she said finally. "Not feminine intuition, Phil. How about just *intuition?* The kind anyone can have?"

Damn you! the outraged seeker within shrieked. *Bitch!*

She *knew,* and wouldn't tell.

But does she know *she knows?* The doctor was back. "All right, I'll buy that," he said. "For now, anyhow." He stood up and went to the window. Looking out, because he couldn't hurt her and see her hurt, he said, "Let me ask you another one."

"Yes?" She was all self-possessed again. That tender amusement bit. *Okay, kid, brace yourself; you'll need it!*

"What makes you think Doug Laughlin was so much like me?" And he held his breath. If he was wrong—or if she lied—he would never know which it had been. The words flew from him, even as he tried to call them back: once spoken, they wiped out all slower safer ways to know for sure.

"Well, darling, there are so *many*— *Did* I tell you that? I didn't mean to. It was such a wild thought— Come to think of it, maybe it is 'feminine' intuition, Phil. Maybe something to do with being pregnant, or—something like that? Because I sure do a lot of it these days. I never used to. Not as *much,* anyhow... Maybe I'm just more relaxed, so that I *know* when I think something, or when I just—*feel* it. I mean, feel it's *true,* so if I wasn't watching, or rather, if I were less *aware* of what goes on inside me, I might think I was thinking, or think I had *heard* it or read it somewhere or actually *seen* it. You know."

"I know," he said. "I know very well. Because *I* thought I *heard* you say that about Doug. And now you think you did. But you didn't."

"I didn't?" It was honest bewilderment... He was *almost* sure it was.

"No, damn it, you *didn't!* I *know* you didn't—because it just happened, by pure stupid dumb good luck that the recorder was on for the whole conversation.

"Which conversation?"

"The one that left me wondering why you should think that. I got out the files on Doug, and decided you were pretty right. Then I remembered something I'd thought about down in New York, and I wanted to make a note of it while I remembered—an insight I thought

I maybe had into Doug's walkout. Seemed more likely to be valid, after I checked some of his reactions against my own. So I went to turn the tape on, and found out it was on, and just for kicks, played back everything we'd said, meaning to wipe it off afterwards, and— you'd never said a word about Doug and me. *Not one damn word!*"

He had turned as he spoke, flinging the words at her in passion. Now he turned from her white face and looked out again.

"Phil—"

"Yes?"

He heard the faint female-rustling sound of her moving, but wouldn't look around. She came up beside him. She too looked out, standing at his side.

"You know," she said slowly, "It *could* be that I'd mentioned it some *other* time? And you remembered it just then for some reason, and *thought* that's when you heard it?"

He nodded. "Could be. When did you first think of it?"

Slowly: "I'm—not—sure."

"But you think it was that day? Don't you?"

"Not in your office. The first time I thought of it, it was out— *there.*" With a tilt of her head she pointed to the Shack.

"You were out there just *now*, weren't you?"

No answer.

"When you knew about Johnny?"

Nothing.

He wanted to grab her shoulders and shake her and make her face the truth. He walked carefully away from her and sat down at his desk.

"I want to tell you about something, Lee. You may have come across some accounts of this kind of thing yourself. It's not too unusual. And you've done some reading in this type of thing—"

"Never mind, Phil." She came back from the window and sat facing him again. "I know where you're going. Clairvoyant and— *telepathic* phenomena under hypnotism. Right?"

He nodded.

"You know any clear-cut case?"

He nodded again. "A couple. Clairvoyance. Not the other." He picked up a pencil, studied it curiously. Just a pencil. He put it down. "Let me add this, Lee: every case I ever heard of that seemed reliably reported and scientifically set up involved a performance under *hypnotic command.* That is, with the help of suggestion. There are at least two or three that seem clear of any suspicion of suggestion as to *what* to see. *Completely* clear, I mean. But the subjects *were* told *to do it.*"

Relay Station—Sunday, October 16, 5 P.M. (C.S.T.)

Once upon a time, the great harbors of Earth used rocket beacons to signal to ships entering and leaving port: ships that rounded the globe, sometimes, under no other power than that of wind and water waves. At the ports of Space, rocket fire moves the ships in and out; waves of sound carried silently on waves of electrons convey the signals now. Otherwise, harbors have always been much alike. Even four hundred miles above ground, men sweat in their pressure suits; swear at the intractable bulk of large masses (with or without "weight"); mill in apparent confusion, behind which incredible achievements of order and planned distribution move endlessly; roughhouse and rag and joke with the blood-and-gut humor (and good humor) of haulers and movers and handlers and drovers and drivers and sailors and truckers and spacers and all men who gain their daily bread conquering space-mass-time with their hands and backs.

Relay Station is many things. Most ports are. It's Earth's eye on the sky and it's the reflex nerve center of radio communication around the Earth. It is also a tunneled labyrinth of intrigue and espionage. But first and foremost, it is Man's greatest port to date. Every ship of all nations that lifts off of Earth stops here for inspection and servicing and then for safe-passage through the vicious rays of the Vanallens, infinitely multitudinous scyllas and charybdises of the Space odyssey.

From Relay, the Belt Balloons, air filled and skin-charged, each with its central pit of a single shuttle ship, are flung up through the twin belts of darting electrons, to meet the great wheel of the *Messenger* in orbit at its 12,000-mile perihelion.

All passengers on U.S.A.A. ships have the option of sleeping through the two first legs of the trip, till the shuttle is safely inside the *Messenger;* but the more knowing ones come out of sedation at Relay, in hopes of traveling close enough to other Balloons to see for themselves the coruscating display of blue fire, as the wild electrons of the Belts are dashed off the charged thin skins of the bulleting spheres.

John Wendt had never seen the Belt Balloons. When he lived and trained on the Moon, and took rare leaves on Earth, the *Messenger,* with its ion drive and thermal exchange power plant, was still a drawing board dream. The thrice he had traveled by shuttle, via Balloon and the *Messenger,* he had made the whole voyage under sedation.

His choice of minimum sleep this time out was not motivated by a desire to see the Balloons. He had avoided exposure to Space talk, Space news, Space views, so thoroughly in his twenty months on Earth that he did not even *know* there was anything worth seeing.

He simply meant to let Pete Christensen, and anybody else who noticed, know that he *could* make the trip. *Wide awake.*

He was a little sorry when he learned that Chris was on the first shuttle, the one that left ten minutes before Mac got him to the St. Thom Port and through the snarl of red tape that wound him up on Shuttle Two. But he assumed there would be communication between the two boats, once on board the *Messenger.* Certainly, the Dome Director would be free to go between shuttles, and certainly, he would be apprised of the change in the passenger list at the first opportunity.

Johnny looked forward to seeing Chris when the time came. The shoe had changed feet, and it fit one hell of a sight better.

He never did get to see Shuttle One crackling spectacularly through the outer edge of the Big Belt, as Two's balloon entered Little Belt; he was much too sophisticated a Space traveler to crowd to the viewports when the others did.

Dollars Dome—Monday, October 17, 2 P.M. (C.S.T.)

"That ought to fix you up now, Miss Trovi." He fastened the buckle that held the miniature set strapped to her suit, and said, "Now if you want to just show me how you'd work it, make sure you got it right...?"

Lisa unstrapped the kit, took out the tape, put it back in, switched the set to *record,* and turned it off again. "I'd better try it with the helmet, don't you think?" she said doubtfully.

"Sure. Good idea." The big mechanic beamed down at her as if he had personally built the whole combination, and not just the small machine. But when he reached to help her adjust the wire trailing from the mike in the headpiece, she shook her head and waved him off:

"I've got to be able to do it myself."

It worked fine. She put three extra rolls of tape in her pocket, thanked him, and left. The big man watched her go, shaking his head.

"Guts!" he said. "Damn but that babe has guts!" He went back into the workshop and told his helper, "That bastard Wendt don't come through, I bet there ain't a single man here wouldn't marry her, the day before the kid's born, or the day after. And mop up the sonofabitch before dinner besides."

"One mistake, chum." The helper was married. "You don't know how easy it is to get a divorce. Don't just say *single* men."

Red Dome—Tuesday, October 18, 9:25 A.M. (C.S.T.)

The Guards Lieutenant saluted with military precision, which was worse than wasted on Dr. Chen. The Director was not even annoyed; the irritation of acknowledging the salute never materialized, because the necessity to do so failed to impress him. Dr. Chen could be exceedingly single-minded on some occasions. He had a superior capacity for crisis action.

He also had a crisis.

And he noted, with some detached part of his mind, that he was enjoying it enormously.

It was a long time since there had been any real emergency or crisis in the Dome.

This one was not in it either.

"Very well," he said crisply. "You will please explain to me how she contrived to leave?"

"She is a good pilot, Comrade Your Excellency. She holds all necessary permits and licenses."

"There are no permits or licenses to leave the Dome," Chen said coldly, "except express assignment from me."

The young officer said nothing.

The Director considered the words that might best express his scorn and contempt for the so-called Guard who had permitted Maria Harounian to leave the Dome. Having considered them and relished them, he filed them in his mind, and said to the dutiful Lieutenant, whose fault it was not:

"I want Harounian found and returned to Dome immediately."

He did not stress the words. He spoke almost softly. But his meaning was deadly clear. "Organize a search," he said. "A full search. I will review your search plan in fifteen minutes. Excused."

The lieutenant saluted again. Dr. Chen acknowledged with the faintest possible nod.

CHAPTER TWELVE
Wednesday, October 19,1977

Messenger—7:45 A.M. (C.S.T.)

He came awake to vicious clarity. The long dreamless pill-induced sleep had left him over-rested, too fresh, too thinking, conscious, and aware.

But this was Wednesday: the last day. He'd be in the Dome that night. He was not absolutely sure he could make it. For the first Goddam time in his life, he was not certain he would be able to come through.

Something strangely like exultation surged through him.

And what in hell was that for? What was so special about not being good enough?

He knew, but damned if he'd tell himself.

One thing he told himself, all right, at the beginning, and that was still good. He got through Sunday and Monday and Tuesday; he could make it through ten more hours and stick with it. Maybe he'd crack up and go tell Chris off or open an air lock or any damn thing. But he wasn't drinking this trip. Not *this* trip.

Whatever happened *after* he got there, he'd get there cold sober. Then it was up to her...

Monday night was the worst. Monday night and Tuesday. He got through that all right, he could make ten lousy hours. But he hadn't had a goddam drink yet, and he wasn't going to. Not *this* trip...

Ten hours?

The bastard was jeering at him. *So okay, laugh. Ten hours is pretty damn long. Yeah.*

He got up, and planned his time. *Breakfast.* That was as far as he could get. *Lunch, later.* And all the time in between.

Sunday, and Monday morning he had seen the control rooms and comm rooms and cargo shuttles and climbed around the massive ion engine. The heat exchangers were old stuff; so was most of the rest. But he had looked at everything, examined, inspected. He could handle this job himself if he had to now. He didn't have to. Basil would. Basil...he'd trained with Laughlin and Wendt, but wasn't tapped for the *Colombo* trip. So now he was a Space ferry jockey...

Good boy, Basil, he made the grade. Didn't go too far out like we did...

Basil would brake into Zeroville orbit. *Should have started by now*, he thought, *shouldn't they?* Then he *felt* the difference, and knew he'd been feeling it all along. Deceleration. Not much yet, but you started easy with ions and let it build. No blast, no sweat.

Monday, after lunch, nothing to do except sit in the damn lounge and watch them all lushin' it up. Hell with that. Hell of a trip not to drink on; nothing else to do. Half the victims got stoned first night out and *stayed* that way.

He spent Monday afternoon in the dining room, drinking coffee, watching out the pretty picture window while the Moon came around and around, bigger each time—if you happened to have micro-calipers to measure with. He stared out long enough so he found out one thing: empty Space didn't bug him at all. He already knew that the birds were okay. He had almost enjoyed it, going through the business end of the wheel with the guys. It wasn't *going* that bugged him; it was *where* the Hell you went.

Which was just what he'd said all along. But now he knew. Chris had kept him knocked out the whole trip up and back before; so they hadn't been so damn sure either...? Well, now *he* was.

He sat there until Chris came in and saw him. Then he sat there long enough to make sure Chris knew he was looking *out*. Then he swung down to the crew lounge and found a poker game getting under way.

He was okay till the game broke up. After that, it was bad. That was the only time he almost broke down. A couple of shots would've put him to sleep at least. He spent the time from two in the morning till six, when they started to serve breakfast, sitting in the damn dark dining room, watching the Moon grow so slowly you didn't know it, except that you *knew* it.

After people started to show up, it was better; he had to keep up some front, when they were watching him.

Chris stayed out of his way; he stayed out of Chris'. He was disappointed, some, but glad; Chris probably knew he came on as Mac's man. So that was that. No battles. Everybody knew what side they were on. At least Mac and Chris knew. Johnny knew what side he was on, too, but it wasn't what *they* thought.

Turnabout, that's all, he thought with silent grim pleasure. *They used me; now I use them. Let 'em all bleed...*

Tuesday was bad anyhow—bad all day long. If he'd had to stay awake Tuesday night, he didn't know—

The Medic asked him, did he want a sleeping pill. Well, Hell, plenty of people took sleeping pills. Only now he was wide-awake, rested, and much too clear in the head. *Maybe I should have stood out of bed...?*

Ten hours... He didn't know what was going to happen, but he *was* sure of this much: he was *not* going to drink; and he was *not*—voluntarily, anyhow—*damn it, not without a fight*—going to sleep out anything the rest of the passengers could take.

Dollars Dome—11 A.M. (C.S.T.)

They stopped at the office to see if Thad had any news yet. He did; but nothing special. If there had been any trouble, or anything out of the way at all, on board the *Messenger,* it was not being broadcast.

"They probably kept him sedated anyhow," Phil pointed out, as they crossed the Mall to the Med Building where his office was.

She shook her head. "No. Not this time."

"Oh?" He looked at her curiously. Under his eyes, she lost some of the quiet certainty with which she had heard both Thad's report and Phil's comment.

"I mean, I don't *think* so. I—" She flashed smile. "—have a *hunch,* let's say."

"Tell me more."

"I will," she said soberly. "That's what I wanted to talk to you about, Phil."

But she said nothing more till they were in his office. Then she took out two small roles of sound tape, and handed them to him.

"I'd like you to hear these for yourself before I say anything," she told him. "I made them out at the Shack. One was Monday. The other's yesterday."

He turned spools over in his hand dubiously.

"You care to give me any notion of what I'm listening to? Or for?"

"I thought perhaps you should just *hear* them first, but—I guess it'll make more sense if I tell you this much first. After we talked about that—telepathy bit, I got to thinking, and I realized I'd just been *scared* by the idea. Kind of foolish, I guess... All this time I've been going around telling people I believe in—or, well, that I think there's a lot of sense in some of the work they've done in E.S.P.—Then as soon as something happens to *show* me, I back off and say, "Oh, no, not for *me*, friend!" She smiled wryly. Phil grinned.

"Honey, I told you to start with, this Shack stuff was spooky. Something makes sense that doesn't necessarily make it *feel sensible.* I still get shivers when I try to think what they mean by an 'infinite universe.' Stuff like that."

"Maybe so. Anyhow, I think I'm over—" She stopped herself. "That's not true. I'm still scared as hell. But I'm scared of having a baby too, and scared of what might happen tonight, when Johnny comes, and—I'm scared of lots of things I know are *real,* and even know I'll get through all right."

He cleared his throat. "Okay, kid. I hope you love me too. Now—what's the bit with the tapes?"

"Well, I tried to think how I might be able to find out scientifi—I guess, *experimentally* is a better word? Anyhow, I thought if I got a recorder fixed up so that I could talk what I was thinking out there—at least *I'd* find out what I do think there—I told you, I'm never positive afterwards just when I got some idea, or just where it came from—?"

He nodded.

"And then, if it turned out to have anything on it that we could *check...* Well, then I'd *know.* Or at least, we'd know there *was* something worth working on. Well, you know what I mean."

"I think so. Just one thing, Lee. You want me to play these, so I gather you do think there's something—" He smiled. "—something 'worth working on?'"

"I'd rather not say what *I* think before—"

"I didn't ask you to. I told you what *I* think, right now. It's just that it's the way *you* talk about the whole business that makes me think so. So I play these tapes, see? And let's say *I* think there's something there—let's say, at a minimum, something that needs to be looked into more?" He paused. "Lee, you're not forgetting that Johnny's coming? He'll be here tonight. I don't know what happens after that. Neither do you. I just don't see the news story on why he's coming. Why in hell would he come up here for McLafferty if he wouldn't for you or Chris?"

"Phil—" She put a hand on his arm, stopping him.

"Listen first, will you? I've heard them. *I know* there's *something* that—well, just listen, will you? We'll talk later. But I haven't forgotten about Johnny, *believe* me. That's partly why I wanted to give you the tapes now—*before* he gets here. And partly why I guess I don't want to talk about it *right now*. I can't decide anything much till he comes anyhow. And—well, whatever happens, I'd like to think that— I mean, let's say I back out of the whole thing and go home and never say bad words like ESP again—*If* there's anything in this thing, I have a hunch it's not *me* especially. I just happen to be the one it—*happened to?* That's as good a way as any to put it. So—so shut up and listen first, will you?"

"Right." He put a hand on her shoulder. "One other thing, Lee— while the saying's still good. Don't forget I made an offer?"

"I won't," she said. She stepped forward quickly inside his arm, kissed him, and turned and left. "I've got a class for the next hour," she said at the door. "Then I'll be in my room till about two or three. After that, I'll be out at the Shack, if you want to talk to me about any of the stuff there."

Zeroville—11:15 A.M. (C.S.T.)

The morning had been all right.

He'd never had more than theoretical training on ion drive; there was no working ship with one when the *Colombo* took off. Now, roaming on invitation between the rocket rooms and control centers, he began to realize just what a monumental accomplishment the *Messenger* was. It was one thing to have the figures in your head: thrust and cost, tonnage, performance, all that. But for John Wendt, at least, nothing convinced but performance. The math told you what to expect—what your chances were. After that, metal and plastic and power, and flesh and blood and brains made it *work*.

If it worked, it was time to believe in it; not until then. He spent the morning acquiring belief in the ion drive.

He made a point of not thinking ahead. But as the drive shut out, and the great wheel, shorn of all velocity, slid onto the Zeroville coasting track, he had no alternative. Eleven-fifteen. TOA Moon Dome announced for seven-thirty. Eight hours, fifteen minutes.

Lunch, of course. Then what? There'd be nothing doing in crew quarters, once the shuttles left—

Sonofabitch!

He wouldn't be on the wheel; he'd be in the shuttle. In Shuttle Two: out like a light. With all the other squares.

All passengers made the shuttle-leg under sedation. *All passengers...*

The speaker overhead came to life: "All passengers please board your shuttles. Prepare for sedation."

Johnny found Basil, and thanked him. "Nice of you to let me hang around so much," he said. "I'd have flipped my top sitting it out with the damn riders the whole way."

"Pleasure, Johnny. I mean it. Hell, it was good to see you again. I don't want to stick my nose where it ain't wanted, but—like man, if you're gonna be around again—oh, crap, you know what I mean."

"Thanks, Bass. Tell you the truth, I don't know yet myself. But you got no one to blame but yourself if they kick you out and give *me* your job. Hell—I felt so much like crew this trip, I forgot all about the shuttle-leg, till they hollered just now." The announcer barked again, and started "Last call."

Johnny took off down the shaft.

He had it *made!*

Red Dome—3:50 A.M. (S.S.T.) (2:30 P.M. C.S.T.)

"...helicopter sighted at base of hill 29.3 kilometers N. 17° E. from Playfair Crater. Flight reconnaissance fully establishes identity of vehicle. No indication of presence of pilot, M. Harounian. No superficial evidence of forced landing. Ground search to be conducted pending permission from U.S.A.A. authorities to conduct same within 50-kilometer zone."

Dr. Chen tapped the stiff paper of the official report thoughtfully on his desk. Then he switched on the phone, and asked for the S.U.A.R. hostel at World Dome.

That seemed probably the best way to go about it. Besides which, Dr. Christensen was not at Dollars Dome, and no second-in-command would want to take responsibility for such a decision.

Dollars Dome—4:30 P.M. (C.S.T.)

Phil Kutler sat at his desk, with a dozen sheets of rapidly typed pages spread out in front of him. He picked up one, glanced at it, put it down, picked up another. He shook his head, marveling or disbelieving, or just dazed: he wasn't sure which.

On each page, he had collected what seemed to be associated bits from the two tapes. Now he began stacking sheets, sorting them into two piles. In one were the "weirdies": what they *seemed* to mean was not even worth thinking about yet, he told himself firmly. The other stack held more coherent and familiar bits, which seemed probable "normal" thought ramblings. He picked up the next page:

"I will come, yes, I come…I hear you call. I know it is time now I will leave this place…come to where love sends the call out…I too love, have warmth, I bring my breath with…come now to know, learn, tell, teach, exchange…come with love to love…"

That was from Monday. From the Tuesday tape: "…came to us…to me…to us, *me-all,* came seeking, not knowing, almost, not-sure…came with openness, with warm-breathing…came to find and to speak and know…"

He put it with the others, then took it off. This one was worth at least *asking* about. He knew in advance what the answer would be. No one had come to the Dome or the Shack; if they had, the whole Dome would know it. But—it hung together too well. He set it aside, separately. The next two went onto the stack. He pulled the remaining page toward him, and sat staring at it.

"…each time around it's closer, bigger…need a damn microcaliper to know it but true, it *is…*Lisa, Lee, love…"

It wasn't till that bit came out near the end of the Monday tape that Phil understood why she had waited till today to tell him, or why she would not stay while he played them. Damn few things that would really *embarrass* Lee—but her own voice talking love-talk to her would be one too much!

"...To you, just to you...screw 'em all...but I dammit I damn I love you, you're too damn good for me but if I still can I'll get you back...round again, bigger, I can't see the difference, but know...too damn many things don't see, don't have to not-know account of that. Don't see you either...baby, babe, doll, *wait*...damn it hurts, scared, Lee, you know?, damn, I'm scared but I'm coming, babe, here I come, *wait!*"

Also on Monday's tape: "...bastard, but not so bad. Smart bastard anyhow...just for now, though...up there, he's the boss...good man, Goddammit, you like the guy or not, good man in his job, and he knows not here, not know...Mac-go-to-hell, who cares which one? Just *you* kid, the rest of 'em drop dead all I care..."

The page was a full one. Tuesday's sections included mentions of someone named Bass, and a man called Kenny, and something about a poker game, scraps on a smashed window, subpoena server, a bit about "Mac"—McLafferty?

Well, *this* page at least could be checked. He folded it, tucked it in his jacket pocket, and left the office.

Downstairs, he turned, without quite planning to, in the direction of the Ad Building. In the back of his mind was the question of whether to speak to Thad about the tapes. He knew he wouldn't; and with Chris on his way back, it didn't make sense, anyhow. But he was not quite ready to see Lisa yet, and he very much wanted to talk to *some*one.

He'd kill some time with Thad, anyhow.

Better that way. His thoughts could work themselves out better on their own, in their hidden places, than he could do by conscious effort.

Dollars Dome—4:45 P.M. (C.S.T.)

The suave exterior of the U.S. Envoy to World Dome, the Honorable Andrew Kenneth Gahagan—a diplomat of the old school—appeared sadly shaken on the phone screen: whether by emotion, bad radio transmission, or creeping senility, Thad could not tell.

When he heard what the Honorable Gahagan had to say, he ruled out the likelihood of poor transmission. The other two choices remained equally possible, since the biochemist had no way of knowing just *how* serious, realistically speaking, a Red "invasion" of territorial boundaries might be.

"It can't wait two-three hours?" he asked. "Dr. Christensen will be here at seven, and I think it should be authorized by him personally."

"My own feeling in the matter," said the Honorable Gahagan "is that it should be authorized by Mexcity or not at all. I felt obliged, however, to determine your attitudes before communicating with State on the matter."

Thad felt an almost irrepressible urge to say, *Oh, hell, tell 'em come on over, if they'll send their bio chief in the party...*or perhaps, *You know, some of the babes there aren't bad. Tell 'em to shoot us a photo and we'll look for ourselves...*or even just, *Oh, fool!* He exercised his will power to its fullest extent and said instead:

"Look, let me buzz you back in five minutes. I've got something here I have to get out of the way, and then I'll see what we can do about it."

He switched off and said to Kutler, who had come in sometime during the conversation, "You get that bit?"

"Just the tailend."

"The Honorable is all worked up because the Reds have asked permission to conduct a search for the pilot—girl pilot, I might add—of a helicopter of theirs that seems to have landed in some kind of trouble inside our zone. I wouldn't've thought twice myself, but Old Horsefeathers has me worried. And maybe with this whole Security investigation bit—"

"Man, you don't read the news. It's sex they're discovering now, not Security," Phil interjected.

"Oh, Well, maybe being as it's a *girl* pilot—Got it!" he said suddenly. "What do you think of doing it this way? Tell 'em sure, and we'll help. Set it up so any search team is mixed? Then there can't be any snooping or anything. What do you think?"

"Sounds good to me," Phil said. "It can't wait till Chris comes, hey?"

"This babe has been missing about twelve hours, and they don't know if she's hurt or in shock or anything."

"Well, we can't very well *refuse* permission then. I guess the mixed search is about the best bet."

"Yeah." He reached for the phone switch, hesitated, picked up a scrap of paper from the desk. "Do me a favor, will you? Get a few guys to run on out to this location right away and look over the plane. That's where it's supposed to be. Meantime, I'll tell Ole Mustachios what the score is, and let—Nope. I'll call Plato *first*, and then tell Gahagan. That way he can't stall."

Phil nodded approvingly, took the paper, and started out. "Hey, Thad," he said first. "Lee's out at the Shack. Suppose I get the squad to drop me off there on the way, and bring her back in? You don't need me for anything around here?"

"No. Good idea. Glad you thought of it."

Dollars Dome—7:30 P.M. (C.S.T.)

When he came out of it, Chris was standing next to the couch, watching him. He got himself unbuckled, stood up, stretched. Chris watched, and said nothing. Johnny straightened out, felt his feet steady under him, and took a stance facing the other man, not more a foot away.

"All right, Johnny, you got here," Chris said. *"Now* what?"

"What I said to start with," he replied evenly. "I want to see Lisa. I hear by the newspapers—" *The hell with that crap! He didn't ask why...*

"I see by the newscasts," Chris picked up on it, "that you are here as a 'special investigator' for Mr. McLafferty—whatever *that* is."

Johnny said nothing.

"Are the newscasts right?"

"Ask McLafferty."

"You're closer."

"Listen, Chris. I came for Lee. You can make it easy or make it tough. We used to be friends, so I tell you this once: I came for my girl. You and Mac can both go to whatever kind of Hell they keep for guys like you. And I'll foul you up as cheerfully as him if you get in my way. I came for my girl. The rest of your politicking fornicating foolishness doesn't concern me at all."

Chris thought it over. "Okay," he said. "I'll cooperate with you in anything Lee wants. Outside of that, I warn you, step out of line just once, just by one toe, and—I'm the boss here. That's all."

"Okay. Now where's my girl?"

"You know the room. If she's not there, try Kutler."

Dollars Dome—7:50 P.M. (C.S.T.)

"He's pretty damn busy," Bourgnese said. "If it's something I can take care of...?"

"You Number Two boy here?" Johnny demanded.

"You could put it that way," the other man said coldly.

"Okay. I'll put it that way. Can you authorize me a half-track?"

"You're kiddin'!"

Well, what in Hell is so special about wanting a car? "What are they, made out of solid gold or something? Nobody but the Big Cheese can sign 'em out?"

"Look, before you flip completely, friend, leave me advise you that there probably isn't even a car in the Dome. If they're not all out already, they ought to be. And what makes *you* so damn eager to get in on it?"

"In on what? I'm looking for Lisa."

"Well, try Kutler if she's not in her room. He brought her back in—"

"He's not here and neither is she."

"You *sure* of that? He went out for her—Hell, it must've been five-thirty or so—"

"I'm sure. She's at the Shack."

Bourgnese stared at him a moment.

"You tried the dining room and dance room and all that jazz? I *know* he was bringing her right back."

"Listen," Johnny said, straining all his nerves for patience. "They're not here. They're at the Shack. Hell, I don't know where *he* is, and I don't give a damn. But *she's* there."

"How do you know?"

"How the Hell do you *think* I—?" He stopped cold. How did he know? "They're *both* there," he said, and *knew* it was true. "I don't know who the hell else is with them, but they're both there."

"Wait a minute," Bourgnese went to the phone and called the Shack Guardhouse. "Charlie! Is Miss Trovi still there?"

"Yeah. Her and the other babe and the Doc. Some half-track dropped him off couple hours ago. They're all in there."

"Right. Thanks, Charlie." He switched off and got Lock Supply.

"Give me the call number on Kutler's suit."

"Hold on. Here it is. Five-nine-cue-six-emm."

"Thanks." He switched off and on again, dialed the helmet radio number. Nothing. "Damn!"

He turned back to Johnny. "Okay," he said. "Let's go."

They strode rapidly across the Mall to Lock Supply. Bourgnese signed out suits for both of them.

Johnny turned to Thad as the other man started away. "Thanks," he said. "I don't know why in Hell you're doing it. But *thanks.*"

"No," Bourgnese said. "I guess you wouldn't know why."

The Shack—8 P.M.—Phil Kutler

The two women sat, one at each side of the tank, gazing into it. Lisa's voice droned as the tape wound from spool to spool:

"...but I-all did not know...idea of unit-body discrete-person too far back with memory haze...and not-alike, even when...but *when? how far back?*...so long I had been one-and-all...recalled haze-memory, but too much lost with no-need-to-know...had to begin, to learn, fresh, new...too slow, too slow..."

"He's coming!"

The words cracked like a whiplash in his helmet; he jumped back, out of touch, put a hand to his face-plate in reflexive feeling for damage, that snap had been so sharply physical.

The plate was intact. Of course. He smiled foolishly, leaned toward her again; found he had to *force* himself to retouch helmets. That crack had *hurt.*

"Johnny?" he asked.

No answer. Then out of the side of his eye he saw she was nodding her head inside the helmet.

"Can you tell if anyone's with him?"

Pause. "Somebody, yes...not Chris...Thad?"

That seemed likely.

"How is he— What kind of a mood—? I mean Johnny."

She giggled. *"Fierce!"*

Great! But *she* didn't sound worried. "That's good?" he asked sourly.

"Depends..."

He backed off to look at her. The half-smile on her face was—in Moonsuit and helmet, in a half-enclosed shack on the Moon's friendless face—absurd, ludicrous...nothing short of outrageously funny with its eternal-mysterious-female. *So laugh already!* He didn't. *Sure*, he thought, *funny, like...crazy, man...but how would it look if she smiled it for you?* Then he realized she could probably hear this as well—or more clearly than?—anything he said aloud through the helmets. And then, with relief, but with bitterness too: *If she were listening, that is...*

She wasn't. She was listening only to one man, the man at the wheel of the half-track, now visibly nearing at full speed across the Moon dustcakes—coming for her.

And the half-smile was gone. A full, lovely smile now, and moist eyes too. *What the hell is he saying?*

None of your damn business!

He started again. It was going to take getting used to: getting to know when you had thought a thing for yourself, or had it thought to you. That one was himself—he thought.

He leaned forward again. "Does Maria know?"

"Of *course*. We were just thinking..." Then it happened again: a sort of stereo-thought in his mind, coming from both, complete, in-agreement, and did-he-agree? Was this the best way?

He nodded, straightened up, and walked through the door to wait outside.

The Shack—8 P.M.—Thad Bourgnese

"It ought to be Phil," he said tensely. "I'll try him again." This time the reply was immediate; nothing wrong with Doc's suit then; he'd just been switched off before.

Switched off? The guy goes out to get Lisa, stays out himself instead, and turns off his set. *Nice going...*

"Hi," Phil said. "Johnny with you?"

"Yeah. What in hell are you doing out here? *And where's Lee?*"

"Right inside. Waiting. Also, we have a guest."

"*Guest?*" If that meant what he thought it did, this was one too much. "Who's the guest?"

"I hate to shout," Phil said. "You dig me, man!"

Yeah? I do, do I? Then what in the name of all-holy have you been sitting out here for? The whole damn Dome goes out hunting, and...

The half-track ground to a screeching halt. Wendt was out almost before it stopped. Thad turned off the ignition and followed. He saw

Johnny's taller figure march like incarnate doom on the man at the door.

"For krissakes, Phil," he started, and would have said, *Let him in!* but it was unnecessary. Kutler had moved before Wendt got there. Johnny went through, and Phil stepped back in front of the door.

Thad walked up slowly. He was trying hard to hold onto the irritation he *knew* he should still feel.

"What gives?" he asked, and managed a frown.

"Lee said, just Johnny, first, please. That's all."

"Just? What's with your company?"

"She'll be out." Kutler's calm ought to be infuriating. But all he felt was: *Well, Phil's got some sense; he must know what he's doing...*

"You wouldn't mind filling me in some?" he asked. "Glad to. Turn off your radio. I don't want to tell the whole world."

The two men touched helmets, and Phil started talking. A moment later, a bulky figure in an ill-fitting, clearly-marked, S.U.A.R. suit came out of the Shack. The three of them headed for the pressurized Guardhouse.

The Shack—8 P.M.—Johnny Wendt

He stepped through the doorway into dimness and a kind of— *warmth?* In the center of the pavilion—that's all it really was—a tank set on the ground bubbled evilly around an enormous hump of moldy grey-white, kneaded-looking, knobbed, and ridged.

Two suited figures sat, one on each side of the tank. As he entered, the one at the far end arose, walked around the tank, came toward him.

Lee?

It wasn't, of course. He would have known by her walk, and when she came close enough, by her face... But before he saw these things at all, he *knew* it wasn't. Lee sat with her back to him. The other woman—*Maria?*—smiled as she passed, and went out.

Lee sat where she was, back to him. But—

Johnny, oh Johnny, my darling, my love!

It was not in words. The thought of the words, the idea of speaking, was there; and it seemed that he heard: but what was most real about it came through without symbols, and surely without any sounds. It was just—

Warmth. Lisa-to-Johnny-warmth. Love.

Nothing to question or worry or doubt or solicit or yearn for or want or need or define. Just love-as-is...love-actuality...love-known, love-before, love-after...a place to rest and be warm through inside himself.

He had felt it before.

He had felt it and it had been false.

He had felt it, not Lisa-to-Johnny, but—

No!

If he screamed aloud, nobody knew it. *He* didn't know. His head ached, either from the resounding scream inside the helmet, or else from the need to scream, kept in his head.

Doug, get out! Get out, damn it! Get out of here! Damn it, you're dead! Don't you know you're dead?

The figure at the tank rose, and began to turn.

Johnny stood helpless, rooted. He would have fled if he could. But the warm flood embraced him, caressed him, held him bound. Frightening, enticing, beckoning, threatening, stiflingly suffocating, vibrantly life-giving. And—

He had run from it before. He could run no more.

The figure turned toward him entirely, and stepped forward.

It was not Doug. Doug was dead.

It was Lee. *Lee, Lisa, Lisa-love, Lisa-loves-John...*

Her walk... *Her* love... *Her* face, smiling up at him, close and closer still, through the plastic helmet plate, tearfully?, lovingly, *hers*.

Lee!

He reached out his arms.

She came into them—almost. His gauntleted hands gripped the backs of her shoulders, and she looked up, laughing. The rigid fabric of his suit was pressed against hers, and there they stood, each one behind his own life-saving column of air inside the pressured suits, in a mad caricature of embrace. Laughter broke loose inside him and bubbled up. He bent his head; helmets touched; and their laughing mingled and merged and grew whole. It raced into the current of love-warmth, and pulled him with it, turning and twisting and sporting in cascading torrents of lovely-Lisa-laughs-with-love...

How long they stood there in the wondrous half-embrace he did not know: two enclosed islands inside their Moon suits, making love through glass walls by the side of a strange pool of—

He shuddered.

—of bubbling putrescence, of—

A friend! she said sharply.

Friend!? He looked at the tank and he shuddered again.

Looked back at his Lisa. "Hey, babe," he said gently, his helmet against hers, "I think we better get you—"

Not yet! She smiled. But she hadn't waited to hear what he said. And she hadn't opened her mouth when she spoke.

Nor had he—the first time.

You know it's true, darling...

Her voice, yes, but voiceless... Their helmets now were clear inches apart. *Listen! she insisted.*

Monday afternoon, she told him, reciting, *you sat in the Messenger dining room and watched the Moon, and you thought you could see it get bigger and bigger each time it went around, if you could have microcalipers to measure with...*

This morning, you watched every step of the ion blast...

Yesterday...

It went on and on. It battered, without hurt; pushed, without tearing; forced itself into his consciousness tenderly, gently, inexorably. It *was* true. It *worked.*

Like the ion engine—like anything—*it worked!* He saw it work, felt it work, knew it worked. So it was true.

Why?

How?

I'll show you, darling... He let her draw him back to the tank, and sat down beside her.

The Shack—8 P.M.—In the Guardhouse

"You are Maria Harounian?" Bourgnese asked sternly.

"Yes."

"You speak English?"

"Only few words."

"You are from Red Dome—from the S.U.A.R. Dome?"

She nodded.

He turned to Kutler.

"How long has she been with you in there?"

"She was there when I got there; two hours, maybe? I don't know if you noticed, Thad. She's—quite pregnant. You might ask her to sit."

"All right. Would you like to sit down, Maria?"

She shook her head. "No-thank." She smiled. When she smiled, her wide blonde face looked remarkably like Lisa Trovi's long dark-skinned face.

"You saw her enter the Shack?"

Some shuffling of feet. "Yes, sir. "

"And you permitted her to enter?"

"Well, yessir. Miss Trovi said—"

"You did not see fit to inform us in Dome?"

"Sir, Miss Trovi said this lady was with *her*. She took all responsibility ."

"But you knew a search was being conducted for Miss Harounian?"

"Well, yes, but we didn't know it was *her*. Miss Trovi come to the door, and said, her and her friend going in to the Shack, let 'em know if anyone tries to call…"

"You didn't ask who her 'friend' was?" Thad shook his head, incredulous. These men were good guards. They knew their job.

"Well, no sir."

"Sir—"

It was the Russian girl. "Yes?"

"Sir—she want us. Calling now."

There was an odd sort of urgency in her voice, in her face, her whole stance.

"Right!" The three of them started back to the Shack, with just one small part of Thad's mind still wondering why neither he nor the guards had called Chris yet.

Inside the Shack, Lisa waited, with Johnny beside her. She smiled a welcome to the Soviet girl; included the two men afterwards. She beckoned Phil. "Start the tape? I'll try to keep talking it."

Mars—April, 1975—Doug Laughlin

The Earthman stood beneath a violet sky, on rusty sands, and turned, inch by inch, slowly, feeling with all his…something he had no word for…exactly as at home he might have felt with a moist finger for the source of wind.

He made three complete turns before he stopped. He nodded, satisfied. That was the way. It didn't change. The tenth time in four days now, and always the same.

He went into the ship, and entered the direction in the Log.

The brother-Earthman slept. The first one sat at the big book and wrote. He covered two pages and went back and read them through, nodding. He then went back to what he had written before, and read that. He nodded again.

He closed the book, and sat thinking. Then he stood up and went to the bunk where the brother-Earthman slept. He reached out a hand and drew it back again. Reached out and drew back. As if a wall stood between them. It seemed like a wall: from the brother-Earthman there was a sort of cloud of *No—Don't touch!*

He backed off from the bunk, somewhat sadly. Got into his heat suit and mask. Went down to the cargo hatch. Checked out a sand-cat. Started it up. Stood out on the sands while the motor warmed in the dawn chill. Made his inching turns again: nodded, deeply satisfied, certain now.

In his mind, he went back inside to the brother-Earthman, walled in his bunk with sleep and *No*. Stood there, thinking, and went back inside and to the Log. Looked through the pages, four of them on which he had written what at last he believed, what he was going to find out for sure.

Wanted to leave what he said, but not leave information to follow with. If he was mad, let one death be enough. Four pages, two sheets, and each sheet somewhere on it had the destination. He thought:

If he was right, explanations would follow. If he was wrong— what difference *why?*

He tore out the sheets. Left the ship. Started out, to find the Mars-people whose love-thoughts, greetings, warm yearnings and welcomes came like a wind, like a breeze, like a flood of light, beam of caresses, from a direction he now knew he knew…

Mars—April, 1975—Martian

I-all waited, eager, sending out callings: joyous, rejoicing, preparing reception; calling in airmakers, calling in watercells, calling in; calling for the Earthman coming...

...I-all, a planet-wide oneness of readying: for new exchange, learning, contact, emotion, give-and-take, take-and-give; from/to/with/alongside/between/together with this unit-body of Earthman approaching...

...I-all, ready now, knowing from last time, from Earth-other-brothers who came in first great ship, knowing ahead this time: air, water vapor—without these the Earth-bodies cannot survive; old memories stirring, from before me-all, once on a time when the I-we who lived before me-all were discrete bodies alive in a fluid of water-air; back, distant-far back before the drying and thinning of atmosphere...

...I-all, descended, evolved, changed, mutated, attenuated, substance of sentience: broken to one-cells; joined in one-thinkingness; stretched out to use all the sparse vapors spread round a planet; combined, united, one-minded but many-celled—starch-makers, water-bags, air-holders, carriers, sun-suckers, thought-senders, soil-savers, moss-tenders, all of the others, all of the kinds of me-us, one-cell and one-cell; and here in the dim place of safehold, the grouped one-cells, planners and thoughtmakers fed, watered, warmed, by my-our other-I's, sending out callings for feeders, airers, for heaters, waterers, all to send extras with carriers to the vault, to tend the Earth-brother...

Doug would have been all right, except that he misjudged the distance. If he had realized he'd have to go all the way to the old city to reach It-Them, he would have done the whole thing differently. He'd have told Wendt where he meant to go—if not why—and taken a heli. If he realized, he would have lived.

If *They-It* had realized—if the two Russians had come to It-Them sooner after the crash, had lived a bit longer to tell more and learn more, if They-It had been able to learn from the first two that for Earth-bodies the life of the brain alone is not sufficient— If It-They had understood the whole human mechanism, perhaps he'd have lived.

Whether the Martian (call it that; call it "it", there is no proper pronoun) could have summoned resources sufficient to keep Doug alive—for years, as it would have been—until help came, the Moon-Martian did not know. But the Martian had too little information to plan ahead, and it took planning.

It *could* have stopped him; *would* have, had it known his supplies would run out before he reached the vault, or that its own preparations were foolishly inadequate. But the centuries—aeons? millennia? How long, Moon-Martian also did not know—of one-ness, alone in togetherness with all just oneself, the long-long loneliness had only been outlined, sharp-edged, and identified, when the two Russians came for so short a time.

Laughlin came closer, and it sent its call stronger and clearer, more endearing. Laughlin's cat sputtered and failed, and without thinking, he strapped the spare oxy tank on his back and set out afoot.

He lived ten days inside the vault beneath what he and Johnny had decided must have been a Martian bank, but had been built especially to guard, preserve, tend, grow, the brain-centre of the planet-wide "body" of the last Martian—the brain into which was poured the memory and knowledge, skill and affections and hopes and dreams and lost beliefs and yearnings and ideals of a race that could not in its own first form survive the stripping of the atmosphere from the old planet.

He lived, intact, ten days; his brain, for which there was enough starch, air, and water, stayed alive and able to communicate—how long?—Moon-Martian did not know—a long time, too-long, till he was sure the Martian knew *enough* now for the next Earthmen; then he chose not-to-live.

It was his choice to make. The Martian did not like it but complied; it had no choice.

Wednesday, October 19, 1977 10·15 P.M. (C.S.T.)

The two bulky figures entered the half-track, and the taller one sealed the door behind them.

When he turned back to her, the woman had already opened the car's oxy valve, and removed her helmet.

Without taking his eyes from her face, he reached up and undid the clasps on his, broke the gasket seal, and lifted the bowl off his head. He stepped forward, and she took one step at the same time, meeting him. For the first time in two months, they met each other's lips.

He stripped off his gauntlets, and held her head in his hands, drinking in the touch and look and scent and feel of her. From the neck down, the limp pressure suits swathed them both in formless fabric armor; but hands and heads were free to caress; a smile could be finger-traced as well as seen; a murmured word was clear to a close ear.

For minutes, they stood close as the cloth barriers would let them be, not thinking anything, not saying anything in words that mattered. Then, still without words, he started the car, and they sat together, his arm around her, her head on his chest, for all the world like two wistful teenagers, while the track chugged torpidly back over the black face of the old Moon, under the gleaming green faced glow of Earth.

Perhaps half way back, the words began. And then they tumbled out, questions on both sides coming so eagerly that nothing could really start to be answered.

It was a curious double-level conversation, too: because while their spoken words explored the wide new world opened up by the events at the Shack, the unspoken dialogue between them continued to re-enforce itself, and re-create their private world of love and close communication. The contact, once made, seemed quite able to function on its own, independent of the—

—*whatever-it-was?* Lisa, in snatches, told Johnny as much as she had been able to figure out, with Thad's help and Phil's, about the growth and differentiation of the Mars-bugs. The bubbling vat was a sort of brain-center. It extended nerve-like networks to all other colonies of bugs. Here on the Moon, where zealous "jailors" fed and tended the "brain," the network was just a sort of habit; on Mars, it served the vital function of connecting the water-holders, the oxygen-makers, the perceptors and proprioceptors and nutriment-synthesizers. The adaptation-or-mutation puzzler, which had first caught the attention of the Dome scientists, was not too different in nature from the sort of "instinctive" decision that sets the sex and functions of each new-made egg in an ant colony. All genes for each caste are present at birth; the environment of the particular cell determines the final role of the member. And the choice of environment for that cell? With a functioning conscious brain, it was much easier to understand in the— Martian? Moon-Martian? *The friend*, was the way Lee thought of it— than it was in an ant colony.

She was telling him how Phil had forced her to recognize and experiment with the *psi* effects, when the call came. It came on the radio—but that was one minute after they had reversed direction, and started back toward the other half-track. It came first in Lee's awareness.

In the middle of a sentence, she broke off, and at the same instant, in the wordless sentence of love she was "speaking" she stopped to say, *They're out of gas.*

Later, John realized that if she'd said it aloud, he *still* would have doubted. But in the inner dialogue there was no space for doubt or disbelief. He heard it, knew it, and acted on it, long seconds before they had switched on and warmed up their radio set, to call for help.

And by that time, he'd had the next thought.

He told Bourgnese, on the radio, that they were on their way, and asked them to stay tuned in. Then he switched off and started to ask Lee if she would try something—then knew she already knew, and before he could tell her exactly what it was he wanted, felt the opening channel between his own mind and the—*friend*—and switched on the set again.

"Bourgnese?"

"Right here."

"Listen, this might be just for laughs, but give your buggy a try again, will you?"

"Tonight I'll try anything, man," Thad said, and then, "She won't catch, John. We're bone dry."

"Forget the starter. Listen—just get in gear and *drive.* I mean—damn it, this sounds nuts. *Pretend* you've got gas. Like, try it once, okay?"

"What can I lose?"

A moment's wait, and an exclamation—hardly more than a *whoosh* of air, but it contained all the bafflement, delight, suspicion, excitement, and fascination that gave them the answer. Then, *very* calmly: "Nice going, John. We'll make it back, I guess."

The new world of collaboration had started.

EPILOGUE

Dollars Dome, Thursday,
October 20,1977—2:30 A.M. (C.S.T.)

In the conference room, Dr. Christensen sat at one end of the table; Dr. Chen sat at the other. Down one side of the table were ranged the U.S.A.A. staff, including Trovi, Kutler, Wendt, Bourgnese. Down the other side were S.U.A.R. men in equal numbers—and Harounian.

The last of the tapes slid to an end, and turned itself off. There was silence. Then Kutler rose and started to speak.

He explained in detail what he knew of the development of Lisa Trovi's ability.

He sat down, and, the Soviet's Gregoriev rose, and told a rather more methodical and experimental tale of the discovery of Maria Harounian's talent. "We came to the conclusion, tentative, that the pregnancy might be a factor," he finished. "It now seems this is justified."

Lisa whispered to Phil. He rose again. "Miss Trovi suggests that the particular pregnancy that was operative was hers—only because the child carried genes familiar to the—the Martian. She understands that it might be possible for a mind, which has not yet developed semantic centers to—receive?—more readily. Thus, she believes her unborn child and Miss Harounian's might have been in contact more easily than two adults."

The first stir of reaction across the table subsided; there were nods of slow agreement.

Bourgnese rose: "Begging the pardon of the two ladies," he said, "I'd like to call attention to another matter. It happens these two infants were conceived prior to a certain—ah, noticeable change in— well, I'm sure you gentlemen have all been aware of the furor in our press about our—ah, *morals*, here? Of course, we don't know how things are at your Dome, but—?" He stood a moment, grinned, found two, then three and four answering grins across the table. "My suggestion was that perhaps the—emanations? *callings?*—from the— Martian—might have been in part responsible for—shall we say?—an extraordinary goodwill in the two Domes blessed with—Martian extensions?"

As he sat down, one of the Chinese delegates leaned forward. "I was just thinking," he said, without bothering to rise, "I wonder how good this Martian is at PK?"

The words raced round the table, with the thought right behind. In a moment, a babble of voices was following. After a short time, John Wendt stood up.

The room quieted slowly. Slowly, and with precision, he told the story of the fuelless half-track.

"Gentlemen," he said. "It appears that we may have at hand a fuel—if you call it that—which will make any kind of space travel more practical. Excuse me; I am doing my best to understate. Assuming this—fuel—does not exist, we now know—" He swallowed, opened his mouth, cleared his throat. "Oh Hell. What I'm trying to say is: I'd like to volunteer three of the crew for the next trip out—anywhere."

THE END

If you've enjoyed this book, you will not want to miss these terrific titles...

ARMCHAIR SCI-FI & HORROR DOUBLE NOVELS, $12.95 each

D-11   **PERIL OF THE STARMEN** by Kris Neville
        THE STRANGE INVASION by Murray Leinster

D-12   **THE STAR LORD** by Boyd Ellanby
        CAPTIVES OF THE FLAME by Samuel R. Delany

D-13   **MEN OF THE MORNING STAR** by Edmund Hamilton
        PLANET FOR PLUNDER by Hal Clement and Sam Merwin, Jr.

D-14   **ICE CITY OF THE GORGON** by Chester S. Geier and Richard Shaver
        WHEN THE WORLD TOTTERED by Lester Del Rey

D-15   **WORLDS WITHOUT END** by Clifford D. Simak
        THE LAVENDER VINE OF DEATH by Don Wilcox

D-16   **SHADOW ON THE MOON** by Joe Gibson
        ARMAGEDDON EARTH by Geoff St. Reynard

D-17   **THE GIRL WHO LOVED DEATH** by Paul W. Fairman
        SLAVE PLANET by Laurence M. Janifer

D-18   **SECOND CHANCE** by J. F. Bone
        MISSION TO A DISTANT STAR by Frank Belknap Long

D-19   **THE SYNDIC** by C. M. Kornbluth
        FLIGHT TO FOREVER by Poul Anderson

D-20   **SOMEWHERE I'LL FIND YOU** by Milton Lesser
        THE TIME ARMADA by Fox B. Holden

ARMCHAIR SCIENCE FICTION CLASSICS, $12.95 each

C-4   **CORPUS EARTHLING**
        by Louis Charbonneau

C-5   **THE TIME DISSOLVER**
        by Jerry Sohl

C-6   **WEST OF THE SUN**
        by Edgar Pangborn

ARMCHAIR SCIENCE FICTION & HORROR GEMS SERIES, $12.95 each

G-1   **SCIENCE FICTION GEMS, Vol. One**
        Isaac Asimov and others

G-2   **HORROR GEMS, Vol. One**
        Carl Jacobi and others

If you've enjoyed this book, you will not want to miss these terrific titles...

ARMCHAIR SCI-FI, FANTASY, & HORROR DOUBLE NOVELS, $12.95 each

D-21 **EMPIRE OF EVIL** by Robert Arnette
THE SIGN OF THE TIGER by Alan E. Nourse & J. A. Meyer

D-22 **OPERATION SQUARE PEG** by Frank Belknap Long
ENCHANTRESS OF VENUS by Leigh Brackett

D-23 **THE LIFE WATCH** by Lester Del Rey
CREATURES OF THE ABYSS by Murray Leinster

D-24 **LEGION OF LAZARUS** by Edmond Hamilton
STAR HUNTER by Andre Norton

D-25 **EMPIRE OF WOMEN** by John Fletcher
ONE OF OUR CITIES IS MISSING by Irving Cox

D-26 **THE WRONG SIDE OF PARADISE** by Raymond F. Jones
THE INVOLUNTARY IMMORTALS by Rog Phillips

D-27 **EARTH QUARTER** by Damon Knight
ENVOY TO NEW WORLDS by Keith Laumer

D-28 **SLAVES TO THE METAL HORDE** by Milton Lesser
HUNTERS OUT OF TIME by Joseph E. Kelleam

D-29 **RX JUPITER SAVE US** by Ward Moore
BEWARE THE USURPERS by Geoff St. Reynard

D-30 **SECRET OF THE SERPENT** by Don Wilcox
CRUSADE ACROSS THE VOID by Dwight V. Swain

ARMCHAIR SCIENCE FICTION CLASSICS, $12.95 each

C-7 **THE SHAVER MYSTERY, Book One**
by Richard S. Shaver

C-8 **THE SHAVER MYSTERY, Book Two**
by Richard S. Shaver

C-9 **MURDER IN SPACE** by David V. Reed
by David V. Reed

ARMCHAIR MASTERS OF SCIENCE FICTION SERIES, $16.95 each

M-3 **MASTERS OF SCIENCE FICTION, Vol. Three**
Robert Sheckley, "The Perfect Woman" and other tales

M-4 **MASTERS OF SCIENCE FICTION, Vol. Four**
Mack Reynolds, "Stowaway" and other tales

If you've enjoyed this book, you will not want to miss these terrific titles...

ARMCHAIR SCI-FI, FANTASY, & HORROR DOUBLE NOVELS, $12.95 each

D-41 **FULL CYCLE** by Clifford D. Simak
IT WAS THE DAY OF THE ROBOT by Frank Belknap Long

D-42 **THIS CROWDED EARTH** by Robert Bloch
REIGN OF THE TELEPUPPETS by Daniel Galouye

D-43 **THE CRISPIN AFFAIR** by Jack Sharkey
THE RED HELL OF JUPITER by Paul Ernst

D-44 **PLANET OF DREAD** by Dwight V. Swain
WE THE MACHINE by Gerald Vance

D-45 **THE STAR HUNTER** by Edmond Hamilton
THE ALIEN by Raymond F. Jones

D-46 **WORLD OF IF** by Rog Phillips
SLAVE RAIDERS FROM MERCURY by Don Wilcox

D-47 **THE ULTIMATE PERIL** by Robert Abernathy
PLANET OF SHAME by Bruce Elliot

D-48 **THE FLYING EYES** by J. Hunter Holly
SOME FABULOUS YONDER by Phillip Jose Farmer

D-49 **THE COSMIC BUNGLARS** by Geoff St. Reynard
THE BUTTONED SKY by Geoff St. Reynard

D-50 **TYRANTS OF TIME** by Milton Lesser
PARIAH PLANET by Murray Leinster

ARMCHAIR SCIENCE FICTION CLASSICS, $12.95 each

C-13 **SUNKEN WORLD**
by Stanton A. Coblentz

C-14 **THE LAST VIAL**
by Sam McClatchie, M. D.

C-15 **WE WHO SURVIVED (THE FIFTH ICE AGE)**
by Sterling Noel

ARMCHAIR MASTERS OF SCIENCE FICTION SERIES, $16.95 each

MS-5 **MASTERS OF SCIENCE FICTION, Vol. Five**
Winston K. Marks—Test Colony and other tales

MS-6 **MASTERS OF SCIENCE FICTION, Vol. Six**
Fritz Leiber—Deadly Moon and other tales

If you've enjoyed this book, you will not want to miss these terrific titles...

ARMCHAIR SCI-FI & HORROR DOUBLE NOVELS, $12.95 each

D-51   **A GOD NAMED SMITH** by Henry Slesar
          WORLDS OF THE IMPERIUM by Keith Laumer

D-52   **CRAIG'S BOOK** by Don Wilcox
          EDGE OF THE KNIFE by H. Beam Piper

D-53   **THE SHINING CITY** by Rena M. Vale
          THE RED PLANET by Russ Winterbotham

D-54   **THE MAN WHO LIVED TWICE** by Rog Phillips
          VALLEY OF THE CROEN by Lee Tarbell

D-55   **OPERATION DISASTER** by Milton Lesser
          LAND OF THE DAMNED by Berkeley Livingston

D-56   **CAPTIVE OF THE CENTAURIANESS** by Poul Anderson
          A PRINCESS OF MARS by Edgar Rice Burroughs

D-57   **THE NON-STATISTICAL MAN** by Raymond F. Jones
          MISSION FROM MARS by Rick Conroy

D-58   **INTRUDERS FROM THE STARS** by Ross Rocklynne
          FLIGHT OF THE STARLING by Chester S. Geier

D-59   **COSMIC SABOTEUR** by Frank M. Robinson
          LOOK TO THE STARS by Willard Hawkins

D-60   **THE MOON IS HELL!** by John W. Campbell, Jr.
          THE GREEN WORLD by Hal Clement

ARMCHAIR SCIENCE FICTION CLASSICS, $12.95 each

C-16   **THE SHAVER MYSTERY, Book Three**
          by Richard S. Shaver

C-17   **THE PLANET STRAPPERS**
          by Raymond Z. Gallun

C-18   **THE FOURTH "R"**
          by George O. Smith

ARMCHAIR SCIENCE FICTION & HORROR GEMS SERIES, $12.95 each

G-5   **SCIENCE FICTION GEMS, Vol. Three**
         C. M. Kornbluth and others

G-6   **HORROR GEMS, Vol. Three**
         August Derleth and others